FOLLOW THE WIND

BO LINKS

SIMON & SCHUSTER

New York • London • Toronto
Sydney • Tokyo • Singapore

Simon & Schuster
Rockefeller Center
1230 Avenue of the Americas
New York, New York 10020

SIMON & SCHUSTER and colophon are registered trademarks of
Simon & Schuster Inc.

Designed by PAULETTE ORLANDO

Manufactured in the United States of America

10 9 8 7 6 5 4 3 2 1

Library of Congress Cataloging-in-Publication Data
Links, Bo.
    Follow the wind/Bo Links.
        p.   cm.
    1. Golfers—Fiction.   I. Title.
PS3562.I536F65   1995
813'.54—dc20   94–36118
                                                          CIP

ISBN 0-671-51058-4

The man was so sick so long, and fought it so successfully, that I think we have finally discovered the secret of Jones's success. It was the strength of his mind.

—BEN HOGAN

Somebody asked me once, "Who's better—Nicklaus or Hogan?" Well, my answer was, I saw Nicklaus watch Hogan practice, but I never saw Hogan watch Nicklaus practice.

—TOMMY BOLT

FOR A.J., forever . . .

May your eyes sparkle with curiosity,
your soul encounter enlightenment,
and your heart beat with enchantment.

· 1 ·

EVEN WITH THE BENEFIT OF HINDSIGHT IT IS DIFFICULT TO EXPLAIN exactly how I found the place. I stumbled upon it years ago, and although the passage of time has worn down the grooves of my memory, I can still recall many of the details.

I was barely twenty years old as I threw my clubs over my shoulder and set out for Lincoln Park Golf Course, which sits on the very northwest tip of San Francisco. Lincoln is a little bit of a golf course, a mere freckle on the great body of the game. If it were a rubber band stretched to its limit, the elastic would snap at fifty-three hundred yards. That's all it is, just a kick-in putt compared to places like Medinah, Oakmont, and Winged Foot.

They will never play a United States Open Championship at Lincoln Park. But then again, those of us who have negotiated Lincoln's hills and scraped shots off her bare lies don't care about that. The course is vivid in our memories for its tumbling terrain and its rock-hard fairways and concrete greens. Most important of all, we remember Lincoln Park because it is where we grew up.

At Lincoln you can't fly a shot in tight or watch the ball suck back to the hole. I have learned from experience that the best way to get around the place is to let your pitch shots bounce a little; you have to punch the thing at the flag, forcing the ball to dance the dance of a hungry rabbit, bobbing and weaving as it hops between daisies and uneven tufts of grass.

The course is tucked into a seemingly forgotten corner of the City, adjacent to a quiet, middle-class residential neighborhood. I suspect the people who live along Clement Street, which borders a couple of Lincoln's fairways, don't care much for golf and are thankful for the wall of trees and the huge fence that work together to keep wild slices from veering into their living rooms. That is not to say nongolfers don't make use of the place. Lincoln is a wonderful spot for a walk and has an excellent museum, the Palace of the Legion of Honor, which features the works of French impressionists and sits in the middle of everything. It is surrounded by the tees, greens, and fairways of at least eight different holes, everything from mammoth par threes to an intimately short par five.

The highest point at Lincoln is the thirteenth tee. From there, weather permitting, a player can see all the way to Contra Costa County and Mount Diablo, catching a glimpse of downtown San Francisco and the Bay Bridge in the process. Even on the dullest of afternoons you can see the Transamerica Pyramid, its thinly tapered top floors jutting above the other skyscrapers, aimed at the clouds like a needle waiting to be threaded so it can stitch the city's rooftops to the sky. And from the tee at the par-three seventeenth, you don't think of the oval green 234 yards away, puckering a bit like a temptress; the only thing on your mind is the landmark that dominates the horizon to the east of the tee box, the Golden Gate Bridge, looming in the distance, stately and still—a huge, mute, inanimate member of the gallery, rigid and tense in anticipation of shots to come.

I wasn't thinking about such vistas on the day in question. All I had on my mind was teeing it up and chasing my ball over Lincoln's hills, hoping to avoid her trees, hoping lightning would strike and I could shoot a score worth remembering. I was alone, so there would be no one to verify the excellence of my effort, should I be lucky enough to get hot.

I didn't have a dime in my pockets, and things were always sort of laid back at Lincoln, so I cut in on the seventh hole. I selected number seven partly because it was the point of entry closest to my mother's home, located nearby on Forty-third Avenue between Anza and Balboa streets. More important, the seventh tee is hidden in a far-off corner of the course, completely out of sight of the starter's window, an excellent place for starting a round of golf if you have no intention of paying a greens fee.

I didn't plan on committing a major crime here. All I wanted was a few holes, a little space, a few whacks at the pellet. After all, a few years earlier, when I was in high school, I was here every afternoon, playing anytime I wanted by virtue of a monthly fee card I would purchase while playing fifth man on the George Washington High School golf team. The school is located only five blocks away, and anyone with any brains knew how to fill out his schedule at the start of every semester: In the morning four "solids" (history, math, foreign language, English) followed in the afternoon by three shots of pure air (lunch, study hall, and physical education). That translated into a school day that began at 8:45 A.M. and ended at half-past noon, leading directly to at least eighteen holes a day because we could leave campus at lunchtime. We never worried about coming back, for our golf coach, the inimitable John "Gravelmouth" McGrath, signed us out of study hall and instructed us in no uncertain terms to hit the links instead of showing up for in-school PE.

I loved golf, so this was heaven. In addition to playing, I had the good sense to soak up the fullness of the game—its history, its heroes, its rules, its lore. And when it came to making the little white pill dance at Lincoln Park, even a player of my limited ability had an edge: I knew the dang course like the back of my hand.

After high school it was on to Berkeley. I played golf—not nearly as often as I had in high school but often enough to keep the flame burning inside me at the right height. While my friends were walking to lecture halls through the smell of tear gas, I was prowling the fairways of nearby Tilden Park, another hilly course not unlike Lincoln. My love of the game continued to grow, with each day bringing some new observation, some new discovery. My progress suggested that if I kept at it, I might just discover the elusive treasure that every player of my meager ability seeks: the secret of the pros. If I ever found it, I knew, I'd be home free—Flush City, ready to bask in a lifetime of shots that went where they were supposed to and stopped whenever I cried out "bite."

The day I cut in was nothing special. The weather was dull, the sky a blotchy wall of battleship gray, the way it is for more than three hundred days a year in that part of the city. There was no wind, and the air was muggy, which meant it was heavy. I could tell in an instant there would be no hang time even if I hit one on the screws.

I didn't stand on ceremony. I looked down the chute of number seven, saw an empty fairway, then slapped a three-wood off the ground and walked onto the course as though I owned it. The ball sailed over a hill that crests 185 yards up the fairway, and I rushed after it, hoping no one was waiting on the down side to rip off what was a pretty fair blow. I knew all about the ball hawkers who lurked over the hill on number seven; after all, only a couple of years ago I was one of them. That, in fact, is how I got started with all of this, for I never even played the game until, at the ripe age of thirteen, I borrowed a friend's wood-shafted, rusty-headed mashie and proceeded to steal an unsuspecting customer's drive that had sailed over the very hill I have just described. I thought about that inauspicious beginning, but only for a moment. I had to get moving.

Fortunately, there was no one around, and I was able to play the seventh quickly. My downhill wedge shot to the green bounced like a kid on a trampoline, but it never veered off line, stopping only twelve feet from the hole. The putt caught the lip and fell. Birdie. I made no outward display of excitement, no fist in the air, no shout to the heavens. All I wanted was to blend into the scenery and play with a natural ease, all the better to deflect any inquiry should someone from the starter's office be prowling around to check if players had actually registered and paid to play.

Had I been thinking straight, I would have realized there was little reason for fear. It was early evening, and the course was almost totally deserted. I moved along, playing five more holes in relative peace. I made an easy three at the eighth, a downhill par three whose green is guarded by bunkers. Then it was back up the hill, climbing the fairway of number nine, panting with every step. Even a good poke down the middle on that hole leaves a blind shot to the green, and my drive fit the pattern perfectly. I fired a nine-iron, which landed safe though not really close to the hole. I escaped with par.

The tenth and eleventh, two short par fours, were birdie land even for a player like me. I almost drove the tenth and sandwedged my ball to six feet. Drain-o. My three-wood tee shot at the eleventh drew a bit, bending its way around the corner, dribbling down a short slope to a decent lie near the green. All that was left was a short chip, which I hit with confidence. The ball did not respond; it seemed to have a mind of its own, bouncing in fear, squirting off to the right. When the ball calmed down and stopped carrying on, it was eighteen feet from the hole. Not a good shot.

I made up for it, though, as my putt caught the grain of the green and rode it as though it were a streetcar whose rails ended at the bottom of the cup. When the putt dropped, I was three under. That's when it started to get scary.

The twelfth is another diminutive par four, all of 280 yards. Even though my tee shot wound up under the trees to the left of the fairway, I could still reach the green with a low punch. It didn't work. I looked up on my second shot, squirreled the ball forward, and faced a tricky up-and-down for par. My third shot, a pitch caught the green and rolled up near the hole. Although I was alone, I was three under, which caused me to feel the presence of a huge imagined gallery roaring at every shot.

I made the putt for par, and that convinced me, as only good rolls can, that it was my day. I began walking slowly toward the next hole, sensing that this was a round I would long remember. If only someone were there to see it—someone to be my marker, someone to attest to the mastery of my effort. Three under after six is as good as it gets for a player like me.

By the time I reached the thirteenth tee, a thick fog had rolled in. I couldn't even begin to think about seeing the East Bay hills or downtown San Francisco or either of the bridges. I was starting to shiver, and under the circumstances I wasn't sure if that was my nerves or the weather talking. I took stock of where I stood: I had parred number twelve and reminded myself for the fourth or fifth time that I was still three under. It was an incredible score for me, so good that I was beginning to wonder just when the hands of fate would wrap themselves around my neck and tighten their grip. The fog hovered around me like cotton fluff, ready to soften my fall, but even in the mist I could make out the fairway.

The thirteenth hole at Lincoln Park is a 495-yard roller coaster of a par five. The fairway runs downhill from the tee, and then back up to a landing area; from there it slopes gently downhill again, all the way to the green. Despite the undulations, the hole is basically straight, and it is very, very easy. The main object off the tee is to carry the ball over two stands of trees that lie 180 yards out, bordering the fairway in clumps to the left and right. With a good tee ball, all a player has to do is blast the second shot at the green and then chip and putt for a birdie. I was staring four under right in the bloody face.

I hit a perfect drive, and my eyes widened with delight as the ball sailed away, straight and true.

The lie for my second shot was a good one, providing no excuse for failure. All I can say is that a sudden, quickening wind at my back proved to be more of a temptation than my young character could resist. Convinced that I could loft one into the stratosphere and watch admiringly as it rode the stiff breeze all the way to the green, I yanked out my three-wood and flailed away. But my grip was too tight, my takeaway too abrupt, and my swing too quick. My hoped-for stroke of majesty looked more like a rotary fan at high speed. I barely made contact. The ball careened far to the right, a toe job if ever there was one. The ball disappeared into the middle of the trees. The last time I looked, the ball was heading straight toward the middle of the Monument.

Everyone who plays Lincoln Park knows about the Monument. It is one of the last remaining landmarks of a Chinese cemetery that covered the land before the City decided this hallowed stretch of earth should be a resting place for wayward golf shots instead of Asian families. The Monument is no mere headstone; it is over twenty-two feet tall. It is made of gray stone, but over time it has broken down to the point where all that remains is a simple archway infested with lichen and covered with creeping greenish moss. Even though the archway continues to stand its ground, it has all but surrendered to the aggressive reach of overhanging tree limbs. The archway is perpetually bathed in shadow now, and the surrounding darkness gives it an eerie quality. The Monument is a marker of death, yet as the greenish moss continues to spread over its surface, it is also the seat of life. I find the Monument and its peculiar setting so haunting that I often sense the presence of ancient spirits hovering nearby.

I feared those spirits this day, feared they had struck me down in the midst of an unforgettable streak, ruining the round of my young life. But I pushed onward, hoping I could salvage something from the wreckage. I trudged into the fog knowing the best I could expect was an unplayable lie, a score of at least six or seven, and no doubt an ignominious departure from the course I loved.

And that's when it happened. I was walking slowly into the trees, the frustration growing, when the fog quickly thickened. I could barely see my hands. I couldn't find my ball, and to this day I have never found the darn thing. The fog soon curled around my feet and began to enshroud my entire body. Then came a wind, much like the one that had prompted me to swing so fiercely at my second shot. But this wind was different. It was guiding me, pushing me forward on a path I could not see.

I didn't know what was happening, and there was no time to

question the circumstances, so I kept going, following the wind and the fog into the trees. I crossed the threshold of the Monument, snaking my way past the overhanging limbs, working my way through the mossy stone archway. The mist was folding over itself, rushing by me like the rapids of a mighty river. The current of fog nearly knocked me down. It felt as if a tremendous force were pushing through a hole of some sort. Even though I was alone, I started to shake my head in disbelief. This is crazy, I thought. But I continued on, drawn by a magnet of curiosity. As I stepped forward, I heard a deep, heavy sound—not thunder but something more subtle. It was a rolling sound, as if someone were pushing open a heavy door that was on wheels, rumbling across stone.

By the time I emerged from the Monument to the other side of the trees, the fog was so thick that the hand I barely saw in front of my face a few moments ago had disappeared entirely. It was a total whiteout. I turned in circles, trying to get my bearings, but all I could hear was the sound of my spikes clicking on a smooth surface that I guessed was concrete. That caused me to look down, and I saw white tile, cut into small hexagons, grouted in place, the type one finds in bathroom floors. And that's exactly what it was—a bathroom in what looked like an old hotel of some sort.

I saw a man at one of the sinks, washing up. I stood by watching and wondering as he cupped the water in his hands, then brought them slowly to his face, wetting it and rinsing the sweat away. He did this several times, finally turning the brass fixtures to shut off the flow of water. When the water stopped, the room went deathly silent. I held my breath, afraid I would startle him if I breathed too heavily or, God forbid, coughed. He was methodical and graceful as he went about his business. When he began patting himself dry, he turned toward me.

I recognized him from pictures I had seen. He was much younger than he looked in the photographs, but there was no mistake. It was the Mechanical Man. The Hawk. The Iceman. Ben Hogan. He just stood there, staring at me. I didn't move, couldn't move. I stood staring back at him as my clubs hung off my shoulder. The room was eerily quiet except for my spikes, which were still clicking against the tile.

"Better remove those shoes, young man," Hogan said. He was talking to me! He was looking, too—a dour, disapproving glance that asked the question that was on my mind as well: *How did you find your way in here, son?*

He kept looking my way as he dabbed the water from his face. He folded the towel neatly when he was done.

"If you have any sense at all, young fellow, you'll remove those shoes. If the bartender catches you inside this place with your spikes on, there'll be hell to pay, and I don't even want to think about what'll happen if old man Fry gets ahold of you."

Who? What was he talking about? And what had happened to my golf ball?

Hogan moved slowly and fluidly. All his movements had purpose, and they all meshed as if connected by a string. He did not say anything else as he passed by and pushed open a swinging door that led to another room. It swung back and forth a few times. He was gone.

The only thing I could think of was that I'd better get those spikes off. When Ben Hogan, winner of nine major championships, the fiercest competitor of his age—maybe of any age—tells you to do something, you don't ask questions; you do it.

I unlaced my shoes as fast as I could. I didn't know where I was, or why I was there, but something was up because I found a pair of slippers, just my size, sitting under the sink where Hogan had been standing only a moment before. They had my initials on them. I put them on and hurried through the swinging door.

·2·

I DIDN'T KNOW WHAT TO THINK AS THE VACUUM OF HOGAN'S departure sucked me along, carrying me after him, drawing me through the door that was swinging back and forth in his wake. The question on my mind was not whether I could catch him but what I would talk to him about. I was sure I'd get the chance. After all, I had removed my spikes.

But if Hogan were to engage me in conversation, what should I ask him about? The grip? The backswing? What he thinks about during a round? Maybe I should inquire about some of the others, about Nelson or Snead or Demaret. Or should I just shut up and wait for him to talk to me? After all, he had already done that, even if it was to rip into me because of the shoes.

The moment I emerged from the swinging door I searched everywhere, but Hogan was nowhere in sight. All I could see was another huge room, much larger than the spacious bathroom I was in a moment ago. There was a long bar, crafted out of mahogany and surrounded by paneled walls bearing paintings, old photographs, and framed newspaper articles, every item somehow tied to the game. The place reeked of tradition. A massive bronze chandelier hung from the ceiling in the center of the room; it was an eclectic fixture, its patina-covered center cast in the shape of a golf bag, with clubs of every sort shooting out in all directions and with globes of light in the shape of golf balls, dimpled and all, perched at the end of every shaft.

I saw tables of varying sizes. Although I was the only one in the room, I could easily imagine the frenzy at the noon hour or whenever the busy time was, with waiters hustling about, rushing hot food and libations to whoever hung out there. Some of the tables were larger than others. This place could accommodate twosomes, threesomes, foursomes, a whole membership if that was the need. But now it was just me. What in the world was I doing here?

When I turned back to the bar, I saw another man, not Hogan but one of the fellows he must have been referring to. With nothing to lose I made an approach, wondering why the bar had matchbooks from all over the world scattered about and a range of cigarettes in an enameled container that bore the logo of the Fairway Tobacco Company of Cedar Ridge, North Carolina. Every generation was covered; there were Pall Malls, Old Golds, something called Flagstick Filters, and even Kools with menthol. There were cigars, too, from Havana, Sumatra, and South America. I decided this must be a men's club of some sort.

"Where's Hogan?" I asked the bartender, the only person around. He was a familiar-looking character, with black hair so heavily loaded down with brilliantine that it looked like licorice. His starched white shirt stood out brightly against his skin, which was as shiny as a lizard and the shade of well-tanned cowhide. Neatly pressed white linen knickers protruded to the south of his apron. He looked ready to tee it up the minute his shift was over.

"Where else," he said to me while pointing at the windows, "but on the range? All the guy does is hit balls. That's all he can do at this point."

When I asked why, I got more than I bargained for. The bartender told me Hogan wasn't even a member of the Club. He was just visiting as a prospective member, checking the place out, trying to determine if he would want to join when the time was right. There were special benefits of membership, said the bartender.

"Like what?" I asked innocently.

"You haven't heard? Didn't anyone tell you about this place?"

"Hey, look, mister," I explained, "I don't know where the heck I am. I was looking for a shot I hit into the Monument right over there. . . ."

I turned to look back at Lincoln Park, somehow thinking I could get my bearings and straighten everything out. But all I saw was more fog and what looked like a driving range. A solitary figure at the far end was hitting balls. The white hat, the repeating motion, and the mechanical precision combined to tell me it was Hogan.

"You look as if you need a drink, junior," said the bartender.

I turned back to the bar and shot the bartender a hard stare. Who was this guy? I knew I'd seen him before, but I couldn't place him.

"What do you want to drink?" he asked.

"I'll have what you're having." It was a stupid reply, but when you're twenty years old and have just walked through a hole in the fog, you tend to say stupid things.

The bartender walked slowly to a small locked cabinet. He was obviously getting ready to show me something special. He looked around the room and then slipped his left hand into his vest pocket, pulling out a set of tiny keys fastened to a long gold chain. He jingled them until he located the one he was after. He held it aloft, his eyes gleaming as though he'd discovered the key to a treasure chest. He carefully inserted the key into the lock. Turning it slowly, he shot a wink my way. What a showman this guy was! Finally, after perusing the contents of the cabinet with painstaking care, he pulled out an elaborate beveled bottle. It was filled with something brown. On his way back to where I was standing, he picked up two small glasses and filled them with chipped ice. The bottle, I could easily detect, was quite old. Its faded label was nearly worn away.

"Glad you said you needed to wet your whistle," the bartender commented. "Junior, this stuff here is nearly seventy years old."

To a fellow my age, seventy years sounded like two centuries. "Is it still good?" I inquired.

"Good?" he asked. He looked at me as if I were crazy. "Junior, this is the best stuff there ever was."

By now I was starting to figure him out. I may be slow, but eventually I catch on. He was somebody I'd seen before, maybe in the movies. I just knew it. Or was he a politician? He looked as if he could convince a garbage man to pay him for the privilege of taking out the trash. The guy was really something.

"Mister," I asked innocently, "haven't I seen you somewhere before?"

"I've been around, if that's what you mean, junior."

"No, I mean . . . I think I know you from somewhere."

"You probably do. I've done it all, you know. Repaired the fastest automobiles that ever took to the road. I was a crackerjack at that. Manufactured pianos at one point. Was a taxidermist when I was just a lad. Like I said, I've been around. Circulated. I've come a long way since Corbett's Glen, and I'll tell you this," he said proudly, "I've smelled every rose along the path."

I tried to circle him, hoping to get a full view of his face, but the bar was a formidable barrier. His tanned skin told me he'd been in the sun. That must be where he did what he did—whenever it was that he did it, that is. The guy had to be from the twenties. He looked like an athlete or something.

I decided to press on with my questions. "Did you play a sport?"

"Shoot, junior, not just a sport. I played and taught 'em all. You ain't listenin'. I've been around."

"Baseball," I asserted with confidence. "I bet you were a ball player. Right?"

"I can see how you might say that. You know, junior, when I had that tryout with the Phillies, the old man, the coach, what's his name, says to me, 'Son, which arm you throw with?' I says, 'Both of 'em,' and whip off a curve with my right arm, burning a hole in the catcher's mitt. Broke his hand clean off. Then I show 'em a change-up with my left. The batter is so far out in front, he falls over. Screws up his nice clean uniform and everything. Embarrassed the man, if you know what I mean. So the manager, the damn fool, he says to me, 'How's about trying the outfield?' I say, 'Mister, are you lookin' at what I'm showing you here?' The sumbitch doesn't answer me. You got that? He leaves me hanging. So I took a hike out of there and never gave it a second thought."

It was quite a tale, but I was still at sea. I just couldn't place him.

"So what did you do after that?" I asked, somehow knowing that whatever the bartender told me, it was going to be good.

"I decided to settle down," he explained. He swirled the bottle, giving its contents an inviting look. "At least for a while, that is. Took a job at a local club outside Rochester, near where I grew up. Became head man before I was twenty. Taught tennis and ice skating in the off-season to make ends meet. Made my money touring, if you know what I mean. Junior, even in those days they paid me a thousand a day to make it fly."

Make it fly? Ice skating? Tennis? Taxidermy? Auto mechanic? Piano maker? Ambidextrous pitcher? Who in the heck was this guy?

"I almost forgot," he continued, interrupting my train of thought. "Did I tell you I pulled a stretch as an assistant to a mandolin maker?"

"What?" I said. When he started to repeat it, I cut him off. "Say, mister, it's all very interesting. Really, I mean it. But can you tell me something more about this place? I mean, I just came through the trees looking for my ball, and there's Hogan, big as life. What's going on?"

"Junior, let me pour you one." He didn't ask my age, and I wasn't about to offer the fact that I was under twenty-one.

"Sounds good to me," I said, gazing down at the shot glasses he was aiming at.

"I started telling you about this stuff," the bartender said proudly. He gazed lovingly at the brown liquid. He poured it slowly, letting it trickle over the chipped ice. "Won it in '21 at Inwood," he explained. "The best damn scotch I ever tasted, though I can't say as I get too many opportunities to drink it here."

"What's the problem?" I asked.

"Well, I hate drinking alone, and no one around this place drinks very much. They're all trying to save themselves or something like that. You'll find out why soon. In the meantime, here's looking at you, junior."

I lifted my glass to his and looked him in the eye. He swallowed the shot in a single gulp. I, on the other hand, sipped cautiously, only to feel the liquid burn my lips like a blowtorch. It was strong stuff, all right.

After I finished coughing, I persisted in the effort to discover what I had stumbled upon.

"What is all of this?" I asked as my eyes drifted about the place. By now I was certain I had done something far more significant than toe the dimples off my second shot. The bar alone started me thinking. It was a sight to see, its finely grained wood surface as shiny as a new penny and as clean as a whistle. Although I knew nothing about spirits, it was obvious even to my untrained eye that the bartender was set up to serve anything to anybody. He could satisfy even the most obscure taste upon request.

Soon I discovered we weren't alone. Off in a corner several men were reviewing documents and arguing over something. A short waiter bussed the remains of their lunch. He winked as he passed us, his stiffly starched white jacket chafing against itself as he scurried by. He was just a kid, no more than twelve or thirteen, with a tassel of hair atop a small round head. His eyes were wide and curious; they appeared to be bulging outward from the sockets, as if he were peering at the world from an embedded lie. I watched him as he scooted off to the kitchen, then I turned back to the bartender.

Suddenly it clicked. It had taken a while, but the tumblers of my mind finally spun into place. Hooch that is almost seventy years old. Won it in 1921. Inwood. Grew up around Rochester. All at once I forgot about Hogan and about my ball. Who cares about them when you're looking into a glass of scotch poured by one of—

"Why, you're—" I whispered, but before I could get it out, he looked down at me, disappointed that I hadn't recognized him sooner.

"It took you long enough, junior. Usually they mark me first thing, come right up and say, 'You're the Haig, ain't you?' 'Yeah,' I say, 'I'm Sir Walter, but these aren't the twenties anymore,' you know what I mean?"

"You look so young!" I exclaimed. "Why, it's been over . . . Why . . . Walter Hagen's been dead for over . . ."

He waved to the men in the corner as if to summon reinforcements to his rescue. Perhaps he didn't need another whippersnapper asking him about all those late nights and fast times or about all those tricks he used to pull when the PGA Championship, which he won five times, was determined by match play.

A tall fellow rose from the corner table and started over our way. I rubbed my eyes as he drew near. He wore a six-gun and a cowboy hat. He did not look like any golfer I'd ever seen. The only thing I could figure was that he must be the old man Fry that Hogan had talked about.

"You the young man from Lincoln Park?" he asked sternly. There was no smile, no outstretched hand to greet me. "Well, are you?" he persisted.

I nodded.

"Good. It's about time you got here. The name's Fry, Jimmy Fry. I come from a little town up in the gold country. Was sheriff there for over fifty years. The old man tapped me for this place, and I said set it up, so here I am. Don't know much about playin' golf, I'm sorry to say. I just watch over all you fellas, keep things in order, you know, sort of like security. We get a lot of intruders here, folks tryin' to get in, crash the gate, that sort of thing. We only let the people we want in this room."

"There must be some mistake," I said plaintively. I could see no reason for my presence here, first opposite Hogan, now alongside Hagen.

"Oh, there's a reason," explained Fry. "But all in good time. First thing we gotta do is introduce you to some of the boys."

"Hangtown, you're gonna like this guy," Hagen proclaimed to the sheriff as they both eyeballed me.

"Hangtown?" I asked, afraid to hear the answer.

"Jimmy here's from Placerville," said Hagen. "Crimony Pete, he's a walking legend. Kept peace right in the middle of the Mother Lode. It was the busy season, if you know what I mean." The Haig let out a belly laugh. "He strung up so many guys between 1850 and 1870 that they started calling the damn place Hangtown. That's my nickname for him here, Hangtown Fry. He hates it, but when you've won the PGA Championship five times, like I have, you can get away with a few things." Hagen smiled benevolently in my direction.

This is just great, I thought. Here I am talking to a ghost, watching Hogan hit balls, and standing nose-to-nose with a man who spends his time between nine and five hanging people who break the law. Suddenly I remembered I was only twenty years old. I nodded at Hagen, dropping my chin so that it pointed to my shot glass which was still almost full. My lips were still pulsating from the one sip I had managed to get down the hatch.

"You'd better finish your drink, Haig," I said with confidence, nodding at my glass, hoping to convince Hangtown that it belonged to Hagen. "And get me that glass of milk when you get around to it."

Hagen bit at the bait and indulged himself. "They don't drink much around here," he whispered under his breath so that only I could hear. He was smiling even wider now with two slugs of Skye whiskey floating in his bloodstream.

"Want to meet some of the boys?" Hangtown asked.

With my hero out there hitting balls, I had only one thought in mind. "Can I just go out and watch Mr. Hogan? Just for a few minutes?" My hopeful eyes looked to the Haig for encouragement.

"Junior," he said softly in the voice of a loving father, "you can do anything you want here. If that's where you'd like to start, make yourself at home."

I looked out the window again and saw that the sky had cleared. Hogan was now hitting with his shadow behind him. The range was fresh and new, the grass as green as an emerald, and Hogan's practice balls were lined up like pearls waiting to be strung on a necklace. He swung with the precision of a second hand but much, much faster. His rapierlike motion propelled the balls one after another, and they seemed to float forever once they were hit, landing as soft as feathers. His shots were things of beauty, hanging in the air like fine paintings in a gallery. Hogan didn't look up. He kept beating balls, except now something was different. A vacant director's chair sat next to him.

"That's for you," Hangtown said with purpose as he pointed me toward the back door of the clubhouse. I wasted no time. I rushed through it, no longer feeling like a stranger, no longer wondering where I was or why I had been summoned or what I would talk to the Hawk about. My only hope was that Hogan would still be there by the time I walked over to where he was practicing.

·3·

THE DRIVING RANGE WAS AN OCEAN OF GREEN, FALLING AWAY FROM
the tee area in gentle waves, then rising back up just as gently at
180 yards. There was hardly a divot in the hitting area, and every
twenty feet or so down the tee line was a small pile of balls, sitting
still like girls at a high school mixer waiting for the boys to come
over and ask for a dance. There were targets in the distance; players could hit a variety of shots, covering varying distances, and in
each case there was a putting surface waiting patiently down the
fairway as a reminder of the great venues of the world. There were
none of the usual markers at 100, 150, 175 yards; the greens that
stretched out to 300 yards served well enough as signposts.

The closest target sat behind a gaping bunker that contained a
desert of sand. The flagstick had a little red basket at the top,
which told me it was Merion, and this was a replica of the thirteenth hole, all 113 yards of it. An easy bull's-eye to hit, but one
surrounded by treacherous hazards.

The next green was 155 yards from the tee, a carbon copy of the
twelfth at Augusta; it sat there in regal splendor, a thin strip of
water crisscrossing the range, serving as a protective moat. Any

shot that was not hit perfectly would most certainly get wet. If something like that was going to happen, it was better to do it here while experimenting than in competition.

The green at 172 yards reminded me of a hole I had only read about. The Strath Bunker sat there like a cyclops, peering back at the player, telling him to beware, to aim elsewhere, to save his courage for another day. The Hill and Cockle bunkers were just as menacing. It was the eleventh at St. Andrews, and when I stared out and drew my focus on the flagstick, I swore I could hear the water of the River Eden slapping the shore behind the green.

Farther behind, just past the two-hundred-yard mark, lay the most famous hourglass-shaped putting surface in the world. The splashes of sand that surrounded it and the rocky crag to the left and rear could only mean that this was where Jack Nicklaus hit that incredible one-iron, the shot that sawed a hole through the sky as it veered down the line, eventually bisecting the flagstick and finishing so close that if the ball's dimples were eyes, they could have looked over and seen the bottom of the hole. His deuce on the seventeenth at Pebble Beach was the final piece of thread that sewed up the Open in 1972.

Although a visitor like me could feel the vibrations of history, it was vastly different for the members. For them there were no distractions, no unwanted complications to interfere with serious practice. Monterey pines, cypress, juniper, and dogwood trees guarded the perimeter like sentinels. The place was as quiet as a chapel.

Not wanting to interrupt, I approached Hogan without making a sound. My slippers moved silently across the grass, and as an extra precaution I tiptoed my way from the bar to the director's chair, slipping into the seat like a hand going into a glove. I sat observing his every move. His fingers came together on the club as if they were sculpted into place by Michelangelo himself. He drew the club away from the ball slowly, his back muscles coiling to precisely the right tension. Then his left hip kicked in, and it all turned in reverse, like the efficient cylinder of a well-oiled revolver. Thwack! Another one sailed off and away.

I watched him for ten minutes. He was a machine, pumping out perfect five-irons the way a punch press turns out parts in a factory. There were no misses. His eyes followed each ball with the keenness of a miner working a mother lode. His lips melted and bent into a subtle grin of satisfaction as the balls hummed into the distance. He was flushed with confidence. He was glowing. He had found it. He knew he was ready.

But ready for what?

Hogan stopped to wipe his brow, and I could feel the heat radiating upward from the ground. He sipped ginger ale from a glass that Haig had left for him. Then he wiped his hands on a white terry-cloth towel. He draped it over a bench and returned to his beloved practice balls.

The towel was bloody, and I could see faint traces of crimson on Hogan's hands as he regripped his five-iron. He was *bleeding*, for God's sake! His callused hands had hit so many balls, they were falling apart. Yet he was going after it again! Hitting, watching admiringly, then grinning after every shot.

I could not resist any longer.

"Why are you practicing so hard?" I asked, hoping not to incur his wrath.

"I practice because I want to get better," he answered.

"But you're practicing so . . . hard."

"This is a hard game."

"But you're as good as anyone. Better than anyone. You're the greatest ball striker who ever was. And they all know it, too. Hagen," I said, looking back at the clubhouse, "told me so himself."

"You can't rest on it, son. You have to keep at it. You have to try and get a little better each day with each shot."

"Are you still looking for the perfect swing?" I knew of Hogan's obsession and was fascinated by it. When I looked at him now, I could see Anthony Ravielli's pen-and-ink drawings that decorate the pages of *Five Lessons: The Modern Fundamentals of Golf.* To hell with Iron Byron; this was the real thing.

"I'm never going to be perfect," Hogan said with a touch of humility. "I just want to get better. I want to do better next time."

Next time?

"I understand why you practice, Mr. Hogan, but why do you practice with such intensity? Don't you ever relax out here? Isn't this supposed to be fun?"

He laughed. Then the serious face returned.

"Tournament golf is not a game of relaxation, son. It's a game of focused concentration, and it's awfully hard work. The only tools I have are these hands, this body, this mind . . . and to get ready, a fellow's got to maximize them, hone them, polish them—and then squeeze the juice out of them. The fun? Son, the fun comes when you get it right."

He turned and grinned. Hogan was talking to me and grinning at the same time! I'll keep your secrets, Ben, I vowed to myself, hoping he could read my mind.

But I was puzzled. The Hawk was never a man of words, and he seldom said much, even to his closest friends. Why was he talking to me?

"You probably heard about the dream I had," he continued. "You know, the one where I went to sleep and dreamed I made seventeen straight holes in one. Lipped it out on the eighteenth hole, and I awoke in a cold sweat. My goodness! I thought I had a tiger by the tail that night! That's the feeling you want. Son, you want to know where it's going to go. And when you've got it going where you want it to go, well, it's just that . . . feeling. When you catch it, son, hang on to it. But don't hold it too tight. Take the time to savor it. Love it. And try to understand it. If you can do that, you'll be smart enough not to let it get away from you. Me? I've caught it a few times, but I just can't seem to hang on to it as long as I'd like. My streaks are getting longer, though."

"Streaks?"

"I understand my body more now, and I know my mind, too. I

can control them. It isn't easy, but it can be done. And the older I get, the more skill it takes for the mind to rule the body. In fact, now I find I have to rely on my mind instead of my body. The only way I can do that is to draw on my experience. I shoot it through my veins, and when I do, it's like a miracle drug. And you know what? The good times resonate, they make me shiver with excitement. And let me tell you something else: Once you control your mind, son, you have something working for you that can't be beaten. Not by luck, not by the elements, and not by another player. When you master your mind, you get a feeling unlike any other a man can possess."

"If you had to hang a name on it, what would you call it?"

"There's only one word," Hogan said. "Exhilaration."

He looked down at his hands.

"Look at these things," he crowed, shaking his head at the carnage.

I shook my head, too, assuming he was in pain.

"That's the price you pay," he observed. "But you know what? It feels great. Heck, I'm hitting it so good, I'll beat balls until my hands fall off. Son, they may need to give me a transfusion before I'm done here."

I felt obliged to share with Hogan my knowledge of his game.

"I read once where you said that if you played a round and hit six shots the way you had planned them, you were really playing well. Do you still feel that way?"

"No."

"Why not?"

"Because it's eight or nine shots now. I am improving, you know." His eyes were bright with anticipation.

"You sure are excited, Mr. Hogan."

"You don't know what excitement is until you get ready to tee it up with everything on the line. When you open a new sleeve of balls, the whiteness blinding you in the sunlight, the dimples sparkling as if they'd been polished. When you walk a course early in the morning, and the scent of fresh grass clippings climbs inside your nostrils. When you hear the purr of a mower on a putting green. When you see a flagstick cut in between a couple of curly-cue bunkers, begging you to attack. The flush of a shot, the flop of a divot—all of this—it flows through me like a river."

He looked wistfully out to the end of the range, as if watching something off in the distance.

"I used to get there at daybreak. When I got to the range, I could look back and see my footsteps in the dew all the way from the parking lot. Oh, how I loved to practice! Once you were ready, once you'd prepared, and you knew you were gonna go out there on the course and turn it loose— Do you know what that feels like, son?"

"It looks like you're getting ready for something right now, Mr. Hogan. But . . . I mean . . . you haven't played competitively in . . ."

Instantly I could see I had made a mistake.

"What? What do I look like to you, son?" He fired the question like a one-iron into the wind. His words carried an edge, and they seared my cheek as they passed. "What am I to you? A washed-up old pro who can't hit it anymore? I'm as fit as ever." Hogan slapped his middle, which was as hard as a rock. I could see that he wasn't much more than forty-one or forty-two years old. He was in his prime, yet he walked with a noticeable limp. He was fighting off a wound of some kind. But here he was, doing what he loved to do. And he was getting ready for something, something big. But what?

I explained weakly that I hadn't meant anything by the last re-mark, but Hogan was fired up now, ready to take on the field, ready to go out and . . .

I looked at Hogan's ginger ale and suddenly felt thirsty. Where was Haig when I needed him? I turned to the right and saw Hang-town in the doorway of the clubhouse, watching me as I watched Hogan. I motioned to my mouth, signaling for a drink. He mo-tioned in return, sending a message that could not be misunder-stood: *If you want something, boy, go get it yourself.*

I slipped away from Hogan, past his bloody towel, the glass, the bench, past a newspaper he had left beside his golf bag. I do not know what drew me to the paper, but I picked it up and slowly began to read. I was careful not to disturb the Hawk, who was busy at work. He continued to bleed and beat balls while I perused the news. I puzzled a moment over the stories until I noticed that this was no ordinary paper. In the upper right-hand corner was the masthead: *San Francisco Express*. And then I saw the date: June 16, 1955.

SAN JOSE STATE COEDS' HOUSEMOTHER SLAIN
EX-HUSBAND HUNTED IN SLAYING

IKE, AIDES "FLEE" CAPITAL AS U.S. TESTS DEFENSE
MOCK A-BOMB ATTACK LEAVES CAPITAL "DEVASTATED"

RUNAWAY AIR COMPRESSOR RAMS HOUSE

FIRE CHIEF TELLS HOW HE BOUGHT JOB

NATIONAL OPEN BEGINS TOMORROW AT OLYMPIC CLUB

There are times when a headline is all that is required, for there are stories that need but few words. Any golf lover, particularly one raised on a course where he could see the Golden Gate Bridge beyond the fairway, would instantly understand the importance of those last seven words. I turned instantly, hungrily, to the paper's sports section.

San Francisco Express
Sports Section Extra
June 16, 1955

U.S. OPEN BATTLE SET:

IT'S HOGAN & SNEAD AGAINST THE FIELD
THE HAWK LOOKS READY—SO DOES SLAMMIN' SAM
BUT CAN HOGAN GO THE DISTANCE?

The question bubbled around in everyone's mind, but the truth was clear: Ben Hogan was ready, as ready as any player had ever been. He had come to San Francisco early to practice and was hard at work a full month before most of his fellow competitors arrived on the scene. As with his preparation for Carnoustie in '53, Hogan forced himself to learn every inch of the golf course. Like Bobby Jones (and Willie Anderson before him), Hogan had already won the Open Championship four times, but his past mastery could not be traded for credit at Olympic; he would have to play his way into the record books. Hogan knew the days of his dominance were dwindling, and he therefore knew that this might be his last real shot at a fifth Open Championship, his last chance at golfing immortality. So he carefully planned and plotted his attack. He was ready to do battle at Lakeside, knowing full well that it would be a struggle, that it was going to be hole-by-hole combat. There was not only Sam Snead but a host of other professionals who wanted this championship badly. The only thing Hogan knew for certain was that they did not want it as badly as he did.

Hogan practiced like a man with his life on the line. He played the course six times in practice, limping every step of the way but never stopping. There were holes where his slow gait caused him to lag thirty to fifty yards behind his playing companions.

When a reporter asked him if he was ready, Hogan said readiness was not the problem. "I don't know if I can go seventy-two holes," he said. "I'm tired. I may not make it." He wasn't kidding. "This tournament golf is tough business," he added. "The preparation is murder. I don't know how much more grinding is left inside me. I'm flat worn out. I don't know how much longer I can do this."

He and his good friend Claude Harmon didn't even play the last two practice rounds. Instead, they went over to the Ocean Course—the Olympic Club's "other" course—and practiced the wind cheaters and the finesse shots they knew they'd have to rely on during the championship. They practiced in obscurity while the galleries crowded around Sam Snead, Tommy Bolt, and the rest of them.

The course would be difficult. Everyone including Hogan knew that. Prior to staging the championship, the Olympic Club hired Robert Trent Jones, the noted golf course architect, to make several important changes. The members knew what had happened the last time the championship was played out west, at Riviera: Hogan took the grass off the fairways and destroyed every U.S. Open scoring record there ever was. Those in charge at Olympic were going to make certain it didn't happen again.

The architect and his crew added 270 yards to the golf course, sprinkling the added distance over several holes. They stretched Olympic from 6,430 to 6,700 yards. They added bunkers and narrowed fairways, and by the time the facelift was finished, the members of the Olympic Club owned more than a golf course. They had become the proud caretakers of a wild beast.

"Ferocious rough is everywhere," the newspaper said. "Even the collars surrounding the greens are over four inches long in some places. There will be no escape for a ball that trickles off the putting surface."

Looking back, it is easy to see that they were playing right into Hogan's hands, for the Hawk knew better than the others how treacherous it was. Although the card listed par at seventy, Hogan ground his teeth on a cigarette holder after one practice session and said, "Par here is seventy-two, isn't it?"

Not everyone was convinced it was impossible. In practice, Tommy Bolt, Hogan's fellow Texan, and Dick Mayer, another tour regular, each fired 66s. Sam Snead, who after eighteen years of trying was still in search of his first Open Championship, peeled off four straight rounds of 70. Then again, there was Gene Littler, the talented young professional from San Diego who had won the Canadian Open while still an amateur. He shot an 81.

The course and not the field will be Hogan's competition, the article said. "The way I figure par," Hogan told those who would listen, "the printed scorecard is irrelevant. It's what you write with the pencil that matters. It's what a man can do that counts. In my book, two hundred and eighty-eight is the number. That could be a winning score."

When the reporters told that to Tommy Bolt, he shook his head. "That's eight over par, isn't it?" he asked. Yes, they all replied; but will it win? "It will if Hogan shoots it," Bolt replied. "I don't care what anybody else says, to win the Open you have to beat the Hawk. There's no other way."

But what was Hogan thinking? Probably that it wasn't called the U.S. Open for nothing. "There are one hundred and sixty-two men who'll tee it up here tomorrow," he said. "Some of them don't have much of a chance. There's a core of talent here that has to be reckoned with. But you can't relax, not for a second. And no matter who you figure to be a threat, well, there's probably some guy out there we've never even heard of who can turn the lights out on us."

Defending champion Ed Furgol was one of the known commodities, having won a courageous championship the year before at Baltusrol playing with a withered arm, weakened as the result of a childhood accident.

And there was a young amateur from Pennsylvania named Arnold Palmer. He had won the 1954 United States Amateur Championship and had just recently turned professional. He would be competing in the Open for the first time.

From the local angle, the galleries were pulling for Harvie Ward, an amateur whose game was beginning to turn heads. No one knew then how bright his future was; he would go on to win back-to-back Amateur Championships, one in September and another the following year. But none of the reporters could have foreseen that; at Olympic in mid-June of 1955, he was just a hot young kid with a lot of promise. Would this be the year an amateur broke through and beat the pros? It hadn't happened since Johnny Goodman did it in 1933.

"The Open can also be won out of the blue," the article said. "Sam Parks, Olin Dutra, and Tony Manero come to mind. They were 100-to-1 shots. Even Ed Furgol and Julius Boros were at least 60 to 1 on the handicap sheets when they walked off with the championship. By Saturday night the new Open champ could very well be a suddenly well-known unknown. The championship will be a pressure cooker. Anybody can blow."

Even though the reporters talked of the unknowns and Hogan warned of them, no one was betting on any of the dark horses to come through. Rather than list the long shots, the writers told their audience about Hogan's new golf club company, which he had started in the early fifties after he split from MacGregor, which had been the leading American club maker for many years. Hogan was now playing with irons forged in his own foundry and engraved with his own name. And he was not the only one; other players, envious of Hogan's success, were eager to play with clubs designed by him.

There was one curious story the reporters missed. It involved a professional from the Midwest who arrived at Olympic with his new Hogan woods and irons. He was getting the hang of them but needed the wedges to complete the set. Bantam Ben Hogan, ever eager to please one of his customers, particularly a hungry young professional willing to trust his clubs, arranged for the wedges to be delivered during one of the practice rounds. They were turned over to an unknown player who would soon show the world he knew how to use them. The player's name, Jack Fleck, would come to haunt Hogan for the rest of his days.

The article about the pending Open shot me backward. I knew what had happened there that fateful week, and all I could think about was the quarrel kindled by the 1955 U.S. Open Championship. Ever since those eerie days in San Francisco, ever since the opening round, the question has lingered: Was it the toughest course ever played?

Merely stating the inquiry sets off the debate. To complicate the matter, there are no accepted standards of measurement; all we have is argument, and when it rages, the combatants in every corner fire off colorful names as if they were arrows. Courses, hazards and holes fly by us, turning our heads as they pass: the Beach, the Quarry, the White Faces, Hell's Half Acre, the Church Pews, the Baffling Brook.

Maybe it's not in the names. Perhaps numbers are the key. If so, is it the yardage or the score? The length of the rough, the speed of the greens, or the velocity of the wind?

The problem with figures is that one statistic can fall behind the shadow of another, and a given group of numbers can easily get lost in a crowd of data supporting yet another venue, at another time, in another year.

So which course was the toughest? The fact is they're all tough under the right conditions, and when they play a major championship such as the U.S. Open on one of these babies, the arm-banded foot soldiers of the United States Golf Association stay up nights making sure the conditions are right.

Let's not worry about whether it was harder than the rest, for regardless of the degree of difficulty, at least one thing is clear: If the Olympic Club's Lake Course wasn't the toughest of them all, it's certainly on the short list. In the first round alone, more than half the field failed to break 80. After seventy-two holes, 161 players had played a total of 440 rounds of golf; only 5 of those rounds were under par. There was no wind to speak of, and the course was only a light pitch longer than sixty-seven hundred yards. But along the narrow fairways and around the small greens was rough so bushy and thick that it could easily hide a bag of golf clubs, not to mention a shot that strayed off line. In the second round of the championship, Ben Hogan shot 73, three over, and gained on the leaders, vaulting from five back to a shot off the pace. He never broke par at Olympic in 1955, but he wound up in the fated playoff with Jack Fleck just the same.

I thought of the Olympic Club and the 1955 Open as I watched Hogan hitting balls. It was so difficult! Yet he must have liked it that way. The tougher the course, the more rigorous the test, the easier for his game to rise above the others.

The golfing world has forgotten about Olympic and 1955. That bizarre week of history has gotten lost in the legacy of Hogan's shadow, which has lengthened with each passing year. He's a legend, a man they tell stories about when sitting around bars. And the legend lives today as much as it did twenty years ago, if not more so. The 1955 Open was a mistake, a historical anomaly, a chip in the furniture that isn't supposed to be there.

I knew all this history as well as I knew the lay of the land at Lincoln Park. But why was this old newspaper lying here? Was it for Olympic that Hogan was out there beating his hands to a pulp? Was there a score to settle? And why was I even here to ask these questions? I had no idea, but I was fairly sure where to go to start getting some answers: Though just a youth, I knew that when a man is puzzled and confused, he can always find help in the counsel of an experienced bartender.

·4·

WHEN I TURNED BACK TO THE CLUBHOUSE, I SAW A BUILDING larger than any I had ever encountered. It was an eclectic structure, the exterior a patchwork quilt of different materials. The main portion was constructed of stone, with irregularly shaped chunks of granite held in place by thin strips of gray mortar. The slanted roof was shingled and gabled from one end to the other. Beveled windows peaked out from under the eaves. On the north side stood a mighty turret, stretching upward like a lighthouse. There were other turrets, smaller but only slightly less majestic, at the other end of the building. What looked like a covered bridge connected the main structure to a second building, which I guessed was where the sleeping quarters were.

The instant I was inside, I saw them. From where they were sitting, they had a bird's-eye view of everything. Whether they had been eyeballing me or Hogan, or both of us, was hard to tell. The shorter of the two, the one with the long white beard, spoke first.

"Aye," he said despairingly. "He's shure t' roon it fer us all."

The younger man remained silent for a moment, his eyes fixed on Hogan.

"No, he won't. No one has the power to do that. But he has a choice to make."

"He'll roon it, he will fer shure," said the beard. "He's a-gwin' t' destroy everythin'."

"Old Tommy," the younger man replied, "you're worrying too much. Hogan has a lot on his mind. He's troubled, and he needs time. He wants to get in here pretty badly, we know that. But which path will he take? It's a doggone important decision, and a player like Hogan can't make it in one day or one week. He may never make it."

"Nae, and I canna rest a' the thought. 'Tis nae gwin' t' be troo wi' Hoogin. He'll skin those balls 'till his hands are blistered 'n' burnin'. He's toonin', he is. He's gwin' t' fight it ou' wi' Fleck. Trust in me, Bobby. I'm ne'er mistaken abou' these things, laddy."

The younger man looked at the older man for a second before speaking. "These things have a way of resolving themselves, my friend." For the next several minutes no words passed between them. Then a thought surged to the surface.

"Wha' if he's dreamin' like so many o' the others do?" the old man asked.

"What if who's dreaming?" the younger fellow replied. "You mean the kid out there?"

"Nae. Wha' if 'tis Hoogin a-dreamin'."

"You mean we might just be figments in Hogan's imagination? Is that what you mean, Tommy?"

"Aye."

"Now that's an interesting thought. You and me as characters in Hogan's dream." The young man paused. "Well, ask yourself this question, old friend: Do you feel alive? Can you touch your own flesh? Because if you can, this is nobody's dream. If you can even conjure up the question, you're outside Hogan's realm and in one of your own. Now you might be dreaming, but what else is new? Tommy, you've been doing that since your days at Prestwick and St. Andrews, old boy."

The two of them smiled at each other.

"Trust me, Tommy. We're here, and we've got to quit fretting over what we're seeing. We'll do a damn sight better for ourselves if we just try to understand Hogan's dilemma and let it take us wherever it's gonna take us."

The old man turned back to the range and continued to look out the window at the Hawk. The younger man patted the older fellow on the back and once again told him not to worry so much. After all, he added, Hogan isn't even a member of the Club yet.

I was barely inside the clubhouse when Hangtown descended on me like a *Daily News* reporter trying to scoop the *Times*.

"He talked to you, didn't he?" Hangtown asked.

"Yeah," I answered. I was not about to tell a lie to a sheriff, even one who'd been dead for almost a century.

"What'd you boys talk about?" Hangtown persisted.

"The game."

Hangtown wasn't a golfer, and he was puzzled.

"What are his plans? Did you talk about that?"

"No," I said. "In fact, that's one of the things I wanted to talk to you about. I'd like someone—you, Haig, anybody really—to tell me where the heck I am and what year it is."

"I can't help you with any of that, son, and neither can Haig. But let me talk to Bobby and Ship. They can tell you what you need to know."

"I give up," I said. "Who are Bobby and Ship?"

"Oh, you know Bobby. At least you've read about him. The best there ever was. And Ship? Well, let's just say he knows all about you. He founded this place a long time ago, and he'll tell you some great stories when you meet him. But all in good time."

I wasn't getting answers, but at least the questions were getting clearer. I excused myself and headed toward Haig and the bar.

If it was 1955 for Hogan, then I was only a gleam in my mother's eye. But when I looked down at my hands, I saw skin that had seen two decades. It didn't compute. If I was twenty, how could Haig, who won his first U.S. Open in 1914, be only in his thirties?

"How's he hitting it?" Haig asked me from across the room.

"Pure as the laws of nature will allow. The man's . . . he's so . . . his action is so . . . How can I describe it? It's like watching syrup pour out of a bottle. It's so slow, smooth, and effortless," I said, trying to keep the Haig's attention with the right image of the Hawk. "The man's a doggone machine." I smiled nervously as the Haig pulled out the bottle of his finest. I was ready to experiment with the blowtorch again, Hangtown or no Hangtown.

"He's the finest striker I've ever seen," said the Haig as he poured. "And I've seen 'em all, too. Nobody hits it like he does. Nobody. He doesn't even need a boy shaggin' for him. Just hits a pile of balls, then walks out to where they've landed and hits the pile he's created back to the practice tee. Pretty amazing, if you ask me."

"Haig," I inquired, "what is this place? *When* is this place?"

"Junior, that's beyond the pale. I can tell you about the people here, tell you what I think of 'em, tell you why I'm here, but beyond that, you have to talk to the man over there in the corner." He nodded in the direction of the same two men I saw arguing earlier.

"Who are they?"

"Bobby Jones and Old Tom Morris. Among the active members, Jones runs the joint. Dominates it, actually, the same way he dominated the game back in our time. He and I mixed it up pretty good, you know. I didn't care for him too much back then, all that rich kid, hotshot amateur stuff and all. Hell, I turned pro when I was in my teens, and I never looked back. Emperor Jones paid to play while I played for pay. Got him in '26, though. Took him over seventy-two holes down in Florida. Just him and me, eyeball to eyeball. Played him like a fiddle. Owned the match from the moment we teed it up." Haig stopped to take a sip of the brown stuff.

"Crimony Pete," he continued. "I never saw much fairway, but once I got myself onto those greens, it was like lightning striking. Made everything I hit. You ever hear 'em say, 'Drive for show and putt for dough'?"

I nodded meekly.

"Well, junior, I'm the one they're talking about. Old Sir Walter. Anyway . . . where was I? Oh, yeah, I dusted off Jones, polished him like he was a coffee table. The man hit every fairway and just about every green. Did him no good 'cause I had it workin' over-time. Jones thought he was comin' down to see some sunshine, but my game was one big hairy storm cloud for him. The putts were fallin' like raindrops. Twelve and eleven, it was. You hear me? Twelve and eleven. Nobody—and I mean nobody—ever took Jones like that. It was pretty, junior. Real pretty. And now I can sit back and smile forever 'cause that's the moment I chose."

"The moment?" I asked. This was all getting progressively stranger with each inquiry.

"Junior, why in the world do you think the Haig here is working full-time as a bartender? The way I strut my stuff, this is the last place any of my pal-o-minos would expect me to wind up. But with the benefits this place has to offer, why, I'd sweep the floors to get in. Can you imagine capturing the high point and holding on to it forever?"

I could see what he was driving at. At least I thought I did.

"You mean to tell me somebody gave you a chance to pick your spot, a high point in your life, your *moment*, as you say, and then allowed you to be frozen there for all time?"

"Bingo."

"Who else is here?" I inquired.

"We don't have enough time to go over it all, and besides, there are others who are waiting to talk to you. But let me tell you about little Eddie. He's the kid you saw bussing dishes before you went out to the range, remember?"

"The waiter?" I asked. "Why, he didn't look more than twelve or thirteen."

"More like ten. In fact, it's ten on the nose. Not a year older. His name's Eddie Lowery. Caddied for Francis Ouimet in the '13 Open at Brookline. Said it was the high point of his life, his little bit of history. He wanted to stay there, so they obliged him. Cripes, the man went on to make a couple of million in the car business, but here he is, with us, still a caddie, bussing dishes on the side."

"Do you all have jobs?"

"Everybody has a role to play, junior. We do our best to complement one another." Haig nodded at little Eddie and tossed him a piece of bubble gum as he scampered by the bar on his way to the kitchen.

"Who organized all of this?" I pressed. "And how'd they do it? And why?"

"Like I told you, you have to talk to Jones, maybe even Ship, about that. Let me tell you, junior. There're guys knockin' on our door every day, every hour. Sometimes it seems like every minute. That's why we've got Hangtown around. Can't take everybody, you know."

The goose bumps on my arms were standing at attention. Jones was here in this very room, and I was going to get to talk to him. It was mind-boggling. First Hogan, then Hagen, now Bobby Jones.

"Haig, I have a pretty good idea why you're here. Jones and Hogan, too. But why am I here?"

"Save the questions, junior." He was gazing out at Hogan again. "Will you look at that hand action, for God's sake? It's beautiful."

Together we watched him. He hit until the balls were gone, then walked off into the fog, which had returned. I started to look away, hoping maybe to catch Jones's eye, but Hagen told me to keep focused on the practice tee. I did that for several minutes, but nothing was happening after Hogan walked away. Then, as if from nowhere, white dots began piling up on top of one another. Someone was firing from afar. Before I knew it, the range balls were back in a neat little circle, like schoolchildren milling about after returning from a field trip.

"Hogan?" I asked.

"I told you there's no one like him," said Haig with an envious gleam in his eye. He stared at the range. "I could hit every practice ball there ever was, and I'd still never be able to hit it like Hogan does."

When I glanced back to the far corner of the room, I saw that Old Tom Morris had left Jones's table. "He's off to the library," Haig said as if I should understand the significance of the remark.

But I didn't. The only thing I could do was stare and gawk at the surroundings, wondering who or what had brought me there and why.

"Jones is ready for you now," said my newfound friend, Sir Walter of Hagen, pointing to the corner. Bobby Jones nodded our way, and my knees trembled. I was about to sit down one-on-one with the greatest player who ever lived.

·5·

ALTHOUGH THE TUMBLERS INSIDE MY HEAD WERE SPINNING WILDLY and clicking like those on a bank vault, I could not yet unlock the secrets of the strange place I had stumbled upon. I knew this was something special, even supernatural, but it was no dream. All of my senses were intact, working overtime to catalogue what was happening. I noticed everything, and at every opportunity I tried to move in closer, as if my alertness was a weapon; against what, I had no clue.

I could smell the wood on the walls, and it smelled good. It was as if the paneling around me had been oiled by centuries of experience, its glow the aura of a millennium of wisdom.

As I approached Jones, I saw he was shorter than I had imagined, only five feet nine if stretched out on a rack. He wore the same clothes he had played in when he was in his prime: a white shirt and tie under a gray woolen pullover and a pair of tweed plus two's loosely draping his legs, hanging like deflated balloons. The hose were nothing flashy, no argyles or fancy patterns, just plain gray matching the sweater. The only touch of flair was his tie, which was a splash of soft blue swirling in a paisley pattern. Wing-tipped brogues completed the outfit, which made him look the part of a chairman, which was what he was here.

The first thing I asked Jones about was the year.

"What year do you want it to be?" he asked in return.

"Can I choose?"

"Would you like to?"

"Sure, but how will I know what to choose?"

"Isn't there something you want to keep, something you want to remember all your life?"

"I haven't lived all that long, Mr. Jones."

"But you have plans to do so, don't you?" Jones was looking me over carefully. As he did, it dawned on me that Jones was answering each of my questions with one of his own. I opted to continue the game.

"What's Hogan practicing for?" I asked.

"What would you do about it if you knew?"

"If I knew what?"

"If you knew what he was practicing for," replied Jones. Then he put it to me again. "What would you do about it?"

"What is there to do about it?"

"Oh, there's a great deal, son," Jones said haltingly. "A great deal." I must have been getting somewhere, because at long last he'd answered without asking me a question.

"I don't understand," I said, still confused.

"You'll gain an understanding here, my friend, and soon. According to Ship, we've got you for only three days. We're just about through the first one, and I don't even know what, if anything, Hogan said to you out there. You're the first one he's talked to, do you know that?"

I told the Master that I didn't, that I was surprised Hogan even gave me the time of day after our encounter in the bathroom.

"Can you share with me what he said?" Jones asked.

I couldn't believe Jones was all that interested in my discussion with Hogan, but I saw no harm in talking about it; after all, Hogan hadn't sworn me to secrecy.

"I could see it in Hogan's eyes, Mr. Jones. The intensity. The fire. Now I know how he got that nickname."

Jones just sat and listened.

"God, he's hitting it pure," I said, as if I could tell the difference. "I mean, all his shots look pure to a guy like me, but those eyes of his—they follow every shot the way a tail follows a kite. Those eyes, crimony, those eyes. They don't just tell me he's hitting it pure, they tell me that he knows it's pure. And that's what he told me, too. Said he was hitting it so good, he'd hit until his hands fell off."

"That's what some of the fellows around here are afraid of."

"Afraid?" I asked the question while attempting to deflect it with a laugh. "How can that be? The way Haig tells it, he's caught the wind and is following it, letting it lead him. Haig says once you get here, the feeling never leaves your fingertips; the wind stays at your back forever. He said something about picking a moment and staying with it. Isn't that what Hogan's doing?"

Jones paused. He was thinking long and hard before responding. I must have touched a nerve, for his eyes darted about the room like an infantryman traversing a forest thick with snipers. Jones wasn't going to take another step with me until he was sure it was safe.

I didn't push the point. How could I? Who was I to put the elbow to the man who grand-slammed himself into the history books? I gave him a moment to himself and gazed about the room, picking up memories as though they were leaves scattered about this enchanted forest I'd discovered.

There was little Eddie, talking with Haig. They'd obviously formed a bond. Maybe the little guy caddies for Hagen in the money matches. In an instant I was sure it was true—they must play for something around here, what with all this talent milling about.

I saw the other room, the library, dark and quiet and lined with books. Old Tom was sitting quietly, motionless, soaking in the stillness of the room as though it were a magic tonic capable of sweetening his every sensation. I held the thought as I stared at him for several minutes. He was alone, but even my untrained eyes could see he was waiting for something.

While Old Tom waited, the range became active again. This time, however, it was not Hogan at the far end. He was gone, but there were others busily hitting balls. Faces and swings from the past leaped back to life as I scanned down the line. The Babe, her powerful and graceful body casting a full shadow, was sending them singing off her driver. George Zaharias sat in the same director's chair I had occupied a short while ago; he sipped lemonade while the woman he adored got down to business with her game.

Eddie ran out to the range and picked up baskets and dropped off fresh balls for the players. There was Walter J. Travis, dressed like an African explorer and chomping on a cigar after polishing off some balls. And right next to him was Francis Ouimet, ripping his mashie the way he had done in the wind and rain at Brookline. Ted Ray watched admiringly, twirling his drooping handlebar mustache; legend has it that the ends pointed upward until that fateful day in 1913. Chick Evans stood a little farther down the line, beaming with confidence, the way he must have in 1916 when he became the first man to walk away with the United States Amateur and Open Championships in the same year.

Closest to the window was a player who was easier for me to recognize than the others. Lema hit with the silky smooth grace that earned him the money to buy the bubbly that led to the nickname Champagne Tony. He had that look about him; I could almost see him holding up the British Open trophy at St. Andrews and then, an instant later, returning the next year at Royal Birkdale and telling them to take good care of the booty because he'd be back for it Saturday when it was over. What a man! I saw him the way he looked at Olympic in '66 when he finished fourth in the Open, behind Casper, Palmer, and Nicklaus. Two months later he was gone.

They'd all come back to life.

With youthful exuberance I attempted to take it all in with one look. My eyes darted everywhere, like tadpoles flitting about in a mountain stream. I saw one hero after the next, and I couldn't decide which of them was worthy of the longest stare.

"Now, don't you go running around here bug-eyed, son. I assure you, you'll get to see it all." Jones could sense my excitement and decided to lower the mercury in the thermometer. "Don't be fretting. You'll meet everybody before you leave. Don't worry about that. But let me tell you something."

Sure, Bobby, I said to myself. Anything you want.

He looked at me hard, the same way he must have stared down Homans at Merion. He was speaking deeply and with purpose. His voice was in slow motion, just like his backswing. "Don't let anything they say affect you. Some of them are worried about Hogan and they'll say things, but you have to pay them no mind."

"What's the problem?"

"It's not a problem, really. It's more a . . . concern. That's what it is—a concern."

"Can't you tell me what this is all about? I know Hogan's practicing, and I know there was a newspaper next to him dated June 16, 1955. Just watching him made me think of the Open at Olympic and—"

"So you do understand." Jones's eyes sparkled like diamonds. I must have said the right thing.

"I know about '55," I explained, "but why does Hogan have that newspaper?" I tried not to let my puzzlement show through, but my face was as transparent as a window.

"Son, that paper did not belong to Hogan. It was left there for you."

"But . . . by whom?"

"Does it matter? The fact is, somebody wanted you to see it. You're being spoon-fed, can't you see that?"

"Mr. Jones, I just got here. You want me to tell you what's going on? Geez, I'm still wondering why I'm here and what I'm supposed to do."

"Do you think there's some assignment for you?"

"I don't know what to think. All I know is I was three under when I nailed it lateral right. I went looking in the trees for my ball, and somehow I walked in here. Then I saw Hogan. Then Hagen. Then you. So go figure. I can't make heads or tails out of all this."

"There's a message there," said Jones. "Has to be."

I said nothing. But my blank stare telegraphed the punch. Jones could sense that I was lost.

"Did you read it?" he persisted.

"Read what?"

"The newspaper. The story. It's got to be a clue."

"All I really focused on was the date. That's what let me know that this has something to do with the Open. I know it was hard on Hogan, but—"

"It was so hard that he wants another chance."

"Another chance?" I gulped. "How could he possibly do that? How can it be? Haig says he isn't even a member. He says all Hogan can do is hit balls. He can't even play the course yet. Haig told me that. What gives?"

"That's the concern. He isn't a member. Somehow, someway he must have found out about us, and he wants in. The display out there is Hogan's way of knocking on our door. Ship says anyone with a record like his gets special privileges, and what Ship says goes. No one minds Hogan using the range. I mean, for heaven's sake, there's plenty of space. We have a passel of practice balls, and around here there's time to burn. None of that troubles us. That's not the problem."

"I thought you said it was a concern, not a problem. Isn't that what you said?"

"Son, you have a keen eye and good ears."

I smiled his way.

"Let me tell you a little more about this place," he offered.

Now it was my eyes that sparkled. Jones motioned to Haig to bring us a round. The drinks arrived, and he toasted me. Jones toasted me! No one will believe any of this, I told myself. But I put that notion aside, along with all thoughts of life outside this place;

for now my eyes and, more important, my heart and mind were focused on Jones.

"You can't belong here," Jones said to me.

"I can't . . ."

"No."

I was instantly crushed, for I had been disqualified by one of my heroes. Jones saw the look of consternation and moved quickly to reassure me.

"What I meant to say," he explained gently, "is that you can't belong just yet. Neither can Hogan. A person has to pass on, if you know what I mean. You've got to be invited to join us. That's the key. It's what all of us have in common. We've left your world behind and been sent here."

"All of you?" I inquired.

"All of us who have been admitted. That's Ship's department. He picks the members. He sets the rules. He is the one who provides all of this."

"Who's here?" I asked, figuring that if I was an outsider, at least I had good company in Bantam Ben.

"Well, you name it. You've met Hagen and little Eddie, and you can see those folks out on the range. You'll probably see a few faces you don't recognize, but don't worry about that. Not everyone here is famous. Actually, we've got a whole bunch of members who can hardly break ninety. You don't have to set scoring records to gain admission here, son. The standards are much tougher than that. As I hope you will discover, a lot of things are more important than your score."

"I don't get it. Are you telling me that there's more here than you, Hagen, the Babe, and all those others I just saw beating balls?"

"Much more. If you love the game enough, son, there's a place for you. The flame burns forever here, but there are obligations. We have a community to run. Someone has to make the food, cut the grass, clean the range balls. This stuff doesn't get done on its own, you know."

I nodded, but inside my head tap dancers were kicking up a storm.

"Let's get back to Hogan," I said, hoping I could be of service. "What's the . . . um . . . concern?"

Jones sighed. "When you come here, Ship interviews you, asks you a thousand questions. He wants to make sure you really want to be here. After all, there are alternatives. Anyway, once Ship is comfortable with having you around, he asks you the most important question of all: Will you play or will you stay? Are you staying or playing? The answer to that one determines everything."

"What's the difference? All of the people on the range sure look like players to me. And they all seem determined to stay here—I mean, why wouldn't a person want to stay? This place is so idyllic, and those people out there look pretty damn—er, darn—content. They must be the ones who have chosen to stay. Or are they players? I mean . . . I mean . . . I don't really know what I mean anymore."

"Oh, my," said Jones with a touch of alarm in his voice. "You are confused. Those folks hitting balls aren't players as I've used the term. They don't plan on playing. They're staying, staying on forever. They'll be here until the end of time."

"Can they go out on the course?"

"There is no course."

"No course?" I looked incredulous.

"Well, not as you know a course. Take Champagne Tony there. He plays St. Andrews anytime he wants. So do I. Hagen, over there"—Jones pointed to the bar, and Haig pointed back, tit for tat—"he plays that course down in Florida. You know, the one where he wiped me out." Jones laughed at himself. "He got me good that day. What a thrill to see him at his best! They always talked and wrote about our rivalry, but Haig and I have worked it out here. He's got his moment, and I've got mine."

"What do you mean?"

"I guess I got a little sidetracked. You see," Jones said as he scratched his head, "if you choose to stay, Ship lets you pick that one moment, that one event, that one thing. Everybody has at least one, so sometimes it's tough. It might be a championship, a game

with friends, something you saw or something you just *felt*. Whatever it is, if it's special enough, you'll choose it. And then you get to
keep it forever." He looked me dead in the eye. He didn't even
blink. "For-ev-er," he said slowly, enunciating each syllable.

"Heavy duty," I replied. Jones looked at me blankly.

I explained in an even tone that I understood the gravity of the
decision-making process he was referring to. But still there was
something I hadn't grasped.

"You talked about stayers and players, and you said all of the
people here are stayers. If that's true, then what's a player?"

"It's someone who doesn't want to stay with us."

"So what? If he up and leaves, who cares?"

"Everybody cares, son, because it may upset the applecart. You
see, if a man chooses to play, he gets only one round. But it can be
any round. Do you understand me? Any round."

"But if he's not staying, why are you so concerned?"

"Perhaps I've chosen my words poorly. A man who plays here, as
we use the term, doesn't just get to play a round, he gets to *replay*
a round. He gets to pick it out—any round, mind you, at any time,
under any circumstances—and do it all over again. You know, a
second bite at the apple. The ultimate Mulligan is the way a fifteen
handicapper might describe it."

Everything went silent for me. The tap dancing inside my head
stopped, and my body became numb. I started to nod the nod of
understanding, and Jones nodded with me. He was obviously worried, but he was smiling because he knew that I'd seen it. He knew
I knew what he was talking about.

"And if he replays it," I explained to the man who already knew,
"he has to live with it. It changes everything. It can change history."

"Exactly. There's no guarantee of success, and that's the rub. If it
doesn't come out the way you want it to, you're stuck with it. And
if you're disgusted with yourself when it's over, your soul will be
shellacked with that feeling for the rest of your days. For all eternity, really."

I could see what Hogan was pondering. He knew the conse-
quences, and that was why he was bearing down with such incredible intensity. He was going to defy the golfing gods and let it rip
one more time at Olympic, one more run at number five. In a
sense, what did he have to lose? All he could do was improve on
the playoff loss to Fleck. In another sense, there was everything to
lose, for who could dare put his peg in the ground with not just
posterity, but all eternity, at stake?

But what about those who'd chosen to stay? Were they at risk?
"Tell me, Mr. Jones, are people here afraid? I mean, if Hogan re-
loads for the '55 Open, will he alter the course of events and—"

Jones finished the sentence as if we were playing alternate-shot
foursomes. "He'll cause such a rumble that it'll bring our house
down. Why, Old Tom is convinced that the tremors will cause the
entire Club to vanish with a puff of smoke. He thinks we're
doomed if Hogan tees it up."

"You can't have that."

"No, we can't," Jones answered. "But Hogan isn't like anyone
else. No one, I mean no one, has his drive or his determination. I
don't rightly know if we can stop him. I'm not even sure if it's our
place to try to stop him."

"But isn't he taking a pretty serious risk?"

"Son, he's putting it all on the line. Everything might just blow
up in his hands. And he'll be stuck with it. So will we."

"But don't you have any records or any experience to draw
upon? Surely this has happened before, hasn't it?"

Jones was shaking his head no before I finished the question.

"No one's ever replayed a round for keeps?"

"No one. We've each chosen our place, our moment, and we've
never had a single problem. For Pete's sake, old Hangtown over
there, he doesn't have to deal with complaints or keep order
among the membership. We don't even have a suggestion box
around here. There's a natural peace to this place, a sense of order.
Hangtown's job is keeping out the intruders, the folks who don't
want to go through the process—the gate-crashers, if you will."

"Tell me again how Hogan got in here. And how did I get here?"

"I don't know which is easier to explain. But it's quite simple, really. Whenever Ship sees a potential member, he summons him here to try the place out, to see if it's up to standard. As for you, I guess Ship must have seen something in you. You love this game, don't you, son?"

"Why, yes, I do. Very much indeed."

"And you've studied its history?"

"I've tried, but I've a ways to go, I'm afraid. I do know where you closed out Homans. Eight and seven on the eleventh at Merion."

"And you know the rules and their purpose."

"I try to play by them . . . but, you know, I'm not perfect."

"We don't require perfection. It's the desire to do the right thing that we look for. Apparently Ship saw something he liked. He must have spotted a character trait, a tendency, an indicator that told him to bring you here. Same with Hogan. Only Ship knows for sure, but my guess is he's brought both of you here for a purpose."

"I just got caught up in the fog and got blown through the trees. It was like someone called me, like that guy Hangtown got out his lasso and pulled me in. Did Hogan come the same way?"

"Not exactly. Have you ever seen Hogan concentrate, son? My heavens, it's like he gives off a radio signal all his own. Straight from his personal transmitter. You'd half-think he had a direct line to . . . Well, anyway, maybe it was Hogan who called Ship and asked for dispensation. Whatever. It doesn't really matter. He's found his way onto the range, and he's here exploring the place, trying to find out if it's suitable. For goodness' sake, son, can't you see what he's doing? He's honing an edge that's already sharp. He's—"

"He's what?"

"Well, to begin with, he's obviously taken a liking to our little place here. My word, the way Hogan's training, the sweat and blood and all, he has Old Tom convinced he's going to go through with it. He's going to tee it up again, that's what Old Tom tells me.

Hogan doesn't seem too interested in staying here. All he wants is one round, one more pass at it. Then he'll be gone, off to wherever you go when you choose that route."

"How can you be so sure?" I asked.

"You saw his hands, boy. Those old paws were bleeding like tomatoes. And you know what else? We asked him to take a room here in the clubhouse, sort of like the one we've assigned to you. He said no thank you, he'd just as soon make his way onto the range by walking through the fog."

"What's wrong with that?"

"Son, it's like being asked to dinner and saying you're not hungry. Why, we offered him a room, and he's telling us he'd rather change his shoes in the parking lot. It's like he doesn't want to have anything to do with us on a social level. Just practice, drink a little ginger ale, and show up for his tee time. That's what worries me so."

"But you don't know he's decided to do it, do you?"

"Of course not. Like I said, you're the only one Hogan's talked to."

"Why is that?"

"Probably because Ship brought you here to talk to him. Maybe Ship knows of a link between you and Hogan. Maybe Hogan senses that link. Maybe that's why he talks to you."

"So Hogan doesn't stay here in the clubhouse?"

"No," said Jones with an air of resignation. "But Lord, we tried. Offered him a room out back in the other building, where most of the sleeping quarters are. Turned us down flat. Said he didn't want anyone bothering him, that he didn't want to bother us. Just wanted to thrash some balls. Ship gave the nod, so he's here. You have the same option, son. We have a room right upstairs for you. I assume you'll stay for a few days."

"You got that right." I was not about to cut this short, not for anything. I was already wondering how I was going to explain this to my friends back home—that is, if I ever got back home.

"Good," said Jones. "We need you." He twisted his neck and looked over his shoulder at the driving range. "Hogan needs you."

"What?"

I was shaken by Jones's last comment. Me and Hogan? Not a likely twosome. I was a no-name kid, my claim to fame being my stature as fifth man on my high school golf team. He was the Hawk, the Iceman, Bantam Ben, the man who conquered Carnoustie and brought the Monster to her knees. "There's no way, is there?"

Jones winked. He knew something I didn't, but he wasn't about to reveal it, at least not yet. Jones told me I'd have to take the matter up with Ship when I met him. In the meantime, Jones said, he wanted me to talk to Hogan again and see where he stood. And Jones had a special request of me: "If Hogan's going to replay," Jones instructed me, "find out which round it's going to be." Jones said he needed to know because whatever Hogan decided to do would affect him, too.

San Francisco Express
June 17, 1955

Bolt's Red-Hot 67 Leads U.S. Open by Three

Fiery Texan Is Only Player Under Par; Unknown Inman Is Second at 70

Hogan Trails by Five

By Dick Yost

For a golfer like Tommy "Thunder" Bolt, yesterday was a surprise. He didn't throw a club. He didn't break a shaft against a tree. Instead, the man with the legendary temper did some throwing and breaking of a different kind. He threw the form book out the window and became the only player to break par during the first round of the U.S. Open at the Olympic Club.

With the golf course playing brutally hard, Bolt fired up his putter and melted par, shooting a picture perfect 67, which gave him a 3-shot lead over former Air Force pilot, Walker Inman, Jr.

Halfway into the day's play, the starting field was staggering around like battle-ravaged soldiers. Of the 162 players who teed off, more than half failed to break 80.

And they couldn't blame it on the weather. Everyone, including a gallery of almost 10,000 people, got plenty of sun. The day was fresh and clear, the air was light, and there was only a hint of breeze. It was a perfect day for scoring.

The only problem was that someone forgot to cut the rough, which looked like wild hay in places. The game's finest players were forced to execute recovery shots out of grass that was up to their knees. Even around the greens, if a player chipped without first rolling up his cuffs, he walked away with stained trousers.

Bolt not only rolled up his pants, he rolled home a wheelbarrow full of putts, too. He needed only 25 of the short strokes to negotiate the Olympic Club's 6,700-yard Lake Course. He cruised, one-putting 11 times, flashing a white-hot 32 at the field on the back nine.

Hogan On Track

Bolt may be leading, but he has a number of pursuers who will give him trouble before it's over on Saturday. Two fellow Texans are within range.

Jackie Burke, Bolt's boyish-looking friend from Houston, shot

34–37—71. He was cracking one-liners all the way around.

More important, Ben Hogan, who has won the Open 4 times already and is fighting for an unprecedented fifth championship, was parked quietly at 2-over 72.

Hogan has been in this position before, and with so much golf yet to be played, he's the man they're all watching.

Hogan himself had no comment. He played methodically, hitting to preselected spots in the fairways that opened up the approaches to the greens. His plan of attack worked to perfection—until he putted, that is. Hogan lipped out one putt after another. He took 19 putts on the front 9 alone, including 3 from 25 feet on the ninth green to turn in 37.

His only birdie of the day was the result of a putt that was too close to miss. His lightning-rod 7-iron finished a foot and a half from the hole at the twelfth. Hogan wound up taking 33 putts in all, 8 more than the leader.

After it was over, Hogan would not engage in any analysis. "My score speaks for itself," he said as he walked slowly away from the scorer's tent after signing his scorecard.

If there was a symbol of the torturous conditions, it was the seventeenth hole, a monster of a four par at 461 yards, uphill all the way. Only one man, Al Besselink, was able to birdie it. Hogan, who has played the hole 7 times—6 in practice—has yet to hit the green in regulation.

EX-CHAMPS IN TROUBLE

While Bolt was smiling as the putts were dropping and Hogan was grinding his teeth on the greens, a host of other top names were wondering if they'd survive the 36-hole cut, which will leave the top 60 players, plus anyone else within 10 strokes of the leaders, around to play the 36-hole finale on Saturday. Sam Snead virtually blew himself out of the competition with a ghastly 79. Snead is still looking for his first Open crown, and he may be forced to wait until next year. He should have plenty of company, as all the former champions except Hogan struggled with the tough conditions. Cary Middlecoff, Ed Furgol, and Julius Boros each shot 76, while Lew Worsham and Byron Nelson hobbled in with 77. Lawson Little went down in flames with 81.

Local Knowledge

Anyone who thinks knowing the course is a sure ticket to success had better think again. John Battini, who has been the head pro at the Olympic Club for 15 years and who qualified for the championship, may be giving himself some golf instruction before it's all over. He shot a horrendous 46 on the front nine. Then things got worse. An incoming 50 left him a sure bet to be watching Gene Sarazen on Saturday when the final day's play will be broadcast nationwide. Battini's 96 is one of the highest scores in modern Open history.

HOGAN HAD VANISHED. I DID NOT SEE HIM DEPART, BUT THE RANGE was deserted and there was no point in my going back outside to sit in the vacant director's chair.

But would he return? That was the question. I asked Haig what he thought, and he delivered his analysis in a way that only Hagen could. "Don't worry, junior," he said as he took a nip of the brown stuff. "The great ones always come back."

It was nearly six o'clock, and although the sun was still above the horizon, it was sinking fast. What was once a crisp blue sky was turning colors as the day faded away. Everything was gleaming and golden, painted by the twilight. The shadows grew longer by the minute, and soon they would walk across the range like a late-afternoon ground crew. Despite Haig's prediction, I concluded Hogan would not be back before nightfall.

With my stomach growling, I asked if it was possible to get something to eat. In an instant little Eddie was at my side. He handed me a menu. I gazed down at the handwritten entries; each one was more enticing than the last. No prices were listed, so I took my chances. Oysters on the half shell, filet mignon, fresh asparagus to keep me honest, and a thick slab of peach pie to top it off.

Eddie was standing by quietly, but something was wrong. The bounce was gone from his step. A closer look at his face told me he was deathly ill. He was as green as an apple.

I leaned in his direction and smelled nothing but tobacco. It was all over him, as if he'd taken a steam bath in a humidor.

"You haven't been—" I tried to inquire, but he cut me off before I could pose the question.

"Tried one a foot long. Got it off Haig. The sucker was browner than tree bark. Big fat Macanudo, thick as a German sausage. Wiped me out."

"That's an understatement, kid."

Eddie had other orders to fill besides mine, and he raised his hand to beg leave so he could get back to the kitchen. I told him to take an Alka-Seltzer to calm down his stomach.

"A what?" he asked.

"Bicarbonate . . . ah, just get something bubbly down there. I'd do it sooner rather than later, if you know what I'm talking about. It'll help you keep your insides on the inside."

"Yeah, right," he answered as he rushed off.

I was alone, but only for a moment. Before I could catch my breath, I sensed someone standing over me. It was Jones. He'd come by to talk some more. He looked at the range first, sighed, and then asked me if I'd been taken care of. I ignored the question and immediately got down to the business at hand.

"Haig says he'll be back," I informed him.

"You never know," Jones answered.

"Well, Haig said it, and he sounded pretty sure."

"Nobody around here is too sure of anything anymore."

"This Hogan thing has really thrown you guys for a loop, hasn't it?"

"More than anything I've ever seen," said Jones somberly.

"I still don't see what I can do for you," I offered, hoping Jones would provide further enlightenment.

"At least Hogan talks to you. It's a start."

For some reason Jones was confident I could turn Hogan around. His faith in my untested ability buoyed my spirits, which were already soaring in this heady atmosphere. I was calm and surprisingly relaxed in Jones's company. I could see that he was reaching out, hoping to probe deeper into my mind. I decided to return the favor.

"You're worried about Old Tom, aren't you?"

"He's such a dear friend," said Jones wistfully. "That man's been through so much. He's a stricken man now. You see, all of this is very threatening to him. I'm afraid he's just plain scared stiff."

"Why should he be afraid?" I asked. "He's a member, isn't he? With full privileges. He's a legend, for God's sake. I know what he did."

"But do you know the full story?"

"I know he won four British Opens in the 1860s. He's the game's original champion. What else is there to know?"

"Shhhhh!" Jones put his hand over my mouth as he looked desperately over his shoulder toward the library. "Don't ever call it the British Open to his face. It's the Open Championship to him, and he's particular about it, too, so be careful. Let me ask you again: Do you know the full story?"

"What do you mean?"

"When you're done with your supper, take a walk into the library. You should be able to figure it out for yourself. And if you can do that, it will have more meaning than if I just tell it to you straightaway."

"Old Tom owned that Championship Belt, didn't he?"

"I'll say he did."

"So what else is there to know?"

"He didn't own it alone. He shared it with somebody."

"Harry Vardon, right?"

Jones did not reply.

"Hagen? He won it four times, too."

More silence.

"Not Peter Thomson, for heaven's sake?"

Jones shook his head.

"Tom Watson?"

All Jones did was point his chin toward the library. "The answer's in there," he said.

I rose from my chair without saying a word.

As I left the dining room, I saw that others had settled in for a meal. There was Lema, regaling a crowd by the window with a story about his early days playing against Ken Venturi. And there were George and the Babe, smooching like teenagers. I saw a few new faces, too. Bing Crosby was singing a few smoothies at the bar, with Hagen beside him, a tad off-key. When you win eleven majors, you can do something like that and get away with it.

Crosby's voice rang in my ears as I crossed the threshold that took me from the boisterous crowd around the bar to the solitude of the library. In the eerie stillness of this room I would begin to unlock the secrets—of Old Tom, of Jones, of Hogan . . . of myself.

·7·

THE LIBRARY WAS A SIGHT TO BEHOLD. THE PANELING WAS PERSIM-mon, not redwood or mahogany, and it brought a special richness to the room, and a touch of wisdom, too. The wood seemed to hold a thousand secrets in its tight grain. Fellows such as Jones must think about what perfect clubheads could be sculpted out of this stuff.

A spiral staircase corkscrewed its way to an upper level, filled with books containing information, some of it well known, some of it obscure, but all of it relevant and somehow tied together. Every wall stretched skyward, filled with words and numbers, stories and statistics, lives, legends, and myths. The game was chronicled here: Every round, every championship, every player, everything that was golf was enshrined.

The room was a giant octagon. Stained-glass windows, spread around at every angle, depicted the moments to remember. There was Jones at Merion. Ouimet thrashing Vardon and Ray. Sarazen's double-eagle. Nelson in '45. Arnie's charge at Cherry Hills. Big Jack was all over the place, and just when I thought I'd seen it all, there he was again, winning the Masters and rejuvenating his career at age forty-six. And there was Watson, his rival, knocking it in on the seventeenth at Pebble Beach to win the U.S. Open. The room was full of history, but there were several plain windows, too, their see-through glass awaiting future glories that would be depicted in new and equally vivid mosaics.

The range may have held a fascination for me, particularly when Hogan was there, but I knew in an instant that this room was extraordinary too.

A warm fire burned in the fireplace on the first level, and when I turned back down the staircase, I spotted Old Tom sitting in a wingback chair, facing the light thrown off by the flames. Surrounded by the silence of the room, he was totally at peace. In the light of the fire I saw the gleam in his eyes; it was as if I were looking at him through a soft-focus filter, the kind photographers use to enhance portraits. Every wrinkle in Old Tom's face had disappeared, and there was not a hint of stress anywhere about him. He may have been upset with Jones earlier and he may be worried about Hogan and the future, but right now, this night, here in this hallowed sanctuary, he was a picture of contentment.

I, on the other hand, was uneasy. Jones's comments caused me to squirm in my chair. What was driving Hogan to practice with such ferocity? What was he getting ready to do? And what was the full story about Old Tom? If ever I had the tools to discover it, they were here, all around me. Clearly Jones had steered me to the right place to do my detective work.

The room was full of what can only be described as Hoganalia. Everything there was to learn about him was inscribed in the volumes that resided here. I quickly plunged into the thicket, flipping through the card catalog until I had an armful of reference citations. When I began to pore over the stories, the thorns of Hogan's life stuck out as if he were a human bramble bush.

They called him the Hawk because of his eyes. He had an unforgettable way of looking at people. He could stare right through his opponents, and he knew how to finish them off once he had them in position for the kill. They called him Bantam Ben because he was a little bit of nothing, all of five feet eight and 130-odd pounds. And when he played in Scotland, they called him the Wee Ice Mon, in tribute to his steely cold nerves under pressure.

It wasn't always that way. He was born in 1912 into a family that was as poor as dirt, and his father, a blacksmith, committed suicide with a .38 revolver ten years later. Times were hard for the family, and when he was only eleven years old, Ben Hogan started caddying to help his widowed mother and his brother and sister make ends meet. He spent his adolescence toting bags at Fort Worth's Glen Garden Country Club. He turned professional after dropping out of high school.

People who knew Ben Hogan said he had no natural talent for the game. He was not born a sweet swinger; he got where he did by learning technique, practicing it endlessly, and then applying it on the course. He never had a chance to play extensively on the amateur circuit; his family had no money for anything like that.

It gave him an invisible pedigree as a player, for there was no college or amateur record and hence no reputation trailing behind him when he set out on tour. During his early days as a professional, he barely put food on the table. At the Oakland Open in 1938, Hogan was down to his last $8; he was in contention halfway into the tournament, but then he got a jolt: In the parking lot across the street from the Leamington Hotel where he was staying, he found his well-traveled Buick, the car that had carried him from Texas to California in search of a paycheck, jacked up on cinder blocks. Someone had stolen the Iceman's tires. He was in tears, pounding his fist against the hood of the car, muttering "son of a bitch!" when he recalled the advice of his good friend Henry Picard. It was he who had imparted words that would become Hogan's guiding star: "Keep playing," Picard had told him in his darkest hour, "no matter what." Hogan did, firing a 67 the next day. Although Harry Cooper took first money, where he eagled the last hole, Hogan finished tied for sixth, putting what must have seemed a fortune in his pocket. The money, all $285 of it, got him to the next stop in Sacramento where he banked another check. He was off and running.

By the early forties Ben Hogan was making serious money playing tournament golf, and his scoring average was making his name familiar to the artisan who annually engraved the Vardon Trophy. He was winning, but the events he captured were not major championships. Hogan knew the value of the majors, and so, despite his outward success, a fire raged within; he was by now well fed, but as the forties wore on and World War II passed, he was still hungry, not for money but for greatness, and the hunger tore at his belly.

Those who watched Hogan play knew a breakthrough would come in time. He was too good for it not to happen. Sure enough, after the war ended and the tour was once again full of the old regulars, Hogan's star began to rise, the added competition pushing him to another level. As Hogan made his ascent to the top, those who saw him play could tell he was different. There was just something about him. Maybe it was the way he carried himself. Or was it the swing? Or the look in his eyes? Perhaps it was just his dogged determination to succeed. Whatever the quality, no matter how elusive its definition, one thing was certain: Hogan was unlike the others. He was more than just a name on the leaderboard. "Hogan" became a mood, a state of mind. More than one observer commented that Hogan gave off an aura when he walked the course, particularly at U.S. Open time. He was a presence out there, a presence for the ages.

Those who saw Ben Hogan play could never forget the expression on his face when he struck a shot: so fierce, so serious, so unrelenting. When Hogan hit the ball, he never took his eyes off it. He was just plain intense, a perfectionist, battling for his life with every swing.

Gene Sarazen said Hogan was "perpetually hungry." To Grantland Rice he was "as soft as a fire hydrant." To others he looked at the ground like a man watching his last dime roll away after dropping through a hole in his pocket. "Those steel-gray eyes of his," someone once remarked. "He looks at you like the landlord asking for next month's rent."

Hogan's glacial exterior chilled many a budding friendship. One time when an admiring competitor whistled after one of his long irons and offered the compliment, "Nice shot," Hogan glared. "How do you know it was nice?" he fired back. "Do you know what I was trying to do with the ball?"

Not everyone was offended by Hogan's stiff exterior. Jimmy Demaret, one of Hogan's oldest friends from Texas, talked of the Iceman's effusiveness on the course, especially during the heat of competition. Demaret couldn't understand why people thought Hogan was so distant. "When I play with him, he talks to me on every hole," said Demaret. "Why, he talks to me all the time, on every shot." What did he say? a reporter inquired. "Oh, it's always the same," replied Demaret. "He turns to me and says, 'You're away.' "

No one, not even Hogan's caddie, was immune from the treatment. Once, during the U.S. Open, Hogan turned to his looper and asked the distance between his ball and the flagstick. "Mr. Hogan," the young bag-toter answered in an uncertain voice, "by my figuring, it's either one hundred and fifty-eight or one hundred and fifty-nine yards to the hole." Hogan stared at him, saying nothing. Then he let out a sigh, lit a cigarette, and took a short walk up the fairway to survey the situation. When he returned, he fixed his eyes on the caddie and asked, "Have you made up your mind yet, son?"

By 1946, Ben Hogan appeared to be on the verge of dominance. And yet, despite his improving record, his game was still fundamentally unsteady. The problem was a wild hook. It was holding him back, subjugating his ambition to a constant inner fear that whenever he struck a tee ball it might suddenly lurch hard left, diving for cover into a briar patch from which there was no escape. Hogan knew a hook could not be trusted, and fear of moving it right to left pulsated inside him with an ominous thumping that only he could hear. People murmuring in the gallery might be a distraction, but Hogan could deal with that; he could simply tune out the whispers. But this hooking business was something altogether different. There was no escape from the ghostly thought of a low-flying duck disappearing into the rough. It was a creeping fissure, one that threatened to crack the wall of Hogan's concentration. It was always there, staring him right in the face, a horrific reflection of lurking disaster. "I hate a hook," Hogan said in one interview. "It nauseates me. I could vomit when I see one. It's like a rattlesnake in your pocket."

The only way Hogan could beat his hooking problem was to tame it through endless hours on the range, through a critical, self-analytical reconstruction of his golf game. Hogan cured his affliction and brought the hook under control not just by tinkering with a move here and there, but by changing everything. He shortened his left thumb. He weakened his grip. He flattened his backswing. And instead of taking the club back well past parallel, the Hawk learned to start down from what appeared to be a three-quarter position. He also learned how to thrash the ball with his wrists, supinating at just the right moment to prevent his lightning-quick hands from rolling over each other at impact.

At the end of 1946, Hogan was hooking so badly that he referred to himself as a desperate man. But within a year his dogged pursuit of the perfect golf swing was producing practical results. He could swing without worry, for he knew where the ball was going to go. Ben Hogan had discovered the answer to the riddle of how to hit a golf ball.

Hogan's erratic hook was transformed into a steady, repeating power fade, a shot that became his trademark. Hogan's perfection of the fade was a turning point in his career, for it brought him control, which was something he desperately sought.

He practiced the new move relentlessly during the 1947 campaign. As the 1948 season loomed, Hogan was so sure he'd conquered the mechanics of the golf swing that he confided his discovery to Johnny Revolta: "I've found it," he said. "This time I've really got it." Those were audacious words for one touring professional to speak to another, but they were true.

Armed with "the secret," Hogan began to collect major championships. Before he was done, he had nine notches on his gun, a record unrivaled by any of his contemporaries. One of Hogan's most glorious triumphs came in the 1948 U.S. Open, which was played that year at the Riviera Country Club in Los Angeles. It was only the sixth time in the fifty-three-year history of the U.S. Open that play was conducted west of the Mississippi River. The USGA's selection of a Hollywood venue was prescient, for Hogan gave the world an unforgettable show. He played with such precision that the course came to be known as Hogan's Alley. His four-round total of 276 was eight strokes under par, and it shattered all previous Open scoring records. His number stood as the standard for two decades; no one beat it until 1967 when Nicklaus shot 275 at Baltusrol. Lee Trevino matched that number at Oak Hill the following year, but those two scores were only five shots under par. Even when Nicklaus returned to Baltusrol and won the 1980 Open Championship, his score of 272, the modern record, was eight under par—the same red number as Hogan's at Riviera. No one has ever done better in the Open.

In 1949, less than a year after his win at Riviera, Hogan and his wife Valerie were driving home to Fort Worth, cruising down Highway 80 in West Texas, when a Greyhound bus, attempting to pass a six-wheel truck, crossed into their lane and crushed their sedan like a tin can, mangling Hogan's body so badly that there was great doubt he'd be able to walk again, much less swing a golf club. He was cut down just as he scaled the tallest mountain. It is impossible to imagine what misfortune like that does to a man.

Somehow, Hogan was ready to return to competition by 1950. The Open was at Merion that year, and he won it in a playoff. He won again the following year at a course called Oakland Hills, a layout so difficult that even the Hawk himself dubbed it the Monster. It would be almost forty years before anyone else would successfully defend the U.S. Open Championship.

Hogan won the Masters in 1951 and again two years later. In fact, in 1953, Ben Hogan enjoyed the finest season any professional player has ever known. Because of his physical condition he played in only six events that year. He won five of them, three of them major championships: the Masters, the U.S. Open, and the British Open. The last title was especially significant, for Hogan had never before crossed the Atlantic to play competitive golf. But he knew that if he was to be remembered as one of the game's greats, he would have to win all the major championships, and the list clearly included the British Open, which in 1953 was played at Carnoustie, a rigorous Scottish course outside Dundee. Hogan arrived early and prepared himself well; in his only appearance in golf's oldest championship, he won going away, his score improving with every round, culminating in a final round 68, a new course record. Hoisting the Claret Jug was only part of the victory, for in humbling one of Scotland's most fabled links, Hogan won the hearts and souls of the Scottish golf fans.

Hogan knew his golf history, and he surely knew the legend of Bobby Jones and the Grand Slam, but he never got his chance to duplicate it, for in 1953 the PGA Championship overlapped the British Open. The scheduling conflict left Hogan with three majors in one year and no possibility of sweeping all four.

In many respects, however, Hogan's feat demands even more respect than the Slam, if for no other reason than the fact that the Iceman did it on bad legs five years after that horrible morning on that West Texas highway. No one—not Jones, Hagen, Sarazen, Nelson, Snead, Palmer, Nicklaus, Trevino, Watson, Ballesteros, Floyd, or Faldo—ever had to overcome anything like what Bantam Ben encountered.

Hogan's 1953 was significant for another reason, although no one realized it at the time. The win at Carnoustie was his final triumph in a major championship. Although Hogan would come close again, his name had been etched for the last time on golf's four most prestigious trophies. Hogan did not know that, of course. He kept playing, kept searching for more glory to add to his already miraculous résumé. Naturally, he continued to compete in his favorite major, the U.S. Open.

In 1955 he came to San Francisco to compete in the Open at the

Olympic Club. He played heroically, and as he sat in the locker room after completing seventy-two holes, the television commentators proclaimed him the winner. No one worth mentioning was even close. It was the first time anyone had won the Open five times. Even Jones hadn't done that.

The only man who had a chance to catch Hogan was an unknown driving range pro from Duck Creek, Iowa, named Jack Fleck. With Hogan sitting across from the showers, Fleck was still on the course at the fifteenth hole; he needed two birdies in the final four holes to force a playoff. He got them, the second coming as he holed a sidehill seven-footer on the final green. As Fleck approached his second shot on the eighteenth hole, Hogan was informed where matters stood. He was so tired, his legs so wasted from the strain of walking thirty-six holes on Open Saturday when the final two rounds were played in one day, that even Hogan knew he would not be able to summon his best if a playoff were necessary. "I hope he makes two or four," he said, hoping it would end right then and there.

Of course it didn't. Fleck caught Hogan at 287, and the next day he was in control the whole way, winning the playoff by three shots. It was one of the game's greatest upsets. Hogan saw a fifth Open Championship slip through his fingers. He never got that close again.

How did Hogan's frustration relate to Old Tom Morris? While the Hawk was on the range shredding his hands, Old Tom sat quietly in the library, just fifteen feet away from me. He was in a fragile state, and with him sitting in peace, I decided it would not be wise to engage him in a discussion of the past. Instead, I returned to the card catalog, which contained a treasure trove of lore about the British, I mean, the Open Championship. Within minutes I located several old Scottish volumes. They were chock-full of articles written in the 1870s. There were several pieces about Old Tom, who by that time was a hero to his people and a legend of the game. A series of old engravings and a few faded photographs accompanied the text.

The books were in good shape, but they were as musty as all get out. When the dust caused me to sneeze, Old Tom turned around and cast a disapproving glance my way. I gave him a respectful look, which I hoped would stand as an apology. He shifted in his chair and once again faced the warmth of the fire.

I could take the hint. I left him to the logs of black oak and walnut, alive with heat, crackling and flaming in the fireplace. As for me, there was the matter of research and the exploration of an unknown path, one that I knew I must traverse. I took the first steps by delving into the books I had selected. I read about Old Tom in his youth when he was under the tutelage of Allan Robertson, one of the early golfing legends to come from St. Andrews and the Old Course. Robertson dominated play at St. Andrews in the 1840s and at the same time ran one of the best-known golf equipment shops in Scotland. Old Tom's main work then was as a ballmaker. Between 1840 and 1842, under Robertson's watchful eye, the shop turned out something on the order of five thousand balls, each one a "featherie," made of a stout leather casing, usually bull's hide, stuffed tightly with feathers taken from local farmyard poultry. Once the casing was filled, it was cured with alum, sometimes with brine, and then stitched as tight as human hands would allow. The entire process was extraordinarily difficult work, and the end products were as hard as rocks. They could be driven great distances, but they were hardly perfect spheroids. They were loosely round, and each was somewhat unique, given the handcrafting that produced them. The flight pattern must have been something to see. I can only imagine the difficulty a player must have encountered when attempting to hole out one of those buggers! Imperfect as featheries might have been, they were all folks had back in those days, and the game flourished as long as dedicated ballmakers like Old Tom turned them out. A productive workman could spin out four good ones in a day. But the slow production was an obvious impediment to the spread of the game, for without ammunition to fire, the budding army of golfers was kept to the size of a small regiment.

As much as anyone of his time, Old Tom knew the sensations of a golfer. He knew all there was to know about touch and feel, and he knew an effective way to communicate his wisdom to others. The books I located were full of descriptions, many of them invented by Old Tom himself, that he used to teach how it felt to play the game with the right implements. One example I found was particularly enchanting. It told of the right feel of a wooden club. "He always likes," it said of Old Tom, "a club with the right amount of life in it, what he himself calls the proper note of 'music.' " One of the great golf instruction writers, Horace G. Hutchinson, elaborated on Old Tom's concept: "A fine steely spring is what the golfer wants to feel, a spring that will bring the club back, quick as thought, to the straight. Then it feels in his hands like a living thing, full of energy, of controlled obedient energy—to do his service." Old Tom often said that when the club feels that way in a player's hands, it is, in every respect, full of music.

By 1849, Old Tom and Robertson were doing much more than making clubs and balls: They were playing in foursomes against the best players in the land. Their most famous matches were against the Dunn brothers, usually contested over the links at St. Andrews, Musselburgh, and North Berwick.

In 1851, Old Tom Morris left St. Andrews for the only time in his life. He spent twelve years working at Prestwick, which in 1860 became the inaugural site of the (British) Open Championship. It was a delightful residence, as one writer described it. Old Tom's reputation grew as a ball and club maker. He also attended to the links, caring for the ground as though it were a member of his family. People came from the surrounding countryside, trekking to Ayrshire to see the "fine grounds" he had prepared for play. He started a family there, and it was the birth of his son Tommy that gave him the appellation Old Tom.

Although ensconced for the time being on the west coast of Scotland, Old Tom did, on occasion, return to the Old Course. Indeed, he returned often to display the considerable playing skills he had honed as a top-flight professional. In 1853, for example, he did battle against his mentor Robertson, thrashing him soundly. By the mid-fifties Old Tom's reputation had grown so considerably that he was becoming known as the King of Golfers, the Lord of the Links.

Despite his success at Prestwick and the admiration and esteem the townspeople there held for him, Old Tom yearned to return permanently to his original home. It was thus with great joy that he returned to Fife in 1863 to take charge of the Old Course at the invitation of the Royal and Ancient Golf Club. His duties were spelled out with particularity. The minutes of the club describe them thusly: "to keep the putting-greens in good order, to repair when necessary, and to make the holes." When required to do what was called "heavy work," Old Tom was granted assistance in the form of one man's labor for two days in the week, and it was understood that he was to work under the supervision of the Green Committee.

A form of reverse déjà vu came over me as I read that last passage. I thought of greenkeepers and course superintendents at modern-day clubs, struggling to please the chairman of the Greens and Grounds Committee. Some things never change.

Old Tom's true love was not horticulture but playing the game. He was a professional, after all, and he played for money whenever and wherever the opportunity presented itself. And the sums were substantial, at least by the standards of the day. It was not unheard of for a man of Old Tom's stature to play for over £100 per match.

As I pored over the books, I gave close scrutiny to the many illustrations, particularly the photographs. They were fascinating, and their clarity was remarkable for images that old. I let the faces burn into my brain, sensing somehow that I was supposed to know these people. Then I came upon the tale of another member of the Morris family, a talented player who by the age of twenty was known throughout the kingdom of golf as Young Tom.

They were the greatest father-son combination the game had

ever seen. By 1872, Young and Old Tom Morris had each won the Open Championship four times. It was eight championships in twelve years—not bad for one family and simply incredible for a father and a son. Old Tom continued to play in the Open Championship until he was well into his seventies, a feat that would be impossible today. Young Tom's name vanished from the record books after 1875. But why? I knew I was on the cusp of the answer. I thumbed frantically through the books, looking for something written in the mid-1870s.

The story, the full story as Jones described it, is sad and tragic, and there is no easy way to recount it. On Saturday, September 4, 1875, Old Tom and Young Tom were playing a match at North Berwick, just south of Edinburgh, against their rivals of the day, Willie and Mungo Park. It was an extraordinary foursome; not only were these the best-known golfers in the world, but between 1861 and 1875, when the Open was contested fifteen times, these four players won thirteen championships among them. The Morrises had eight, as noted; Willie Park, who won the inaugural championship at Prestwick, had won it three more times by 1875, and his brother Mungo had also etched his name into the history books, winning in 1873.

The match between the Morris and Park clans was a nail-biter of the first order, a contest filled with drama and uncertainty. It attracted a massive throng of interested spectators who bet feverishly on the outcome. The competition was in the usual format of the day: alternate shot. If Old Tom "foozled" one into the gorse and whins, Young Tom had to play the recovery.

The Morrises finally prevailed, but only by the narrow margin of a single hole. At that point one could easily say all was right in the world; Old Tom was reigning supreme as the Master of St. Andrews, and Young Tom, still in the early stages of his professional career, had already far eclipsed his father's prodigious talent. He had vied for the Championship Belt as soon as he was able, winning his first Open at the ripe old age of eighteen. Then he followed the initial triumph with two more victories in succession.

He retired the belt, the stipulation being that if a man won it "thrice in succession" it would become his property forever. With Young Tom's retirement of the belt, the Open was suspended for a year while the organizers sought a new trophy worthy of their champion. They settled on a Claret Jug, which is still in use today over a hundred years later. It cannot be retired. It continues to be passed on each year to the new champion.

Although the badge of victory changed in 1872, the victor did not; Young Tom captured the Open Championship for the fourth time in a row that year, and as his fame continued to grow, his latest prize, the Claret Jug, sat next to the Championship Belt, both trophies resting prominently atop his mantel. He was hailed far and wide as the greatest player who ever lived, the Champion Golfer, the King of Golf. Little could his father have guessed that Young Tom's reign would be such a short one.

The books described what happened in elaborate, chilling detail. Before leaving St. Andrews on September 2 to make the journey to North Berwick to face the Park brothers, Young Tom devotedly kissed his bride and gave her a warm embrace. He had been married only a year, and he was deeply in love. She was, as one account described, "a remarkably handsome and healthy young woman; most lovable in every way." She was carrying Young Tom's first child. On Saturday, September 4, while battling it out against his rivals, Young Tom expected to became a father at any moment.

As the Morrises and the Parks were leaving the final green, a runner approached Old Tom and delivered a telegram advising that Young Tom's wife was desperately ill in childbirth. Old Tom said nothing of it to his son; he simply instructed him that they were obliged to depart at once. For all Young Tom knew, he was going home to hold a son or daughter in his arms.

Father and son bolted from the course and made swift use of a fine yacht that was placed at their disposal. They completely bypassed a wearying rail journey through Edinburgh, sailing instead directly across the Firth of Forth to St. Andrews. Upon docking, the two of them walked through the streets of the town, hurrying toward home. It was during that walk that Old Tom broke the news to his son. By the time they reached the house, all was lost. Young Tom's wife lay dead, and next to her was a stillborn baby. And with that, the lives of Young Tom Morris and his loving father changed forever.

There is no way to recapture the melancholy of the scene. The best I can do is to read what I pulled off the library shelf. A friend wrote: "I was in the house when they arrived. What can one say in such an hour? I will never forget the poor young man's stony look—stricken was not the word—and how, all of a sudden, he started up and cried, 'It's not true!' I have seen many sorrowful things, but not like that Saturday night."

It was a crushing blow, one that would fell many a man, and it did just that to Young Tom. "He lived as if in some trance—all his lighthearted buoyancy gone." He tried to play on, but it was evident to all who watched him that his soul was not in the game. He played several exhibitions, and in one last blaze of glory he even ventured out into the snow to play a man known as Colonel Molesworth who had issued a challenge that he could defeat any professional. From what I read, Molesworth was one of the craftiest and most feared bettors in the kingdom. Young Tom was talked into the match, and the game was on in late November and early December 1875.

In all my young life I had never read of golf like this. It was a thrashing, pure and simple. Young Tom put old Colonel Molesworth in his place, besting him six rounds out of six. The margin was a whopping fifty-one strokes. The number looms even larger considering Young Tom had to gift Molesworth thirty-six "handicap" strokes.

But the match did not end there. They played on for three more days, through snow and frost. Local writers described the weather in terms that would make Vince Lombardi and his Green Bay Packers proud. "So thick was the snow on the links," one account relates, "that the umpire thought the match should be postponed. But to this Mr. Molesworth would not agree, and, accordingly, the greens were swept." All the sweeping in the world could not change the result. They played six more rounds, and Young Tom delivered six more thrashings to his opponent. It must be said that Colonel Molesworth did a bit better this time around: He lost by only forty-five strokes.

Later the same year—on Christmas Eve, in fact—Young Tom retired to bed after dinner and never woke up. Some say he died of too much liquor, but those who knew him best said it was a broken heart that cut him down.

A flood of tears came to my eyes as I retraced Young Tom's footsteps from the confrontation with Molesworth to his deathbed:

> Especially during the last three days' play the conditions of the weather were adverse to scoring. But, besides this, it was evident to all that Tommy was in no condition to play a great match. His play lacked all its old characteristics of spirit and determination. His heart was not in the game. It was, indeed, not very far away—in the snow-clad grave in the old cathedral churchyard, where his wife and baby had been so lately laid. During the progress of the match he repeatedly said to his friend, Mr. Denham, that but for the interest of his friends and backers he would not have continued it.
>
> After the match was over, he continued to be seen on the links and in his old haunts, looking ill and depressed. Then he went home for a few days. He returned for the Christmas week. On Christmas Eve he supped with a private party of a few friends. Returning home about eleven o'clock, he conversed with his mother, who was by this time an invalid, for a little while, and then retired to rest, bidding his father Goodnight as he went to his room. He did not appear at the usual hour for breakfast, and on his being called, there was no response. When they entered his room to see what was the matter, he was found lying as if asleep, but alas! it was the sleep of death. Examination proved that his death had been caused by the bursting of an artery in the right lung.
>
> The news spread like wildfire over the links and in the city. Consternation prevailed everywhere. Christmas greetings were checked on the lips by the question, "Have you heard the news? Young Tommy is dead!" or the whispered "It can't be true, is it, that Tommy was found dead in bed this morning?" Everywhere there was genuine grief for so great a loss—

the loss of one who had been the joy and pride of the whole golfing world; everywhere the sympathy with the bereaved father and mother was keen and great. The telegraph conveyed the news to the evening papers, and next morning to some of us among our belated Christmas cards and greetings came this:

OBITUARY NOTICE
THOMAS MORRIS, JUN.

DIED HERE THIS MORNING AT TEN O'CLOCK.

He was only twenty-four years old.

Old Tom played on, but he was never the same. The loss of a son like Young Tom was too great for any individual to bear, and when one considers what the two of them had achieved in such a short time, it's easy to see why the intensity and fervor were gone from Old Tom's game.

I paused a moment, contemplating what had happened to Old Tom and Young Tom. Then suddenly, out of nowhere, something tugged at me and caused me to look in the direction of the fireplace. I saw Old Tom standing alone, tending to the fire, stoking the embers. He threw on another log to rejuvenate the fire, and as he dusted off his hands, he looked back to me.

He was the same Old Tom, but something had happened. No longer was there a soft-focus filter between him and me. His image was sharp and clean. It was vibrant with color, the redness in his cheeks reflecting the embers, his white beard somehow turned golden in the glow of the fire. He paused to exhale. It was not the pant of an exhausted runner but a breath of apprehension. He was gazing away from me now, peering worriedly into another large but vacant wingback chair that adjoined his, facing the fireplace.

His eyes had a look of fear, of anticipation, as though he expected some untoward event to occur. He continued to sit alone, and the only thing he transmitted to me was despair. Despair that I won't be able to deal with Hogan? Or was he still bearing, even here, a father's grief?

Old Tom sighed again, and I needed no words to tell me what he was thinking. He was convinced that Hogan would ruin everything, that something would go wrong when the Hawk re-teed with Fleck. He feared what Jones and I had discussed earlier that afternoon, that Hogan would alter the course of events and cause everyone's dreams, not to mention the entire Club itself, to vanish. If anyone here knew how fate could turn even the purest happiness to the deepest sorrow, it was Old Tom Morris.

I could see that there was nothing more I could do in there, so I decided to make a quiet exit. As soon as I found Jones I told him what I had learned about the Morris family. He slapped me on the back, said something about good work, but I didn't have time for that. Something was happening out on the range. I heard noises, and I saw an image. Even though the sky was dark, the balls were flying once more. I looked toward the window. Hogan was back! Except this time he was under the glow of a full moon, his white golf shirt and pleated slacks iridescent in the moonlight. The shaft on his five-iron radiated and sparkled at the moment of impact. He was at it again. The balls looked like light bulbs on a scoreboard, and they streaked like tracers once they were hit. What fireworks! The whole range was crackling and popping like the Fourth of July, as if someone had decided to unleash a full arsenal of pyrotechnics. Flashbulbs of light bloomed like wildflowers in the sky. The air was an exploding spectrum of red, green, blue, silver, and golden embers, giving life to the fertile darkness that hovered over the range. Hogan stood alone at the center of the action, putting on a gala performance at midnight for our benefit.

I shot from my seat as if the gun had gone off for the hundred-yard dash. I bolted straight for the director's chair, torn between the urge to watch Hogan up close and the desire to keep talking with Jones. I was sure Jones would be there again; Hogan was quite another story.

IN MID-FLIGHT, TEARING OUT OF THE CLUBHOUSE TO REVISIT THE Hawk, my conscience got the better of me. I stopped at the door and turned back to Jones, worried that I had insulted him with my desertion. I at least owed him a question, and there was one nagging at me now. There was something I needed to know, something to bring me full circle before I faced Hogan. Jones held the key, and it was to him that I turned.

"I know about all these other folks and the moments they've chosen, but what about you?"

"What do you think?" he asked.

Darn! What a time for him to start asking me questions again.

"The Grand Slam?" I inquired.

Jones shook his head, then laughed to himself.

"You're kidding," I said. "You mean to say you wouldn't want to be there, closing out Homans at Merion and having all those fans grab you and carry you off on their shoulders?"

"Oh, it was a great time," observed Jones, "but it didn't linger."

I looked at him with amazement. The Grand Slam didn't linger?

"You don't understand what all that did to me," he explained.

"It was the hardest part of my life. The pressure was indescribable, and it never let up. The competition drained me dry. And the expectations! Do you have any idea? They all expected so much from me, and I was so committed to achieving it, that, well, it just like . . . ground me up. Chewed at my insides. Cut me to bits. I couldn't eat. Couldn't sleep. Didn't sleep. I had to shut the door on everything, everything but golf. Do you know what that does to a man? Do you know what it can do to his family, to his friends? It narrows your vision—and it narrows your life."

"You sound as if you wish it hadn't happened."

"Not at all. I'll take my immortality, don't get me wrong. It's just that there's a steep price to pay for all those trophies. Major championships don't come cheap. The adoration, the fame, the greatness, if you call it that, it all costs something, and I wasn't willing to continue paying the price after Merion. I was content to return to my family, to my career, to my life. It was like going out in the afternoon and playing nine great holes and then packing it in when you realize it's time for dinner. A lot of fellows would stay out there, firing away, trying to shave another stroke off old man par. Not me. I just went on home, and never looked back. Never worried about where I'd been or what I'd missed or what I would have shot if I'd kept on competing. I hung up my record along with my clubs. I kept playing, of course, but only for casual enjoyment."

"You weren't happy with the Slam?"

"*Relieved* is a better word. By the time 1930 rolled around, I had enjoyed so much success that if I didn't win, they wrote about how I blew it. They couldn't fathom that maybe, just maybe, there was a pretty darned talented player who whipped the pants off me. Now you take Johnny Goodman. That old boy just plain tore me up in the '29 Amateur Championship, knocked me out in the first round. The sports writers—most of them, I should say—wrote about how something was wrong with my game. That was true to a certain extent, but really the only thing wrong with me was Goodman. He was better than I was that day, and he deserved to win. It was that simple. And I wished that once they could've writ-

ten it that way. Shoot, Goodman was a legitimate player in his own
right. That boy won the Amateur and the U.S. Open before he was
through. Darned if he wasn't the last amateur to take the Open.
Did it in '33 at North Shore outside of Chicago."

"So what did you choose?"

"Can't you figure it out?"

Another question, for which I had no answer. My guess about
the Slam had put me one down, but I played on, hoping to get hot
somewhere along the line.

"The British Open in '26? The shot out of the bunker to beat Al
Watrous?" It was a bit obscure, I knew, but I hoped the inquiry
would impress Jones with my knowledge of his deeds.

"No." That's all I got, just one word. Two down.

"How about the day you won for the first time at St. Andrews?"
He shook his head. Three down.

"Your first club championship at East Lake?" I was clearly
stretching at this point, but when you're this far behind, you tend
to start pressing.

Jones put his fingers to his chin. He thought back to his youth,
then laughed. "Not even close," he said with a grin. Four down.

"I know," I said, springing to life. "When you first set foot on
the nursery property that became the Augusta National? Right?
How about watching the Masters come into its own as a major
championship? Oh . . . oh . . . I know! When you returned to St.
Andrews in 1958, and they made you an honorary burgess of the
borough? That has to be it."

I was really getting desperate, for I had just fired off three inquiries at once.

They were all misses, but I must have been close, for the series of
questions, fired like darts, prompted Jones to straighten his back.

"Augusta was, and still is, a special memory for me," Jones responded. "My trip back to St. Andrews in '58 was wonderful, too,
but I was in so much pain that night, what with my ailment and
all, that it sits better as a memory than it did in real life. You know,
I wish I could have walked up there to receive that honor and then

walked out among the townspeople. It was a powerful and fulfilling moment, one you wait a lifetime to experience, but they had to push me in there in a blasted wheelchair, and then they pulled me out in the darned contraption when it was over. My heart was full that night, but I was not my real self. I was only a shadow of what I once was. Oh, what I would have given to have walked in there the way I walked through the Valley of Sin!"

A beautiful, rich sadness came over him. The mere memory of the Old Course and the town around it touched him deeply. He looked up at the ceiling, perhaps hoping I would not see the water welling up in his eyes. But I did see it, and my eyes teared up, too.

"What a town that is!" Jones exclaimed, regaining his composure. "And those people! Their friendship is what makes St. Andrews my favorite place on the Earth."

I felt as though I knew a bit about Jones now, and I sensed he was dropping hints my way. After all, I was seven down with the questions, so what harm could I do? He was always known as a gracious champion, and perhaps he had decided to let me lose this battle of wits with dignity.

"There's something about that place, isn't there?"

"You bet there is," he said. The tears were coming back, and this time he let them flow. He spoke with great hesitation, and his voice quivered as the words tumbled off his lips. "It's hard . . . for me to talk about such a place . . . without feeling . . . a . . . a great deal of emotion. Part of me . . . is buried under those fairways . . . and part of me rests . . . in the hearts of the townspeople."

"So when was your moment?" I asked politely, hoping he would keep talking.

"Six years into retirement."

"Six years into retirement?"

"That's what made it so special."

"That's what made *what* so special? Tell me."

"Not now," Jones whispered as he shook his head. "You have some work left to do tonight. Hogan won't be out there much longer."

Oh my God! I'd totally lost track of the time. It was nearly twelve-thirty in the morning, and Bantam Ben was still swinging away. He somehow reminded me of John Henry, his hammer ringing as he pounded away at a mountain that would soon consume him. The range was crackling as the shots cut through the darkness. Smoke was everywhere. The sky was still on fire.

Jones put his hands on my shoulders and gave me a gentle push in Hogan's direction. I told Jones I'd be back later as I streaked a beeline for the director's chair.

Jones walked slowly upstairs to the members' lounge, which was above the library and overlooked the range. The entire membership was assembled there, with noses pressed against the bay window—even little Eddie, who was still awake despite the fact that it was long past his bedtime. He perched atop a chair so, like the others, he could see what was going on.

All eyes were on Hogan. The sparks were really flying, and perspiration cascaded off Bantam Ben's face. But he didn't stop, not even to wipe himself dry. He kept on firing, rat-a-tat-tat, until all the balls were up and away. Then he gathered his things and walked slowly over to where I was sitting. When he said good night, I asked him how he was feeling. There were no words; he simply nodded. I told him Jones and the folks at the window had asked me about 1955 and Olympic. He acknowledged the comment with a subtle grin but said nothing. He started to walk away, heading off for the night, when suddenly he turned around and spoke. "They're worried about me, aren't they?"

This time it was I who nodded. "What do you want me to tell them?" I asked dispassionately. Hogan is not a man to plead with. I would ask only once, and I did my best to ask the question in a calm voice so that Hogan would not detect how desperately I sought his reply.

"Tell them to read my message," he said, choosing his words with care.

"Your message?" I asked.

Hogan said nothing more, but he stopped and pulled out his

shirttail. He reached behind himself and unlaced the corset that protected his back. Then he rolled up a pant leg so he could take off the brace that guarded his right knee. He swallowed two aspirin tablets, stowed his gear away, and grabbed his satchel. As he turned to leave, he slung his five-iron over his shoulder.

"Where is it?" I asked in a slow, serious tone. "And when will we see it?"

"You'll know it when you see it."

Hogan limped slowly toward the trees. For the first time he looked tired, which was understandable considering that he had been out here for over an hour drilling balls as only he can. But he was done now, and he departed as quietly as he had come. The Hawk is a man who lets his clubs make the noise. They make his statement for him; they play his music; they beat his tattoo into the wind.

Hogan's message. Where was it? Where could it possibly be? Had he dragged his club through one of the practice bunkers, leaving a word or a string of words in the sand? I couldn't find anything.

Did he leave me a note? There was no paper anywhere out here.

How, then, had he done it? And what was he trying to tell us?

A distant glow caught my eye as Hogan faded from view. It wasn't the moon, which had slipped under a cloud cover. In the inky darkness the balls Hogan had hit with such ferocity glowed like hot coals embedded in the upslope of the range 180 yards distant.

Off in the distance, a full five-iron away, I could see that Hogan had hit his shots with remarkable precision. The balls were in little circles; to the right they seemed to be in a pattern that wrapped around itself. A curlycue? No, it couldn't be.

In the middle of the range were even more of his shots, pulsating with light in the shape of two circles, a smaller one on top of a larger one.

It was only when I looked to the far left that it hit me. I began to detect a readable pattern. Hogan must have started with the left side of the range, for the balls over there were hit into a tighter group than the others. They radiated in the darkness. The shape was familiar: the number two. No question about it.

It took a few more moments for the full image to coalesce for me. When I realized what he'd done, I knew he had sent word as only he knew how. Hogan, the perfectionist, had written an unmistakable message with his five-iron. There was the number two, on the left; that much was easy. But I was wrong about the middle cluster of balls. A closer look told me that Hogan had not crafted a snowman out there; he had drawn an eight. And there could be no other interpretation of the curlycue to the far right: It was a six.

Two eighty-six. I had done my research, and I knew what it meant. I spun around to find Jones. He knew, too. So did Haig. And Old Tom. Oh my God! Old Tom saw it. He was throwing a fit, bouncing up and down like popcorn popping. Little Eddie was tugging at Haig's apron, begging for someone to explain it to him. He must not have known about 1955 when Fleck and Hogan tied at 287. This time, Hogan obviously had vowed to himself, there would be no playoff.

•9•

To say that I lost all track of time and space is an under-statement. I did not know the hour or the day of the week or even the year. My only markers were the faces I saw. In them I could read more than any timepiece could possibly tell me. To some of these people, folks such as Haig and little Eddie, the precision of a Rolex was irrelevant, because for them it was eternally springtime, and that was all they needed to know.

But even for them there was reason to pause. It has been known to rain in April—yes, even in the middle of springtime—and Hogan's looming shadow was to the Club what thunderheads are to the sun that hangs over Augusta. In a matter of moments the light can be blocked, a blue sky can fade into an ominous shade of gray, and a day's triumphant achievements can be washed away in a torrent of raindrops. I could sense just such a weather front building now, and it scared the living daylights out of me.

Fortunately, my fears were soon replaced by another sensation, that of total exhaustion. The day's events, going all the way back to that three-wood toe job that brought me here in the first place, had taken their toll. I was completely whipped, and all I could think of was sleep.

But my imagination was stronger than my body, and it continued to run riot, forcing me to look, search, and seek a cure for the fears that were beginning to drown me. The effort caused me to fight the impulse to close my eyes, and I flailed hopelessly against a force that was rapidly overtaking my every muscle. I sparred with slumber, struggling valiantly to stay awake—to think, to pray, to hope, to discover what I had been brought here to find. But with all I had seen and learned during this first fateful day, I could only telegraph my punches. I was out cold in no time at all.

My sleep was deep and peaceful, at least in the beginning. The dreams were rich. The images were at once vivid and real, and I saw them in technicolor. Almost as soon as my eyelids fell, I became convinced that I was dead . . . and I was not at all worried if that were true, for if it was death that had brought me to this threshold, it can't be all that bad. I longed for family and friends, and perhaps for one heroic season when the hard-luck eleven from my alma mater, the California Golden Bears, those Chicago Cubs of college football, would turn back the clock to 1920 and the wondrous era of Andy Smith. No . . . No way! . . . a smidgen of reason left inside me said that would never happen in my lifetime, but then again maybe, just maybe, this wasn't my lifetime anymore. Maybe here, in the rarefied atmosphere of . . . of . . . wherever in heaven's name I was, the miracles of which I dreamed could and would come true. . . .

I see a long tunnel, with light glowing at the other end. No, that's too simple, too ordinary; I force my subconscious mind to conjure up something more creative. Instantly I see and smell brown loamy soil. It's only dirt, but it's so . . . so rich. I hear the sound of people, lots of people, from above, and I crane my neck, straining as if all I have to do is get out of a deep leather chair in order to see where I am. But I smell loam, not leather. I'm buried somewhere, under the surface, pushing up daisies; now I know I'm a dead pigeon for sure, but where have they buried me? The footsteps come rumbling. People are yelling in a frenzy.

Pow! The ground above me explodes as though someone just stepped on a land mine. A huge chunk of turf sails away, cutting a window for me to see through. What a divot!

I am alert to all that is on top of me. The first thing I see through my porthole is a little boy holding a standard that says three under after three. The sign atop the standard says it's 1960. It's the Open. It's Cherry Hills. I'm watching the charge of charges—from under the fairway! I've just seen Arnie take a swipe at one of those six front-nine birdies that catapulted him from seven shots back into the thick of the chase.

At this juncture he's only en route. The King is on his way, but he has a long march ahead before he reaches the throne. I know how this journey ends, but the crowd standing over me, surrounding me and Palmer, doesn't know exactly where the coronation march is headed or if it will ever reach the castle. At this point in the Open, the King is still trailing Mike Souchak. Hogan is on their heels, and so is a young amateur they're calling Ohio Fats. Hogan will fade and so will young Jack Nicklaus, but Arnie will keep on marching today and for several years to come.

Palmer was 135 yards from the green when I heard the explosion. Up in these Rockies, he must have hit a nine-iron or a wedge, something like that. Man, does he have power! He dug the ball out of the grass like a human steam shovel, unearthing a slab of sod larger than some counties, lifting it skyward with his follow through, firing the ball at the flagstick with the keen eye of a gunfighter who knows he can hit anything he aims at.

Instinct driven by adrenaline takes over, and I shout through the gaping hole, through the personal bay window that Palmer carved for me. I yell at the top of my lungs: "Go get 'em, Arnie!" But Arnie can't hear me. The exhortation echoes in my secret chamber beneath the fairway. Then, just as fast as the porthole was opened, it is slammed shut. I am thwarted by Palmer's caddie. Everything goes dark again as the King's looper replaces the divot.

My slumber-shrouded mind will not rest. It races off to another fateful encounter. Without bearings I cannot place the venue, but I feel as flat as a pancake. I'm stretched thin. Stiff as a board. So stiff, in fact, that I can barely breathe, but I guess that's the way it is when you're only a tablecloth. Is this some sort of dining room? No, it can't be, there's too much noise. But wait—the arm bands! They're my first clue. The USGA's blazered battalion is here. I strain to look about, but the fact that I've been reduced to the thickness of barely one-sixteenth of an inch inhibits how I move and what I can see. There is white everywhere—it's blinding—and people are scurrying in and out.

Off in the distance I hear intermittent roars of applause. The noise is totally irregular, there is no rhythm to it, but when it happens, when the sound travels and echoes, it grabs your attention. What's all the ruckus?

Ouch! That hurts! Get that needle out of me! You think I'm a pincushion?

I force my mind to analyze the data, and the pieces come together slowly. I hear numbers being recited, all in voices that belong to women. From my angle I see . . . Oops! I'm blocked out by something. A piece of paper, a postcard, or at least something that looks like that, covers me. Ouch! There it is again! Take that needle out of my belly, will you? Good heavens, this is painful!

Now the piece of paper moves, and I can see one of those USGA officials up close. Stern-looking son of a gun. He's collecting the pieces of paper after the ladies sign them. They're not postcards at all; they're scorecards, that's what they are. And those darn needles are not needles at all, just sharp, prickly pencils, drummed into me by women golfers who are fidgeting nervously as they busily check their—Saaaay! I'm part of the scoring tent. But where? When?

The answer is right in front of me. She is short and plump, and she is sitting down to review her round. I can hear people nearby offering congratulations. Someone says she shot 72. Her four-round total is 298. It's hers, all hers, they say. She has beaten everyone, even Betsy Rawls, who beat her in that playoff back in '53 at Rochester. It's different now. The trophy belongs to her, and on this day the best Rawls will do is finish second, a shot back.

Almost out of nowhere I spy a napkin on the table, embossed with a monogram or logo or something like that. A wing and a— yes! That's it. Winged Foot. The women. The USGA. The Open. It must be 1957.

Suddenly, as if someone has thrown water on the coals in a sauna, the heat swells and rises. I feel it. My body throbs, and my heart is beating so intensely, it feels as if it is outside my chest. I am gripped with tension because I know what is about to happen. A startling, unbelievable tragedy is set to occur right on top of me.

"Nooooo!" I cry out in futility. "Don't sign it! Don't sign it!" She obviously cannot hear me, and that makes it all the more frustrating. How do I stop her? Can I stop her? I don't know, and the uncertainty causes me to panic. Raising my voice as high as it will go seems like the ticket. It had better be, for it is all I can think of. I fire commands in her direction like machine-gun bullets: "Check the score, Jackie! . . . Remember the shots, remember them all! . . . For crying out loud, remember the blasted fourth hole, will you? . . . Don't listen to all of those backslappers; for God's sake— *focus your eyes!*"

My thoughts flash over to Hogan for a moment, but I shake loose. I can't leave the table, not now. I have work to do, at least that's what everything indicates to me. Yet I continue to question the surroundings: Is this still a dream, or have I been transported again and handed a new assignment?

I don't know. I may never know, I tell myself, and if I have to act, well, I'll do it based on a leap of faith. I force myself to assume this is reality, not fluff. A playoff with Rawls? Not this time. No, sir. This time she's won it! Her weeping fifteen-year-old daughter Barnette embraced her after she putted out on the seventy-second hole. She's so excited, so ecstatic.

Alas, that will be her undoing. Too caught up in the emotion of the moment, she succumbs. The euphoria of victory renders her

powerless to recall the details of her round. Watching this is unbearable! Checking a card is so simple! She's done it a thousand
times before without incident. What's to worry? she tells herself as
her eyes float over the numbers, numbers she looks at but doesn't
see. All she thinks about is that calligrapher inking her name onto
the pages of history. United States Women's Open Champion. This
is her moment, and she will bask in it for the nation, for golf, for
herself. She's part of the record book now, and she'll leave the
bookkeeping and her fate in the hands of her trusted marker, the
woman who accompanied her throughout the final round. She
blindly accepts the scorecard that was prepared by fellow touring
professional Betty Jameson.

But Jameson has made an awful mistake, one that will cost her
fellow competitor dearly. Oh, it will put her in the record book all
right, but not at all in the way anyone could have imagined. Jameson has written down a five for her on the fourth when she really
took six.

"Nooooo!" I cry out again, every thread of me quivering, hoping to slide the card away from her hand. But I cannot succeed. She
signs on the line marked "Competitor." Even though her total
score actually was 298, good enough for a one-shot victory, Jackie
Pung has signed a card that inadvertently gives her 297. Either
score is a winner, and everybody who was there knows she did
win, but when a player signs a card and verifies a score lower than
what she actually shot, the penalty is swift and sure.

In an instant the great Hawaiian-born player from San Francisco
goes from winner to loser. The record book will show Betsy Rawls
the champion at 299, with Patty Berg a distant second at 305. All
Jackie Pung gets is three rounds and a word. When bookworms
like me peruse the record book, all we see is a 78, followed by a 75
and a 72, and then "DISQUALIFIED." In the eyes of the record book,
Jackie Pung never even completed seventy-two holes.

"Aggggh!" I cry out in anguish, wrinkled and wet—I don't
know if it is my sweat or Jackie's tears—and one of those stone-
faced arm bands abruptly pats me back down into place. Not so

hard! I complain as he beats on me like a tom-tom; but he, like the fated Jackie, cannot hear.

I don't know if she'll ever be asked to join Haig and Jones and the gang, but I'm fairly certain what she'll do if that day should come. I've just witnessed the moment she'll choose, the redemption she will pursue if only she gets a second chance.

With no time to fret over Pung and her personal disaster, I drift again, this time into a stream of some sort. All around me the water flows by. There must be five thousand people across the way, and it is hot and muggy. Wisps of steam rise silently from the brook as the crowd claps to signal the arrival of another group that will play through. One glance at the green reveals a wicker basket atop a pole that anywhere else would hold a flag. It must be Merion. The players are wearing white shirts and ties, some are in knickers, some in light pleated trousers. It's going to be Jones and Homans, I just know it. I'm going to see the end of the Grand Slam!

Even in the heat I feel as cold as stone. Then I look about and see that I *am* stone. I'm a mere rock in Cobb's Creek, otherwise known as the Baffling Brook, that guards the eleventh green on the fabled East Course. Although this is the spot where Jones closed out Homans 8 and 7 to win the 1930 U.S. Amateur Championship, that will not happen this day. This looks like stroke play, not match play, and it must be another Open. It seems that Opens are all I'm drawing tonight in dreamland.

I cannot tell which year it is. I try to see who's approaching, but there are no scoreboards, no standard-bearers following the golfers. I've gone pretty far back, since the portable placards with the players' names and scores were used at the Open as early as 1939 at Spring Mill. I know my golf and my golfers, but unless it's Jones or Hagen or Sarazen coming, I'm going to be lost out here.

The buzz of the gallery helps. The hum of excitement can mean only one thing: The leaders are approaching. I sit stoically in the midst of the rushing waters, contemplating the landmarks. When did they play at Merion? I know they played at the old Philadelphia Cricket Club in 1907 and again in 1910, but that's a different course, in a different neck of the woods. This is not the Philadelphia Cricket Club but the Merion Cricket Club, which is located not in town but in the nearby suburb of Ardmore. The first Open there was 1934 when—oh, nooooo! I've been selected to watch lightning strike again!

He strides into view, walking the walk of a man who is leading by two, moving with the determination of a player who is about to be crowned Champion Golfer of the United States. Bobby Cruickshank has driven perfectly and has only a short pitch over the brook, my brook, in order to reach the putting surface at number eleven. He takes a mashie-niblick from his caddie's hands and addresses his ball. He swings and—yikes! He's hit it fat! Reeeeeal fat. So fat, in fact, that it's coming right at me.

What to do? What to do? I can't exactly get out a fielder's mitt and make the play. But I can do the next best thing. I thrust my chest out the way a soldier does when a Congressional Medal of Honor is being pinned on him. It is almost imperceptible, but I am able to raise my rocky crest out of the shoaly creek a good four or five inches, just enough to provide a runway for Bobby the Crook's shot to home in on. *Plink!* I've done it just in time! I manage to impact the ball at precisely the correct angle, and I send it careening off toward the flagstick.

It is truly amazing what I've managed to do. I've saved his round from a watery grave, and maybe, just maybe, I've saved his life. After all, how many players leading a national championship like the U.S. Open fire the old pelota into the drink, only to have a friendly slab of stone leap into the breach and provide a rock-hard trampoline so the ball can somersault into birdie range? Cruickshank was looking back at his pursuers, padding his lead, pulling away, when he misfired that missile in my direction. If I don't rise to the occasion—no pun intended—he winds up slashing his wrists in his hotel room that night.

But he's safe! Or so I think. As I watch the ball rolling toward the hole, I turn away from the Crook, and that is our mutual undoing. He can't believe his stupid shotmaking error, nor can he fathom how it is that he's been rescued miraculously by the hand (or rock) of fate.

I know my game and I know what's coming and I am quick to shout, even though I was unable to make contact with either Palmer or Pung in the earlier dreams. "Hang on to it!" I plead in desperation. But it is no use.

In his delirium Cruickshank opts to celebrate his good fortune with a spontaneous gesture of frivolity. The fortuity of his fate a sight to behold, he gleefully tosses his mashie-niblick into the air, dancing a jig for an amazed gallery, telling the world that he is not only lucky but that he'll always be lucky. Ah, luck; it can turn corners on you, sometimes with alarming speed, and what goes up must come down. Unfortunately for Cruickshank, the club he so happily tossed to the heavens happens to come down directly on top of his head. The blow to the noggin knocks him cold. He manages to regain consciousness, but he isn't the same man with a welt the size of a chestnut sticking out of his head. His two-shot lead disappears like the morning fog. Olin Dutra, an unknown pro from Los Angeles, deftly plays his way to the clubhouse with a masterful final thirty-six-hole score of 71–72 and ends up beating Gene Sarazen by one stroke. Cruickshank finishes 77–76 to tie for third, two shots back.

It is like this for the rest of the night. Fits and starts. Glory, then ghosts. The dreams continue to come forward, crashing against my subconscious like waves thundering into a seawall. I ride out the stories, the visions, the circumstances one by one, the way a surfer angles his board and stretches his ride, squeezing thrills, excitement, exhilaration—and a little bit of terror, too—from the salty foam.

All I can figure is that the dreams must be some sort of message. They're there to tell me something, trying in some allegorical sense to teach me a lesson. But what is it? Why do I see Arnold Palmer at his best and Jackie Pung at her worst? Or Cruickshank's dance of doom? Why couldn't they hear me? Why am I continually placed on the doorstep of history yet relegated to the status of an outside observer, a golfing Elijah, unable to affect events that are swirling all around me?

Questions like these flit in and out, punctuating my dreams. It is as if the visions are fragments of sentences and the queries semicolons at the end of them. I cannot summon forth the answer to the riddles, so I drift aimlessly in reverie, awaiting the dawn.

The dreams grow increasingly vivid. One image fades away, replaced by another that is even clearer, brighter, drawn in sharper detail. Finally, after all the images have washed together, I hear the drawl of West Texas. I find myself standing in a line with a ticket in my hand. People are boarding slowly as the engine on the big Greyhound starts to roar. The driver is letting the motor get warm before heading off down the road. Once clear of Pecos, he'll open her up. The gears will be humming as he heads due west toward El Paso, which he'll make by noon.

We're on the road a couple of hours, peeling down a two-lane highway, when the driver decides to pull off at a service station near a town called Kent. He drops off a load of newspapers, then gets us back on the road. Traffic has picked up a bit, and we're behind an Alamo Freight Lines semi, slowing to a crawl as ground fog creeps over the West Texas hills. The road begins to twist and turn. We're falling behind schedule, and the driver knows there's no way to make El Paso on time unless he tries to pass. But there's nowhere to do it.

Everyone on the road has his headlights on. The driver suddenly shifts into third gear and jams down on the accelerator pedal as he pulls out to go around the semi. We're picking up speed, filling the lane reserved for oncoming traffic as we finally pull ahead of the truck. The bus is really rolling now, but in the fog no one is too sure what lies ahead. All we can feel are our stomachs dropping as the road shoots down into a hollow. I begin to make out a bridge spanning a culvert.

"Slow down, will you?" I shout the question from the fourth seat back on the driver's side. But the message falls on deaf ears.

We're accelerating, not slowing down. The wheels are spinning so fast, I fear we're out of control. I know we're out of control. Then I hear the incredible screech of the tires. I smell the awful scent of burning rubber. I hear the bus driver shouting. "Can't get back! Can't get back! Oh, nooooo! . . . We're gonna hit that carrrrr. . . ."

That car!

I snapped awake, startled, in a pool of warm sweat. My pajamas and the bedding were sticking to me. I heard the grandfather clock in the lobby below bang out eight bells, and out of nowhere, before I could shake off the terror I had just confronted, I felt something fiery brush against my left leg, which exploded with pain.

"Get that scalding iron away from me," I shouted to no one in particular. "I'm not a calf, and I don't need branding. Knock it off!"

Then I looked up into Hangtown's eyes.

"Sorry, kid," he apologized, looking down at his six-gun, which he had used to prod me awake. "This old Colt gets that way every morning after I fire her some. Gotta keep sharp, y'know. Dang if that barrel ain't hot as a furnace after I get done shootin' with her. Y'know, you ain't the first to be scarred by Old Betsy here." He blew on the barrel, then gazed upon his trusty revolver as though she were his kid sister.

I am not a morning person, and this little episode was doing nothing to change that circumstance. "That thing's as hot as . . . You gotta be more careful, Hangtown."

"So do you, young fella. You can't just sleep in like that. There's work to do, and there ain't much time in which to do it. You've got only two days left—you know that, don't you?"

I told him I recalled Haig or Jones or somebody saying something about there being only three days to look around. But the looking had turned into investigating, and the casual conversations had grown progressively more intense. What was at first a curiosity had turned into a grim race against time.

"I'm not so sure this is fun anymore."

"C'mon, kid. You gotta get goin' here. Jones is waitin' on you for breakfast. You'll see Ship this mornin', too. You'd better get cleaned up."

I rose from the bed in a groggy state. The shower was a good pick-me-up, but as I started to regain my bearings, the worries, the doubts, and the fears crept back. They plagued my mind like gophers tunneling beneath a virgin fairway. Where's the greenkeeper when I need him?

The doubts were serious business. They were no mere rodents burrowing in the grass. No, these doubts were more like a mechanized reaper cutting down everything in its path. The blades were gaining on me as I came to a startling realization: If Arnie and Pung and Cruickshank and that damn bus driver couldn't hear me, if I couldn't reach them, how in the world was I going to get through to Hogan?

San Francisco Express
June 18, 1955

LOCAL AMATEUR HARVIE WARD CATCHES BOLT AT 144

SNEAD COMES BACK WHILE HOGAN CONTINUES TO HOVER

36 HOLES TODAY FOR OPEN TITLE

By Dick Yost

Golf's own version of Mount Vesuvius erupted yesterday, as Tempestuous Tommy Bolt blew to a 77. While steam was spewing sideways out of Bolt's ears, young Harvie Ward, San Francisco's brilliant amateur, fired a spectacular even par 70 to catch him and share the lead at the halfway mark of the 55th U.S. Open Championship. They are tied at 144, four over par.

CROWD AT THE TOP

Ward and Bolt will have plenty of company. Close enough to pick their pockets are four-time winner Ben Hogan, who tacked a 73 onto his opening 72 for 145, and Julius Boros, who won the Open Championship himself in 1952. Boros, who shot 76 on Thursday, turned things around yesterday, firing a second round 69.

First-round phenom Walker Inman kept his plane in the air yesterday with a 75, while another unknown playing with him in the same threesome, Jack Fleck of the Duck Creek Golf Club in Davenport, Iowa, quietly moved into the group at 145 with his own round of 69.

SNEAD COMES BACK

By far the day's biggest turnaround was Slammin' Sam Snead, who bettered his opening round 79 by 10 shots. His 69 left him at 148, only four off the pace. Snead may be playing the best golf all of a sudden: He hit 11 of 14 fairways and was putting for birdie on every hole on the back nine.

It may seem like the course softened up during the second round, but Boros, Fleck, and Snead were the only ones to break par, and Ward was the only one who matched it. While there weren't nearly the number of outright disasters the first round produced, the Olympic Club's Lake Course hardly surrendered to the field. The cut was at 155, a whopping 15 strokes over par, the highest figure anyone can remember in an Open. Anyone making the cut is still in the thick of it.

BOLT DIGS DEEP

Everyone knew that Tempestuous Tommy Bolt's serendipity could never last. He was out in 39 and was in danger of dropping yet another stroke to par when his 5-iron second shot came up a good 20 yards short of the fourteenth green. Disgusted, Bolt slammed his club into the ground. The throw was one that had to be measured in depth, not distance. Despite the outburst, Bolt deftly chipped up for his par.

It was the final hole that killed him. His drive hooked out of control, hit a woman in the gallery, and then bounded deep into the trees for an unplayable lie. He wound up with a double-bogey 6, a back nine 38, and a second round of 77—10 shots higher than Thursday, just the opposite of Snead, who lowered his score by the same count.

It was Hogan, however, who proved to the fans why he is so dangerous a player. On the sixteenth hole, a 603-yard par 5, he hit an uncharacteristic hook off the tee. His ball struck a tree branch 175 yards out and dropped straight down into the high rough. From there he gunned a fairway wood and then hit a 2-iron to the green. The iron shot cut a hole in the sky and spun to a stop 25 feet from the hole. He made the putt for 4, much to the delight of the gallery.

NO-NAMES STAY CLOSE

Fleck and Inman, the two golfers no one seems to know much about, were an interesting pair. Fleck was deadly on the greens. He one-putted 6 times on the back nine alone. He canned a 20-footer at the twelfth, an 18-incher on the long sixteenth, and a 10-footer at the final hole. His only real lapse occurred—where else?—at the seventeenth, where he lipped out for a bogey.

Inman played steadily and refused to crack. He was out in even par 35 and seemed ready to sprint away from the pack, but then he stumbled, bogeying the last three holes for a round of 35—40—75.

Today, when two rounds will be crowded into one day, the United States Golf Association has them playing in twosomes instead of threesomes. It makes for some interesting pairings: Harvie Ward (144) will play with Inman (145) at 8:30 and 1:00. Hogan (145) gets Bobby Harris (148) an hour later, at 9:30 and 2:00. Boros (145) and Snead (148) tee off at 9:00 and 1:30. The volcanic Bolt (144) will match up with mild-mannered Jackie Burke (148) at 10:15 and 2:45. Fleck (145) and young Gene Littler (149) will bring things to a close at 10:30 and 3:00.

They're all alive. Anything can happen.

·10·

THE EGGS LITTLE EDDIE BROUGHT ME WERE GOOD—SCRAMBLED firm, not too runny—but the hotcakes were even better. The buckwheat and syrup went down the hatch in a freefall as I gulped my way through a pile of eighteen dollar-sized beauties. The number of flapjacks may have been a coincidence or it may have been an omen; whatever the circumstance, I was too busy stuffing myself to contemplate it. A full round of the little jessies was just what the doctor ordered.

The coup de grace to this welcome repast came in the form of a mug of steaming hot coffee. Even though I was only twenty, a mere college lad unaffected by the pressures of adult life, I had already developed a taste for the stuff. Java. Joe. The Mud. The darker the better had become my motto, and this brew was so dense and thick that even light could not escape the pull of its gravity. The stuff seeped onto my tongue with such agonizing slowness that I attempted to accelerate the process by swallowing hard, but it seemed this *arabica especiale* was determined to come my way one precious drop at a time. Once inside me, the opaque java pushed off from shore and navigated the entwined tributaries of my nervous system, eventually shooting the rapids of even my narrowest capillaries. My entire body began to tingle as I was jerked from semiconsciousness by the jolt of caffeine. My inner juices started to flow, and as they surged, I felt as though I'd been jumpstarted. I swore I could hear a low-pitched humming noise, the type one hears when standing near high-voltage wires.

I had come downstairs to eat and rouse my senses, and, quite clearly, I did both. I was certainly no longer a hungry and drowsy kid who had overslept. Suddenly, with a full belly and the bean jumping around inside me, I was dancing with energy, ready to take on the world.

The dreams? They were now firmly embedded in my psyche, along with my observations of the surroundings and the people I had encountered at the Club. I tried to make sense of the jagged pieces of the puzzle. I saw Hogan's gear, and I instantly thought of his pain. Then I leapfrogged to Jones at St. Andrews in '58. More pain. Then there were Cruickshank and Pung. Even more pain, albeit of a different sort. I could see the Babe being cut down by cancer. God, that must have been awful. And then there was Young Tom Morris, fading from life like a nineteenth-century table lamp plumb out of oil, and Old Tom, forced to see his son taken long before his time. Everywhere I turned I saw all this heartache, all this sadness, all this hurt.

My only instinct was to shake it off and get away. Escape now while you have the chance, I told myself. Even if it is for just a moment, take a break. I knew I could revisit the hard knocks later, but for now, with the sun still on the rise, I tried to get my mind on something else.

Quite frankly, I didn't bother to notice who else was in the room when I entered. My one-track mind was barreling down the breakfast straightaway, and I paid no heed to who might be seated nearby. As I looked around, I saw virtually none of the regulars. The room held a smattering of new faces.

The scene was shifting daily, it seemed. I did not see Hogan anywhere. Nor did I see the Babe or Old Tom. The only mainstay, outside of Haig who stood guard behind the bar, was Jones, who sat nearby in animated conversation with a bald, mustachioed gentleman in a tartan kilt who was arguing with him about the condition of the greens.

"Doc, they're too blasted fast!" complained Jones. "Why, those things run like jackrabbits. You have to use more water or more fertilizer or something. You've got to slow 'em down, or else it's going to be frightful out there."

"I canna' do tha', Mr. Joones. What I've come here fer is t' be in charge o' fairways 'n' greens, and tha' I am. Ye canna' be a-tellin' me how t' be a-cuttin' 'n' a-waterin' the buggers. These are all me courses, 'n' 'tis me who's gonna be dictatin' the playin' conditions. Ye got tha'?"

"But, Doc—listen to reason. This is a game we're playing, not a blessed exercise in futility. The object is to present the player with a challenge, something within the realm of possibility. A decent result must be at least achievable. These courses are impossible the way you've set them up. Those greens are like greased lightning!"

"Ah. I'm beginnin' t' see what is happenin' here. Ye're all cryin' like babies, ye are. 'Slow 'em down,' ye're weepin'. 'Please, oh, please be a-cuttin' the rough now, Doc. Move the boonkers, they're in me way.' What d'ye think this is here, a piece o' paper t' be drawin' on? Well, if it 'tis, I'll tell ye this: I've drawn all I'm gonna, 'n' I'm nae a-totin' an eraser for ye t' correct what ye dinna like. Play her the way ye finds her. Treat her wi' respect, and she'll return the compliment, and dinye e'er ferget tha'."

They continued to argue, but Old Baldy wasn't budging. I never thought I'd see the day Jones would be cornered in this place, but apparently it happens. Indeed, I was witnessing it right in front of me.

When Jones finally realized he wouldn't get his way, he did not whimper or remonstrate. There would be no yelling, no arm waving from him. He simply thanked the man for his time, then rose from his chair and excused himself. He headed straight to Haig for consolation. The two of them talked for a moment, until Haig roared and bellowed, caught his breath, then laughed like a hyena. He slapped Jones on the back and sent him off. Then he looked over at me.

I responded to the summons. "What was that all about?" I asked.

"That? Oh, that's just the Macker laying down the law. You thought old Hangtown was a tough bronco? You oughta see Mac when he gets up a head of steam."

"Mac?"

"You couldn't pick him out? Junior, you must've played something by him. Crimony, the man's designed or remodeled a couple of hundred tracks at least. Ever drop your peg at Cypress? That was a new one in my time, but it has sure grown into something, hasn't it?"

"Wait a minute," I replied. "You mean to tell me that the green-keeper here is—"

"You got it, junior." Haig laughed at himself and his surroundings; it was a deep, hearty, rolling laugh, one of pride and satisfaction. "This is really something, ain't it?"

"Yeah," I answered, my mind a full three-wood down the fairway from Haig. He had just pointed out one of the greatest golf course architects of them all, and he was telling me that Alister Mackenzie was the Club's man for course maintenance.

"If he's heading up Greens and Grounds, which course do you get to play? One of his?"

"Nah. We play just about anywhere, 'cause everything's reciprocal. If I want to knock on Jones for some cash, he comes with me down to Florida—you know, Sarasota and St. Pete. The game's on at Whitfield Estates and Pasadena Country Club, the same joints where we duked it out in '26. I own him down there, junior." The Haig was glowing like a light bulb. "And hey, if Emperor Jones over there wants to hit on me, he takes me to his place across the pond."

"St. Andrews?"

"Right on the noggin', kid. And Old Tom's got North Berwick.

Little Eddie over there has Brookline. We've got a regular rotation working here. But you've gotta be invited."

"By whoever has privileges?"

Haig winked and pointed his finger at me. He was playing the role of a teacher and telling his prize pupil that he was acing the midterm.

I could see the gleam in his eye as he explained how things worked. Despite Haig's air of nonchalance, he was getting excited. So was I. I began to itch with anticipation. I had questions, though, lots of them.

"Doesn't all of this get boring after a while?" I put the query to him gently so as not to burst the bubble. "You're all cooped up here, Haig. It's as if you're confined in a prison. It's not like you're in jail, I know, but a person can't exactly leave, can he?"

"Sure he can. You wanna take a hike? Hit the trail, junior. Just go out the way you came in. But you'll have a devil of a time re-tracing your steps once you're over the line. We've had a few who have left. Then they thought about it and changed their mind. But by then it was too late . We've never seen them again."

"Why did they go?"

"Who knows? I'm afraid it was like you said. They got bored. But there aren't many of 'em, I'll tell you that. Once a man gets here, once he drinks it all in, once he sucks it down deep into the pores of his skin, he comes to know what this is. And if he's like us"—Haig looked around the room at his friends and clientele to make sure no one could overhear—"he doesn't ever want to lose it."

"I still don't get it, Haig. How can a man be frozen into a moment?"

Hagen looked at me like the bartender he is; I couldn't tell if he thought I needed another drink or if he'd concluded I'd had one too many.

"Don't you see it, junior?" he asked, looking at me sideways. "These guys ain't been frozen in time. They ain't petrified fossils, you know what I mean?"

"But if a guy wants to preserve a second or two in time, a brief spell, a moment, as you put it, how can that be enough?"

"For Pete's sake, kid, it's not just a second or a moment. It's a time of life, a period, maybe a run of two, three, four days. Maybe it's a week, a year, a decade. You ask a man what was best for him, he's apt to say just about anything. Me, I just got those couple of weeks down in suntan land. Getting ready for some Jones hunting, then going out for the kill. For crying out loud, junior, I tied one on down there a few days before the match, you know, partying and all. . . . It was so bad I thought I'd die of the hangover if Jones didn't get me first. I carry that around, too."

"The bitter with the sweet?" I asked, trying to figure this thing out.

"Not exactly. It just came with the territory." Hagen shook his head and laughed. "I didn't start sipping the brew until I was over twenty. But junior, let me tell you something. I made up for lost time in a hurry. Hell, my elbow got so bent that it swelled up. There were people who didn't know me who thought I played *tennis*, for God's sake."

"But if you're surrounded by more than just a moment, you have some ups and downs to deal with, don't you? Don't the bad spells overcome the good ones sometimes?"

This can't be perfect, can it? I whispered that question to myself as Hagen poured a drink. He sipped the scotch as if they were the last drops that would ever touch his well-lubricated lips.

"I suppose that's possible, junior, but you gotta understand this is different. Here, you know it's somehow gonna work itself out. It just gives you confidence, patience, a gentle sort of feeling. Crimony . . . will you listen to me talking like this, junior? But think about it. I mean, take me and Jones down there in Florida. Did I hit 'em all on the screws? Heck, no! I hit the devil's pellet flat sideways a couple of times. But I knew if I could get it to the green, it was anyone's game. And then I made everything I looked at. Now here, in this place, even if I hit her crooked, I know I have some weapons left. A hot little putter can give a man a lifetime of patience, you know what I'm saying? I have no worries about what's gonna happen. I know I've got what I need to do the job. Can you begin to see what I'm getting at here? This stuff is like a banquet for your mind, kid. It don't need no waiter, no kitchen, no cook, no menu. It just feeds off itself. Now I just feel so good out there, so relaxed, so ready that there ain't no way to hit it bad. Damn, it's fine. That's just what it is, junior. It's fine. It ain't much of a description, I know, nothing fancy and all that, but that's just what it is."

The emotion was beginning to show even though Hagen, that Houdini of Match Play, the Potentate with the Poker Face, was known for cleverly disguising his true feelings. He grabbed me by the collar. "You know what it's like to go out there when you're hitting it on the screws?" His voice had dropped to a whisper, and his chin pointed westward to the range, which lay empty and still.

"P-p-perpetually pure, right?"

He released me. "Hey," he said, "I like the way you said that, kid. *Per-pet-chew-alley pure.* That sounds nice. Reeeeeal nice. Shoot, I let it slide once in a while, but there ain't no one around here gets into my pocketbook, no siree bob. Hell, out there I can lay a Hoylake on 'em, and they don't laugh. I mean, I can have 'em remove the flagstick when I'm coming in from one seventy-five, and they don't ask any questions. They pull it because they know I mean business. Sank four on der Bingle last week. Old Crosby was shaking like a leaf by the time the last one went down. The Bing Cherry couldn't even sing us a song at dinner, he was in such a state."

"But wouldn't you like just a little bit of uncertainty? Just a little bit of excitement?"

"Junior," Haig said as he shook his head, "you're not listening. If it's excitement you want, just match me up at my best against Jones at his best. Or match me up against the Babe at her best. Sometimes we just play on through the night, one great shot topping another, birdie matching birdie, eagle for eagle. You know how it goes. Anything you can do, I can do better. Oh, someone wins in the end, you can bet on that." He looked around, knowing that that's exactly what happens. "What I mean is, we beat each other's brains out, but who can complain when everyone plays his best?" He laughed again at his good fortune. "I can't begin to tell you the feeling in words because it ain't like anything I ever felt. Back then, when I was alive, you know what I mean, if I got beat, I always groused that I could've, that I should've done better. But who knows? Maybe I played as well as I could. Maybe it just wasn't my time. But here? Kid, here it's *everybody's* time. Every day of the week and twice on Sunday. It don't get any better than that."

The hair on my arms was standing at attention just listening to him. Jones at his best. Hagen at his best. The Babe at her best. All of them, the freaking Hall of Fame, at their best.

But what about Mackenzie? Where does the Master Builder play?

"He has a little course out west called Pasatiempo," said Haig. "Down in Santa something in California, halfway between Frisco and Pebble Beach. Some kind of layout, I'll tell you that. Load up on pellets before you take on that back nine."

The questions were starting to leapfrog one another.

"If he built Augusta and Cypress Point and Royal Melbourne and all the rest, why did he settle for an out-of-the way place like that?"

"Ever teed it up there?"

I confessed that I had never heard of the place even though I lived only about sixty-five miles away from it.

"Well, let me tell you this. One trip around, and you'll know why a guy like the Doc said it was his favorite spot on the face of the Earth. And old Doc is a real bulldog about it, let me tell you. He and Jones got into one of their discussions a while back, something about Jones wanting him to move a bunker on a two-shotter, and the Doc took Jones by the shirt collar and literally dragged his fanny out to the sixteenth at Pasatiempo. Said it was the greatest par four in the world. And he's one guy who oughta know."

Haig also told me about his equipment and that used by the others. "Hell, I remember the first time Lema asked me to tour the Old Course with him. Thought he had me with his steel shafts. I had to use 'em, you know. His course, his time. That sort of thing. Rules are rules, even for guys like me. Well, he was a rookie, and I let him have a few bets. Then I said, Tony, boy, how's about you coming down to my place for a rematch? He said I'm on, and out he came with those steel shafts. When Jones made him put 'em away and play with a set of Wilson Sure-Flites, hickory and all, his pants got heavy on him. Dropped a load, he did. Spent the rest of the day worrying if the blasted shaft was gonna break in half. I told him hickory was just as strong as that steel crap, but he wouldn't have any of it. I left him talking to his fool self with his pockets picked clean as a whistle. He protested to Jones and even to Ship, but rules is rules, junior."

So that's how they do it. They can exchange course privileges—after all, Haig did say that everything was reciprocal—but they have to use the clubs of the host's era. No wonder Haig and Jones wanted Hogan here. Forget the fifties; they wanted to see what he could do in their time.

Yet I was still uneasy, unable to fully assess what I was hearing. "I think I understand what you're talking about, Haig, but there's so much pain around this place." I decided not to tell him about my dreams.

"Junior, you're running your mower with the blades set too low. You're chopping up the grass like it was poison. Jiminy Christmas, you've got to stop and smell the flowers while you're walking along."

"What do you mean?"

He smiled like a ball that's been sliced in half by a topped five-iron. Quick as a cat, he checked to see if Jones was around. When he verified to his own satisfaction that no one was present to countermand him, Hagen put his arm around my shoulder and said in a whisper, "I've got something working in a little while. Cool your heels for forty-five minutes, then meet me out back."

"What's cooking?" I asked, hoping to get a preview of what was in store.

"Just be there," he said. "It'll be something you won't want to miss."

The parking lot behind the clubhouse was made of compacted gravel, and it began to crunch beneath my feet the moment I set foot outside the rear door. Haig was waiting as promised. He was sitting at a portable garden table, next to a long black Austro-Daimler limousine. Haig was eating a late breakfast, in the open air like an aristocrat.

The rear door of the Austro-Daimler was open, and I could see Haig's long camel's hair polo coat splayed across the backseat. He ate nonchalantly. A liveried chauffeur, who must double as his valet, attended to his every need. "A little more coffee, my good man," he said to his manservant, who dutifully came to his service. They both smiled when they saw me coming their way.

"What is all this?" I asked, admiring the linen tablecloth and the sterling silver radiating in the sunlight. "I thought you were taking me to watch you play. Food we can get inside."

"Now don't go getting impatient, junior. I'm just showing you how it's done. You have to live a little out here, you know what I mean? It ain't all slashing through the jungle." He turned to the chauffeur. "This really brings back the memories, doesn't it, Spec?"

"Yes, sir, Mr. Hagen. Sure does."

"Junior, this is Spec Hammond, the same guy who was with me at Deal for the British Open in '20. The sumbitches wouldn't let us in the clubhouse, so we showed 'em something, didn't we, Spec?"

"You bet, Mr. Hagen." Spec poured the coffee without a change of expression.

"You have to understand what a statement old Spectator and I made. Me finishing a round in the British Open and having my man Spec here pull this thing up behind the eighteenth green."

Hagen looked over at the limousine admiringly. "Had them bug-eyed and flapping their jowls, it did. Spec served me lunch right there on the spot. Right behind the eighteenth green. Just like this—fine linen, fine wines, crystal, and all. It was sweet, junior."

Haig was wearing beige knickers, argyle hose made of cashmere, and a light-colored sport coat. His white shirt was freshly ironed, and a bright red cravat was the centerpiece of the outfit. His gold cuff links were engraved with the symbol of the Professional Golfers' Association of America, which he helped organize in 1916, only two years after he had won his first U.S. Open, little more than five years after he had turned professional.

Hagen looked like a champion, like a man who had won eleven major championships in his time, not to mention seventy-five other tournaments including five Western Opens, which were among the most significant championships in those days. In the bar yesterday, he proudly told me that he had never lost a playoff and had never three-putted a final green in his life. He was full of ebullience on this morning; he must have been ready for some serious action.

"Junior," he said, "did I ever tell you about the time they set me up to play with the Crown Prince of Japan? Akimoto, Sukimoto, something like that. It was before the war, you know, number two. I got tied up doing something and showed up a couple of hours late. Some low mucky-muck to the high mucky-muck comes to me, all bent out of shape, and says the Crown Prince is waiting. He's been waiting for two hours, the guy tells me, and he claims His Holy Highness is getting splinters sitting around waiting on me. You know what I said to him? I said, 'Well, if he's still here, it just proves one thing. He ain't going nowhere.' I get no answer, nothing but a blank stare. So I tell him to beat it, that I'll be along in a minute, that his boss will still be there when I'm ready to let her fly. And you know what, junior? We teed it up, me and His Highness, like it was a regular game. Had a swell time of it, too."

"Haig," I pleaded, hoping he would get on with it.

But it didn't work. "And let me tell you about old Sarazen," he continued. "We were paired together in '35. You know, the Masters, fourth round. Yeah, that shot. We get to the fifteenth hole, and there's hardly anyone around, see? And you know me, I've got serious business waiting for me when we're done. So I says to him, 'C'mon, hurry it up, will you, Gene? I've got a big date tonight.' Darned if the Squire didn't hole the thing out. Boom! Just like the doctor ordered."

I was now impatient, for I could not risk being gone for too long. Soon Jones would come looking for me, and he was bound to be all over me with questions about Hogan and my plan of attack. "Am I going to be able to see you play?" I asked, trying to pry Haig off his chair and onto a golf course, "or are you just going to talk about it?"

"Sure, junior. But take it easy, will you? There's gonna be plenty of action. Just don't be rushing me, okay?"

"I really don't have all that much time." I looked as if I was on my way to a funeral. "You know that."

"Yeah, but you can't rush these things. Besides, this is gonna be worth it, son. I've got me a slippery eel to hook today."

"Who's the victim?"

"It's actually a fellow I've never played with before. Just heard a lot about him, so I wanted to see him in the flesh."

"Who is it?"

"Ever hear of Titanic Thompson?"

"No." But the name alone promised to be worth hearing about, I thought to myself.

"You ever made golf bets, junior? I take that back. Ever made any bets?"

"I've played for a five spot, if that's what you mean."

"That isn't what I'm talking about, unless of course that five spot had some zeros on it."

"Then I guess I never did," I replied. How many zeros, I began to wonder.

"Don't worry about it, junior," said Haig, "because there aren't too many who have. At least not like this guy bets. Anyway, Titanic and yours truly are lined up for a little something today. Just an exhibition, but I thought you'd like to watch. And don't be sweating it, kid. You don't have to stay for the whole thing. Give us a look see for a few holes, and if it ain't your style, beat it back in there." He motioned to the back door of the clubhouse.

"Where are you going to play?"

The Haig wiped his lips with the napkin and then sipped some coffee. He squinted into the morning sun. The day was clear, the air crisp and bright. Haig set his coffee cup down gently, the china barely making a sound as it clinked against the saucer.

"You've been to the Beach, haven't you, son?"

"Only played it once, in high school. Pretty special. But why there?"

"It wasn't my idea. It's Titanic's joint. I hear he asked to be sent there. I don't know as he had a right to it, mind you. I think he's from down South, Texas or someplace near there. All I know is they've all been talkin' about him spending time around Tenison Park, hustling the daylights out of anyone who crossed his path. He must have worked a deal with someone, and there he is, playing the Beach, working the vines of a rich man's vineyard. Junior, if what they say is true, Titanic Thompson has to be pulling off the grapes with both hands."

"He must've been there at some point in his life, wouldn't you think?"

"I suppose, but I don't know as he spent much time there compared to other places. And he's never told anyone I know of why he chose it. The only thing I know about him is that he was there at some point along the way. Worked some of the swiftest slides I've ever heard of."

"Slides?" I asked.

Haig looked at me as if I was supposed to know the term. "Slides his hand into another guy's pocket and removes some money," he explained.

"How exactly does this guy Titanic do that?"

"Well, the way I heard it. . . . This is just a story, mind you. I have no way of knowing if it's true or not. But let me say something right now, junior. There's enough legend surrounding this character that at least some of it has to be true, you know what I mean?"

"So what did he do?"

"It was the dead of winter. Now you see, there's no snow at Pebble, but it can get pretty damn cold there. Back then, at Christmastime they sold roasted chestnuts from a cart just outside the lodge building, you know, the joint where everyone stays."

I nodded, unsure of the precise physical setting. I have only seen Del Monte Lodge as it looks today, a large hotel flanked on one side by elegant shops and on the other by one of the world's most famous—and perhaps most beautiful—golf links.

"Well, old Titanic, he bets this guy he can throw a chestnut over the lodge. 'No way,' the guy says. Titanic bets him something like a hundred dollars. Whistles to a kid near the chestnut cart and says for him to bring over a bag. The kid does it, and Titanic slips him some change to take back to the guy workin' the cart. Then he pulls out a chestnut and eats it. Then he pulls out another and says, 'Here goes nothing.'" Haig let out one of his heartiest laughs. "The wind is in his damn face. The thing sails over the lodge and comes down near the eighteenth green. An incredible throw even for Titanic. I mean, I know he used to play semipro ball, but this was really something. The poor slob who made the bet with him, he must have been a high roller from somewhere. He peels off a big fat hundred, slaps it into Titanic's palm, and hightails it out of there."

"What's so special about that? The guy didn't know Titanic was a ball player?"

"Junior, you're not getting it, are you? There ain't no one, not even Babe Ruth, who can make that throw, into the wind and all. And with a chestnut. The damn thing'll come back in your face if you don't pitch it just right."

"There must have been some trick," I said, stating the obvious.

"For openers, junior, Titanic and the little kid were partners. At least, the kid was paid off in advance. You see, Titanic had one of those chestnuts filled with lead. Then he paid off the guy with the cart to stick it in a bag filled with regular chestnuts. Told the guy to just hang on to it until he gave him the high sign. Then when the kid buys a bag of the things, the cart guy hands him the lead number. The kid brings it to Titanic like he's never seen him before in his life. Then old Titanic, he eats one of the babies for effect, just like I already told you. He heaves the leaded chestnut, and it soars like an arrow. Easy money, kid."

"He made a living doing stuff like that?"

"Junior, he made a *very good* living."

The image of Titanic Thompson brought to mind an old phrase: There's no limit to human ingenuity when it comes to one man making another part with his money. He was living proof that the old adage rings true. "Did he pick Pebble Beach," I inquired of Haig, "because of all the money that hangs out around there?"

"You're catching on fast, junior."

"But when was he there? What year was it?"

Haig put his fingers to his chin. "I don't know exactly, 'cause I never trust the stories. He's never consented to play me, you know. So this is going to be a new experience for me, too. I'm planning on it being the late twenties, or the thirties, around there sometime. At least that's when I've heard of him hanging around the place. Junior, the way I hear it, you've got to see this guy in action to believe him."

Haig continued to tell me stories about the man he would face in a matter of minutes. His favorite story about Titanic Thompson was about his driving along a Texas highway outside of Dallas. Titanic passed a road sign saying it was seventeen miles to town. He stopped, got out, walked back to the sign, dug it up, and put it in the trunk of his car. Then he turned around and drove back away from the city to a point that was nearly twenty-two miles out. He pulled out his shovel and reset the sign. Then he waited. Several weeks later when he was driving the road with an unsuspecting customer, he struck up a conversation about distances. Then they came to the sign. "You know," he said to his companion, "I'll bet you it's over twenty miles into downtown Dallas. Those state highway boys don't know nothin'." When the other fellow disputed him, relying on the sign, Titanic was ready to sink him. "I'll bet you a hundred dollars," he dared. Yes, Titanic Thompson made a very good living for himself. Haig said he drove that road for years, playing the same ruse on the uninitiated. According to Haig, Titanic Thompson called that sign his own private annuity.

Then there was the time he let a guy beat him out of a couple of hundred dollars on the course. Let him win on the last hole. Then the show began. "You ain't that good, fella," Titanic moaned, "so don't be parading my moolah all over the place here." The winner called him a sore loser. "What?" exploded Titanic. "Why, I can beat your lame ass left-handed. Bet you a grand. Make that two grand. Or are you chicken?" The bet was on, and so was Titanic. He had once qualified for the United States Amateur Championship left-handed—under an assumed name, of course.

"I can't say any of these yarns are true," Haig said. "But I'm believing 'em just in case. It's like insurance with this guy. And, junior, no matter what the guy says, if it sounds too good to be true, it is. So keep your hands in your pockets. Don't bet him he can't do something he says he can."

"C'mon," I argued, "he can't be that good. Can he?"

"Junior, you don't realize what we're dealing with here. This guy once bet a man he could hit a ball a quarter mile. The money got laid down, and he trucks the sucker to the rim of the Grand Canyon. Bats it out into the wild blue yonder. It went a quarter of a mile and then some."

My smile broadened as Haig explained the hustle.

"That ain't all, junior. The guy who was betting with Titanic started protesting, saying it wasn't fair. Now old Ti, he's cagey with this fella. Ti apologizes, says he wants to set it right. Tells the guy he can do it on flat ground. He says—now get this—that he can belt the thing a damn mile without cliffs and all that."

"What?"

"That's right, junior. A mile on flat ground."

"No way," I protested. "No one can hit it that far—unless the fairway's made of concrete."

"Not bad, kid. You're already thinking like Titanic does. But get this. He doesn't need concrete or a highway to beat this guy. He goes out to Michigan, of all places, and in the dead of winter. See, he never told the guy where or when he was gonna do it. Just said it'd be someplace flat. So he teed it up on Lake Erie. Right on the ice! The ball started out in Michigan and didn't stop bouncing till it got to Cleveland. Old Titanic, he made the guy deposit the dough with a third party, escrow like, before he even told him where he'd be hitting the shot. Wanted to be sure he could collect. The man thinks of everything."

"So how are you gonna beat him?" I asked, wondering if Haig would follow his own advice and refrain from betting.

"Oh, we ain't gonna play for anything major, maybe just a few hundred or so. I'm doing this for you, remember."

Spec the chauffeur looked at his watch and coughed to attract Haig's attention. "Is it time, Spec?" Haig asked. "Okay, then, let's get going."

Spec disposed of the table, folding it neatly and placing it, along with the linen and china, in the trunk. Everything was secured tightly, the vehicle having been outfitted with a compartment for the paraphernalia a man like Haig needs to bring to his exhibitions. There were several sets of hickory-shafted clubs and at least a dozen pairs of golf shoes.

"Take her out slow and quiet, Spec." Haig gave the instruction in a calm voice through a glass partition that separated the passengers from the driver. "I don't want them to know we're coming just yet. Pull her to a stop just after you crest this rise up ahead."

We were on a gravelly road that wound up a hill and into the trees behind the clubhouse. I had no idea where it led, and before we'd gone very far, the mysterious fog that surrounded the Club engulfed us. If I didn't know better, I'd have sworn Haig had double-crossed me and was taking me back for an unceremonious dumping at Lincoln Park. But when we cleared the fog at the top of the hill, the sky had changed. Although it had been clear and blue only moments ago when we were back down the road at the rear of the clubhouse, it was now gray and slightly hazy. A cooling breeze floated in and out. Monterey pines bordered the road, shooting upward. I rolled down the window to take a look outside, and when I heard waves crashing, I knew we were somewhere near Carmel-by-the-Sea, a stone's throw from Del Monte Lodge and the Pebble Beach Golf Links.

Spec Hammond coasted the limousine to a quiet stop. The partition slid open. Haig leaned toward it. "You have the other suit, Spectator, old boy?"

The chauffeur handed Haig some rumpled clothes. They were almost the same color as the ones he had on, but there was a vast difference: While they, too, were decidedly handsome, they were also decidedly unpressed. Haig started to undress; he was changing his clothes in the backseat of the car.

Unbelievable. The Haig changing out of his best duds to go eyeball to eyeball with Titanic Thompson? "I thought you always did it with style," I commented. "You're dressing *down* for this gig?"

"I don't exactly get how you're putting it. A gig? But here's the point, junior. Why do I want to look fresh for this guy? I've got an image to keep up. I want him thinkin' old Haig here just got out of the love loft with some dame. I want him thinkin' I can't hit my hat. Say, Spec," he said, turning his attention away from me. "Shoot me some of that scotch back here, will you?"

Drinking at this hour?

Haig splashed the stuff on his face liberally as if it were cologne. Then he answered my puzzled look with a simple explanation.

"Got to smell the part, junior."

This was the Haig they tell stories about, the man enshrined in legend. In an instant he had transformed himself from a member of the landed gentry to a morning-after caricature of a good-time Charley.

"You'd better get cracking, Spec. We're going to be hopping when we get there."

The chauffeur was also changing his clothes. The breeches and boots came off and were replaced by baggy pants and an old woolen sweater. The pants were rumpled, and the sweater had more holes in it than a practice putting green. A ragtag cap replaced the black captain's hat he'd had on only a moment ago.

Spec restarted the engine. It purred in a low hum, and the car started to move slowly. Ever so slowly.

"Pull up behind the putting green. Make it look as if you're lost and have been looking for the place for a while."

I knew in an instant what he was doing. It was the old Hagen molasses treatment, usually applied to a match play opponent: Never show your mug until the last possible moment. Get 'em to think you forgot, that you overslept, that you ain't gonna make it. Do whatever you can to rattle the cage. Then when you do show up, they're knocked off kilter, right out of the box. But keep it going. Make sure your rhythm, or lack of it, drives them crazy. If you have a simple shot, take some time. Make it look as if it's impossible. Even the strongest opponent will crack sooner or later.

Spec Hammond followed Hagen's directives like an actor playing a role. The limousine came to a stop behind the putting green. Haig spied the first tee, which was only thirty yards away.

"There's Titanic, all right." Haig was checking him out, right from the start. Titanic Thompson was a tall, thin man, and he was pacing the first tee like a man who has to go to the bathroom.

"He's waiting for us, junior."

When he saw us walking his way, Titanic Thompson stopped his pacing to greet Haig and welcome him to Pebble Beach. "Glad to have you, Walter, my boy." His voice was loud and deep, and it carried like a long tee ball. "Some of these folks here asked if they could watch us play," he boomed over at us. "You don't mind a small gallery, do you?"

I don't know what Titanic Thompson's concept of "small" is,

but there were over five hundred people ringing the first tee. If their clothing was an indication, the vast majority of them were staying at the lodge. The men wore tweed jackets and ties. The distinctive odor of pipe tobacco was in the air. There were a fair number of women in the gallery, many of them with their hands on their hats as the breeze picked up. The ladies had their eyes fastened on Haig.

Haig walked briskly to the tee and shook hands with Thompson, who towered over him by a good four inches. With their hands joined, Haig looked up into his opponent's soft blue eyes, trying to measure him, as if that were possible. But Titanic Thompson was not a man to assess with a yardstick; he defied definition. Even his eyes were misleading, for their pale azure masked their keenness. He was the sharpest of the sharpies, perhaps the best surveyor of a situation there ever was. This was a man who knew how to size up and take advantage of an opportunity the instant it appeared. He was a prairie dog who knew how to scramble for food.

As caught up in the confrontation as I was, there was still a question that I needed to have answered: What year was it? What would Haig's equipment be? Hickory or steel?

I began casting about for clues, and the answer came sooner than I had expected. Off to the left and behind us, hanging from the entrance to the lodge, was a banner, sewn in blue and gold, announcing Pebble Beach as "the first West Coast venue for the United States Amateur Championship, to be contested here next summer, September 2 through 7, 1929."

Well, I'll say one thing for Titanic Thompson: He wasn't afraid of anything. He was taking on Walter Hagen in his prime, at the peak of his powers, fresh off his fifth triumph in the British Open.

This was going to be a command performance, and the mere thought of it evoked a question that has traveled the ages, from the days of the Knights of the Round Table to Wyatt Earp and Doc Holliday, to the days of nuclear triggermen: Who was going to blink first?

"So, Titanic," Haig said as he turned to the crowd, playing them as if they were clubs in his bag. "How many strokes shall I give you? One a side is all you're getting, so don't go begging on me, okay?"

The crowd roared. "He's a bumpkin, Haig," shouted someone. These folks were a bit rowdy for so well dressed an assemblage. "You can take him, Walter," yelled another. "Let's go," said someone else.

"I've never begged for anything in my life," boasted Titanic Thompson to the crowd. "I'll play you flat, old man."

No strokes? How could Thompson hope to succeed in a contest like that? I mean, the guy might be good, but this was the Haig he was up against. The Haig in his prime. Titanic Thompson couldn't be that good.

"Be my guest," said Titanic, turning to Haig and motioning to the tee. "Let 'er fly, champ."

Hagen wasted no time. He strode confidently to the hitting area and put his peg into the ground. He waggled and got set. He was hunched over a bit and deadly serious; the look on his face told anyone curious enough to notice that he was going to tear into the ball.

Then he backed away. Was he too nervous to hit?

He walked over to one of the women in the gallery, a real looker. "My darling," he said, admiring her flowing auburn hair, "you look like a woman of inestimable taste. Where can I buy some fine champagne around here?"

She blushed and turned to the man whose arm she had been holding only a moment before. He was not amused. She looked only at Hagen, at his jet black hair, his weathered but handsome face. She was peering into the eyes of a man who had seen every continent on the face of the Earth and had experienced all the pleasures human ingenuity can create, flexing his virility at each and every location. She was smitten. "Why," she said softly, "Mr. Hagen, I believe you can purchase something right over there. I'm certain they can satisfy ... ah ... your every need." She gave him the hairy eyeball. He leaned over and put his arm around her as she pointed him to a row of well-appointed store windows that faced the putting green, opposite the lodge.

"Thank you for that advice, my dear. I won't forget it." Haig winked at her as he pulled away. Now the guy next to her really was not amused. "Easy, buster," Haig said to him, attempting to defuse the dynamite. "This is all in sport. It's going to be a contest of skill, a little exhibition. I'm a professional, you know. Just trying to please the home folks." Then he looked into her eyes. "Take care of this little lady, my friend. She looks as if she's worth hanging on to, if you know what I mean."

The man now had to hold her up, her body having fallen limply against his. She had fainted dead away.

Back at the tee, Haig wasted no time. A fast, lurching swing got his shot airborne. It careened far to the left, barely staying in bounds.

I couldn't believe Haig's opening drive. "I thought you said you were going to turn it on for me," I complained. "You almost knocked that thing out of the yard."

"Relax, junior. You haven't seen my short game yet."

"Be careful, will you? Something tells me you're going to have to hold more than a hot putter in your hands to whip this guy."

"Not to worry, lad. I've got it covered."

He sure was confident. But so was Titanic Thompson. His swing, in contrast to Haig's, was as smooth as glass. He pumped one out there 235 from the tee. He was in perfect position to come into the green.

Both men moved quickly down the fairway. The spectators, unrestrained by ropes or marshals or officials of any kind, surrounded the players, roaming where they pleased. Haig's drive had them buzzing like a swarm of bees, but the gallery grew quiet when the players began studying their second shots.

They were equidistant from the green, but their lies were as different as tall fescue and creeping bentgrass. Thompson was in the open, while Hagen had to play from the trees with a restricted backswing.

Haig got down to business before Titanic did. He was playing as if he were rushing to get to the bank before closing time, but his hurry-up tempo did not inhibit his ability. He produced an approach that was an incredible piece of shotmaking. He took a mid-iron and punched it low, hooking the ball around the trees that stood between him and the green. His ball, a Wilson Sure-Flite, bounced over a bunker, coming to rest three feet from the hole.

Titanic played a short iron that finished well short of the hole. He was twenty-three feet away, so he putted first. When it lipped out, I figured this was going to be a long day. I mean, he almost made birdie right out of the box against one of the greatest players ever. Hagen knocked in his short putt for birdie. One up.

As we walked to the second tee, I tapped Thompson's caddie on the shoulder. "How in the world can Titanic hope to compete with Haig straight up?" I inquired. "Is he that good?"

"Yeah. He's that good. He can shoot whatever he needs to, kid. But Hagen can do the same. We might be out here all night."

I didn't have that kind of time, but he didn't know anything about that.

"How much has Thompson bet today?" I was dying to know what they were playing for.

"Enough," he said. "Enough to buy us dinner—for the rest of our freakin' lives!" He let out a raucous laugh and started hurrying to catch up with his man. I ran alongside him.

"But how can Titanic expect to win? He can't beat Hagen straight up."

"Well, let me put it to you this way, kid. He's already up over a thousand dollars."

"No way!" I corrected him fast. "He lost the first hole, or can't you count?"

"You really don't get it, do you?" He walked off without saying anything more.

Hagen ripped two immensely long shots on the second hole and got home in two. Thompson was in the fringe with his second, but a poor chip took him out of birdie range. Hagen two-putted. Two up.

"Junior," Haig said to me on the way to the third tee, "I probably should have more dough riding against the sumbitch, but I'm content just to let you watch this. But don't you get too google-eyed now, 'cause I can't keep this up for eighteen holes. Just relax and enjoy the show."

For the next four holes I watched Hagen mug to the crowd. His technique was fascinating. He played quickly; the most interesting part was the way he hit the difficult shots so fast. He scarcely took time to line up. He just approached the ball, secured his footing, then ripped it, lurching into the ball like a lumberjack trying to fell a tree. But give him a knockdown shot, something simple, and he would take all day studying, posturing, gesturing, posing, thinking, changing clubs, doing anything he could to prolong the moment of uncertainty, the suspense, before he hit. The easier the shot, the longer he took. But the results were always the same. He knocked 'em stiff, one after another. And on the putting green he was as delicate and precise as a brain surgeon. He moved carefully. He saw it all. And he rarely missed.

Haig birdied the third, to the delight of the gallery. His drive—a monstrous hook reminiscent of the screamer he almost knocked out of bounds on number one—left him deep in the tall grass. Undaunted, he burned a six-iron onto the green and proceeded to tank the putt.

But Titanic got hot, too, birdieing the short, well-bunkered fourth with a niblick that almost went in for an eagle. Then Titanic drained one from thirty-five feet at the uphill par-three fifth. Haig returned the compliment with yet another birdie on the par-five sixth, where he chipped in from off the green. Haig was four under after six, and Titanic Thompson, two under and two down, was hard on his heels. What a start!

The seventh hole at Pebble Beach is one of the most beautiful par threes in the world. At only 107 yards, it is a downhill wedge shot that must land on a tiny, kidney-shaped green. To the right and back is the Pacific Ocean. Bunkers are everywhere. It may be the most gorgeous golf hole I've ever seen.

As short as it is, it can be a terror in the wind. When it's blowing hard, it requires a long iron to get there. But today, with the sky gray and relatively calm, the players could choose from a variety of different shots. There was wind, to be sure, but nothing that would knock anyone over. These two could navigate it with anything from a mid-iron knockdown, coming in low, to a full wedge, flying high and landing "soft," as Haig would say.

Haig, who won the honor with his birdie at the sixth, played a seven-iron, keeping his ball underneath what little breeze there was. He punched it in there to about ten feet. It was a solid shot, an eminently commercial play. Titanic had his work cut out for him.

Thompson eyed Haig's ball and looked over at Haig himself. "Let's double it right here," he bellowed. Haig nodded at him.

I tugged at Haig's sleeve to get his attention. "What are you guys up to now? How much is on the line?"

"Five hundred," he said matter-of-factly. Until this moment I had never seen anyone play for more than $20. I was hypnotized by the action as I stood there like a kid in a candy store.

Titanic, on the other hand, was all business. He scanned the gallery, checking the faces of people he had markers with. Finally, he bent over and pulled up a tuft of grass, tossing it into the air to check the wind, which had picked up. It was getting stiff, and it was blowing right into his face. He squinted at the green and at the ocean beyond it. Then he called over his caddie. He reached for his clubs and slowly pulled a driver out of his bag. Wait a minute. It was windy, I knew, but . . . a driver?

Haig and I watched in disbelief as Titanic Thompson laced one but good. He grunted at impact, sending his poor Spalding Dot out over the green, over Haig's ball, over everything. It landed at least seventy-five yards out in the water, drowning in the sea beyond the green. It was a goner if ever there was one.

"What was he doing with that shot?" I asked Haig.

"My boy, he was going three down."

Titanic didn't show any emotion whatsoever. He turned to Haig and said "That's good," referring to the ten-footer that awaited Haig on the green. Hagen took two at the seventh, Titanic Thompson an X.

Hagen was five under after seven, and he was starting to pound his opponent into the ground like a stake. It was time, I decided, to make another attempt at diplomacy with Titanic's caddie.

"You guys are three down," I whispered to him. "What's Titanic going to do now?"

"Don't you know anything, kid? Titanic's got only pocket money bet with Hagen. His real dough is sprinkled all over the gallery here. That's where the action is."

"Yeah, but he's three down and sinking fast, fella." I was still whispering so as not to disturb the players. "Even Titanic Thompson isn't going to get rich betting on that."

"Listen, genius, he didn't bet on that. He told everyone here before Hagen even showed up that he'd be late. Won two hundred and change right there. Some of these idiots actually thought Hagen would get himself to the church on time." He chuckled. "Then Ti said Haig would offer him strokes. That's five hundred, clean as a whistle. Then"—the caddie was almost hysterical now—"then he tells 'em all he'll play Hagen straight up. I mean, they went nuts. Must've thought old Titanic Thompson rotted his freakin' brains out drinking bathtub gin. They figured he'd be tying his own noose if he played Hagen on the level, so they bet he'd never play Hagen even up. Picked up about three hundred lickety-split by stiffing your guy on the strokes."

My jaw was down.

"What these folks can't get straight," he continued, "is that old Ti ain't really playing Hagen at all. He's playing them."

And now he had to play the eighth, the hardest hole on the course. It is a massive par four that forces players to fire their second shots over a deep chasm across Stillwater Cove. It was here that Titanic Thompson started to come back. He caught the fairway with his drive, then rifled a brassie onto the green and made the putt. He won against Haig's bogey, three versus five. "He wasted that birdie," Haig told me as we departed the green.

At the ninth, a 450-yard par four that parallels the Pacific and is a slicer's nightmare from start to finish, Thompson won with a par as Haig played the entire hole from the right rough.

After nine, Haig had hit it in every direction, was two under par, but was only one hole ahead. Let them say what they will about Titanic Thompson, the man can flat play golf. Hagen was at his peak, playing his fanny off, and Titanic was right with him.

The back nine starts along the ocean, and then, after one hole, it takes them back into Del Monte Forest. Away from the pounding surf, the golf grew quieter, and Hagen slowly numbed Thompson with a series of scrambling pars. He won the tenth with a four, and Titanic never got any closer to him than two down.

At the seventeenth tee Haig stood dormie. He had the honor, having kept it since the tenth. But he was uneasy, for he knew it was a long way back to the clubhouse. And he also knew that even though Titanic was two down with two to play, he was a dangerous adversary, especially if he could manage to force the action to the final tee, for on Pebble's legendary oceanside par-5 closer anything could happen. It would be prudent indeed for my man Walter to zip up the pouch right here.

The seventeenth, like the seventh, is a world-famous par three. The green is in the shape of an hourglass, surrounded by an assortment of odd-shaped bunkers and bordered on the left and rear by the ocean. The main difference between the two holes is that number seven is the length of a football field, while seventeen is more than twice as long.

Haig slammed a brassie toward the green. His ball was hit well, but the wind shifted as he made impact. Instead of quartering, it suddenly followed from the rear, giving Haig's shot an extra push, sending it into one of the back bunkers.

Even though he was two down with two to play, it was advantage Titanic. Thompson pulled out his driver, just as he had done on seven. This time, however, there was no murmur from the gallery. In this fickle wind the club selection was eminently reasonable.

But all that changed when he uncorked the shot. It soared like Lindbergh for Paris, but in the opposite direction. Headed due west, this was a golf shot that looked as if it would carry Hawaii. This baby wasn't coming down until it hit Japan.

Haig looked over at me and shrugged. We both fixed our eyes on Titanic. With his shot drowning in a watery grave, Titanic had to concede the match. He paid Haig several hundred dollars the same way a banker hands out greenbacks to a patron making a withdrawal. It was only business.

The crowd applauded both players, and everyone walked the eighteenth fairway back to the lodge where, no doubt, Haig planned on taking that woman's advice and procuring some bubbly to celebrate the occasion.

"Have you figured it out?" I asked him in a whisper as we walked along northward, with the Pacific on our left and tall pines and immaculate mansions on the right.

"I'm thinking, I'm thinking," Haig said as he looked over at the waves, which were crashing against the seawall that prevents the fairway from eroding onto the beach below.

"He's pretty good, I'll tell you that," said Haig. "But he probably picked this place 'cause they don't know him around these parts. He is from Texas, you know."

"You figure he wants to be just another guy out here? A vacationer, a guest looking for a friendly game?"

"Yeah," said Haig. "The less they know about him, the easier it is to hustle. One thing a hustler can't handle is a reputation. Me, junior, it's my life's blood. To a guy like Titanic, though, it's death."

I was looking over the crowd, noticing the clothing, the long dresses, the hats on the men and women, when Haig snapped his fingers. "Gotta be," he said, turning around to find Titanic.

We both watched him among the crowd. He was smiling like a

stockbroker invested in a bull market. They were all handing him money, some more gracefully than others, and to each of the losers Titanic simply said, "That's the way it goes, boys."

When we made it to the lodge, Haig found the woman he had made eyes at on the first tee. She was standing with the same fellow, the two of them part of a vast crowd that had swelled massively in the two and a half hours since Haig and Titanic teed off. There were over fifteen hundred people here now. They applauded Haig and Titanic vigorously, the roar rolling like a wave over the throng. It was the third ovation in fifteen minutes.

Haig asked his favorite spectator where that shop was again, the place where they sold booze. She pointed down the lane of shops to the third place on the right. It was a spirit house, appropriately situated between a pharmacy and a haberdashery shop. One fixed you up before the drinking began, the other after.

Haig sent Spec over to pick up some champagne. He returned with several magnums, and Haig adjourned to the ballroom inside the lodge where the people had gathered. He toasted everyone: Titanic, the lodge staff, the crowd, the Wilson Sporting Goods Company, the United States of America. After several rounds he cornered Titanic Thompson and asked him about the driver.

"I understood the shot on seventeen," said Haig. "Hell, Titanic, I can see you hitting a driver under those circumstances. The club can get away from you anytime, it's just one of those things. But that one on seven? What were you doing out there?"

"I bet a guy."

"That doesn't help me, Titanic. What was the bet, for crying out loud?"

"Some loudmouth. World traveler, he was. Said he'd seen you at St. George's, at Deal, and at Muirfield. You know, the Open."

"So what? Lots of guys saw me there. What makes this fellow so special other than his big mouth?"

"Well, that's just it. He said he'd seen you. Said you were long, as in l-o-n-g. The old starched collar tells me to go get Jim Barnes, Arthur Havers, and Mac Smith. Says I could stretch their drives back-to-back-to-back, and even then I'd never be close to Sir Walter. I mean, he's telling me this like he's a professor or something. Now, you can guess where this is going, boys. The son of a gun says I'll never outhit you in a million years. Shoot, Walter, I couldn't resist. Had to make the bet. Darned if I didn't bet the bastard I could do it twice in one day. I bagged one at seven and could have tied the ribbon on it at twelve, you know, when you knocked it on there with a mid-mashie." He lifted his champagne flute and took a long sip. "Hell, fellas, I just waited until seventeen for some drama."

"You mean you weren't even trying to win?" I asked, interrupting him. "You were two down at seventeen. You could have pulled it out, especially with Haig in the sand."

"Son, I had five hundred bucks bet with your buddy Walter here. I had five thousand bet with Mr. Great Britain over there. And look around this room, kid," he said, craning his neck. "I bet these folks that your friend's first shot would be a hook." His eyes were darting everywhere, searching for new pigeons like a newly licensed hunter out to bag the limit the first day of the season. "I bet he'd smell of scotch when he showed up. Bet he'd talk to a dame before he hit a shot. Oh, he had me a little worried when he addressed that thing, but when he backed off . . . kid, when he backed off, I knew it was my day. I mean, I even bet Mr. British Open over there that the Haig would birdie number seven. I gave your pal the damn putt, for Pete's sake. But trust me, kid, it was for a good cause. I got over ten thousand dollars in here." He gently patted the right front pocket on his plus fours.

Haig looked at Titanic, then he leaned over and whispered in my ear, "Isn't this guy beautiful, junior?"

In all the frivolity, Haig showed me that he was truly a professional. It was not the golf or the social graces that did it but his attention to detail. The instant I reminded him of the time and the burdens that Jones had placed upon my shoulders, he excused himself from the crowd and steered me out of the lodge and back toward the limousine.

Spec was there, ready to roll. Once we were away from the lodge, we wound through Del Monte forest, back into the fog. When we emerged, the sunlight was blinding. Spec pulled up to the back door of the clubhouse as if no time had passed.

Hagen was out of the car as soon as it stopped. I rushed after him, chasing him back inside, trying to catch up but losing ground with every step. By the time I reached the bar, he was already back to work, the unaffected expression on his face a clever cover for our covert mission.

The moment he saw me sliding onto a bar stool, he motioned with his palm, telling me not to speak. "That little jaunt, junior," he cautioned me, "was on the quiet. So mum's the word. I don't know what Jones would think of me and Titanic putting on that show out back, and besides, even if he didn't mind, Jones might object to my horning in on his territory—with you, I mean."

Haig drifted back to the stories about Jones and their match in Florida. He continued for several minutes. When he talked, there was not a hint of worry in his voice; there were no second thoughts, no compunctions about our visit with Titanic Thompson. Haig was free and easy, floating on air; it was as if telling stories of his exploits against Jones down in Florida had shot him full of helium.

But the euphoria didn't last, for Jones himself reentered the room. Haig squelched the stories, smiling my way as Jones asked me about last night and about my plans for the rest of day two.

I was afraid he would ask about such things. I didn't exactly know how to explain the dreams I had last night or if I should even try. After all, they were a trifle strange. How many people—even wide-eyed college juniors—hallucinate the way I did? Discretion quickly won out. "Slept like a baby," I told him. On Haig's advice I didn't drop any hints about the morning's adventure at Pebble Beach.

"And Hogan?" Jones asked, persistent in his effort to learn of my plans. No wonder he was a killer at match play. The guy never lets up.

"I don't know," I said. "There ought to be a way to reason with him, but I'll be a monkey's uncle if I know what it is. I feel like it's the seventy-second hole. I'm dog tired, staring down a tight hole location right behind a deep bunker, being asked to rip a long iron in there close."

Jones smiled. "Your lie may be better than you think."

"What do you mean?"

"For one thing, son, are you sure that reasoning will do the trick? Have you considered the man's emotions? He has them, you know. We all do. Maybe that's the way."

"I can't reason with Hogan. No one ever could. He thinks for himself, has a mind of his own. Emotions? He keeps them all bottled up inside. He's locked as tight as a fortress. You know that."

Jones was thinking, searching for the right way to make his point. "Ever lined up a sidehill putt, son? If you have, you know how difficult it can be. But it can be done. Just because the job's hard doesn't mean it can't be accomplished."

"But I can't intrude on him," I pleaded. "Hogan'll brush me off like pine needles in his line. I'll be cast aside in no time."

"But you've got to read that line, son. It's not a moving target."

"I'm not worried about moving targets. I'm worried about moving Hogan. He seems pretty darn sure of what he wants to do. No one could stop him before. What makes you think I can do it now, here, in this place?"

"I'm telling you, son," pressed Jones, "you aren't looking at an impossible shot here. You're closer to the green than you think. There's a purpose to all of this, a reason behind it." Jones looked me over like a putt he could not afford to miss.

I didn't know how to respond to him.

"Didn't you tell me," Jones asked intently, "that Hogan opened up to you somewhat when you were talking out there on the range?"

"Well, yes, but—"

"Then you have to get him to open up again and find the spot at which to bore in deeper. He'll let you in if you can find it."

"How will I know?"

"What did he tell you when you asked him about that message he knocked out last night? Remember?"

"He said, 'You'll know it when you see it.' "

"And you will. It's like picking a club for a shot into a swirling wind. Just use your best judgment and then trust it to be right."

I pleaded with Jones that I was not ready to climb this mountain. There was so much more that I wanted to know, that I needed to know. I asked about the library, and Jones said it was completely at my disposal. Anything I needed was there, he said. He also told me there was someone else I had to consult before proceeding further. He said he'd never known when the right time was with Ship but that my time had come.

When I asked who he was talking about, Jones went silent, almost as if he didn't hear the inquiry. But he did. He helped me out of my chair and walked me around the room. Saying nothing, he pointed to a parchment map on the wall. From the lettering, the thing appeared to be several hundred years old. The only place that was at all familiar was Auchterader, a little town near Gleneagles in the foothills of Scotland. As I strained to read the details of the topography depicted within the frame, Jones pulled at me again, this time dragging me over to a painting of rolling fields of green. Next to the canvas was a glass case in which an ancient walnut crook had been preserved. A card next to it said USED FOR BAFFING, CIRCA A.D. 1450.

I stood there, taking it all in, and I realized he had led me on a grand circle tour of the room. I was standing across from the library now, directly in front of a plain unmarked door. When I looked at Jones, he stared into my eyes with an intensity that I cannot describe. It was as if he knew what lay behind the door and how it would affect me over the course of the precious few hours and minutes that remained. Without hearing any instructions, I knew I was supposed to walk on through the passageway and follow it wherever it led.

Adventure is a funny concept. It is at once a noun, a thing: *an adventure*. But it is also a state of mind, a feeling, a force that can surround and engulf a man who is only halfway willing to let it get inside him: *the spirit of adventure*. Once it imbues the senses, it overtakes them, leading people where they would not otherwise tread.

Even within the generous bounds of my experiences here, I knew I was venturing into uncharted territory. What would I find behind the door? Fire-breathing dragons? Friendly elves? There wasn't time to worry about which it was, good or bad, friend or foe. Whatever it was, I had to confront it, for I had opted to travel the full distance, and if this sojourn, this side trip, was part of the itinerary, so be it. Little did I know then that behind the door was the pathway to enlightenment, the crucial stage of the journey that would lead me to the answers to my questions.

·11·

THE STAIRWAY WAS MADE OF STONE, SO COLD AND HARD THAT IT must have been as old as the ages. And yet, despite the enduring character of the masonry, time had taken its toll. Many of the steps were cracked, and the edges were well worn, almost rounded, by generations of climbers. The surrounding walls had a chiseled appearance, as if they had been carved out of the side of a mountain. The passageway looked like a mineshaft.

The well-traveled stairs were shiny and slippery, but fortunately for me, my shoes had soft rubbery soles that gripped perfectly. I made the ascent quietly, without incident, winding around and around in a dizzying spiral. By the time I reached the top stair, I was aloft in one of the turrets that framed the clubhouse. This had to be where the man they called Ship had his office.

There was no way I could have been ready for what I encountered there. Through a rounded stone archway I came upon a room that took me back several centuries. The only light came from a candle sitting on an unfinished wooden table, which was weird because I could see that the room had been wired for modern appliances. Several outlets were in plain view.

The first indication that I was not alone came from a clicking sound, the type made by one of those ejector putting devices—some people call them "playback" machines—that allow you to putt across the living room carpet and have the balls automatically propelled back to your feet. And that's exactly what he was doing when I first spotted him: working on his stroke.

But this was no mere ten handicapper hoping to get better. There was no pipe to puff on, no cardigan, no BullsEye Old Standard, no Titleist 384 Tour 100s rolling across the clean pile of a woolen carpet. No, this old fellow was something altogether different.

He wore what I first thought were rags, but which upon closer examination turned out to be a tunic or robe of some sort. He was old—ancient, really—with long white hair rolling in curls over his shoulders and down his back. A thick beard hung off his chin like unkempt moss.

He held a crook, one that looked as if it had been crafted from the same tree that yielded the specimen on display downstairs. He was swinging at small stones, knocking them in the direction of the electric putting cup, one manufactured in the 1960s by Eagle Enterprises, Ltd., of Topeka, Kansas. Whenever he hit the contraption dead center, it sparked and smoked, the ejector rod pumping like a piston as the machine tried madly to repel the pebbles that were lodged in its jaws. After a dozen or so jolts, the machine went dead, and the old man cast it aside, throwing another one onto the floor—a replacement of sorts—into which he continued to fire more of his rocky projectiles.

This fellow was more than a little eccentric, I quickly concluded, but he had a collection of golf clubs the likes of which my young eyes had never seen. Being something of a club freak, I was instantly captivated by the array of implements he had at his disposal in this golfer's aerie. There was one that looked like Calamity Jane, another that was the spitting image of Old Betsy, Palmer's favorite weapon of the late fifties and early sixties. There were offset heads, center-shafted blades, and any number of odd-shaped mallets that weighed anywhere from a couple of ounces to several pounds. He even had a Zebra.

When he saw me gravitate to the hardware, he broke the silence.

"Those are nae guid fer playin'. Me crook 'n' these wee stones, the featheries o'er there, they're wha' 'tis used fer gowlfin', laddy. Aye, they are."

I said nothing. A man with a long crooked piece of timber and a handful of rocks was not someone to be trifled with, especially on the off chance that he knew how to use the first to propel the second in my direction. I bided my time before saying anything. Who in the blazes was this guy?

"Ye're lookin' at me hittin' here like I'm some sort o' fossil. But I'm a gowlfer, indeed I am." He gestured toward the putting machine. "Laddy, this . . . this . . . catapult 'tis nae guid fer playin' and 'tis a menace t' me practicin'. It canna be guid fer anythin', but the Leemur Man's sayin' I should be usin' it."

"Lema?" I asked. "You mean Tony Lema?"

"Aye. The Leemur Man has himself an eye for such things. He's always a-comin' t' me t' help wi' me strokin'. Brings a bottle, too. Tha's the best part o' the lesson. I'm gettin' better, I am, but I'm ne'er a-gwin' t' threaten Crenshaw. I could be practicin' forever and ne'er be a-strokin' like him."

If only the company that made these putting contraptions could see this! To see their ingenious device so roundly defiled by an old Scot would surely drive them crazy.

I knew I had been sent here by Jones to make inquiry and I knew I must inquire of Ship soon, but I sensed it would not be prudent to attempt to get inside his mind by entering through the front door. Instead, I would have to work my way around, through the mental thicket that lay between us. If I was lucky, I would be able to slip in through a side entrance.

"Why don't you use golf balls with that thing?" I asked. "They'll work much better than the stones you're shoving in there."

"Aye, tha' they will. But ye dinna know wha' the game is I'm playin'. Joones 'n' Haggin, them two says I've got t' start playin' their way. But I'm nae a-gwin' t' do tha'. They'll come t' be playin' as I do, if they wanna be baffin' wi' me in the fields."

"Baffin'?" I inquired. This fellow obviously was not the Haig's typical Wednesday pigeon; Haig wouldn't waste his time on an old-timer who hits rocks into a putting cup.

"They're playin' a game tha' I canna ken. I've ne'er been one t' be a-countin' when I'm gowlfin'. 'Tis hittin' the stones 'n' feath-eries tha's the game. An' I'm a far bounder, I am. Bounded o'er the far hillock last time on th' green. E'en Haggin canna do tha'. An' Joones! He canna e'en strike wi' me baffin' crook."

The old man must have played Jones and Hagen in some sort of challenge match out behind the range, something like that. But who was he? And why was he cooped up in this Tower of London?

The only thing I could see with certainty was that the man in front of me was very, very old. He walked about the room slowly, as if he were tired, ready to doze off the moment he let down his guard. When he paused to sit down, I decided to take the plunge.

"How long have you been playing?" I asked, hoping I could get him to talk expansively.

"Well now, I'm o'er . . . o'er . . ." He never made it through the answer; his voice turned into a slow grating buzz in mid-sentence as his chin nodded downward and softly touched his chest. He was fast asleep before responding to my first question.

I gently attempted to rouse him, hoping I could figure out who he was and why Jones had sent me to his lair. As I shook his frail body, I noticed a delicate quality about him. His robe was thin, al-most like tissue paper. I was careful not to tear anything. His skin and bones were just as fragile, and it made me worry that he'd crack and crumble if I exerted any pressure on him at all. Around the room were ledger books and quill pens, bookshelves stuffed full of records. This must be a clearinghouse of some sort. But that was not all. Against one wall stood a score of assorted crooks, each a different size and shape, each made out of a different type of wood. I could see ash, hickory, persimmon, maple, and hazelwood, and this was just one batch of his equipment. He must be a craftsman, too, for at the far end of the room was a workbench that ran the length of the end wall. Works in progress competed for space there, vying with an array of hand tools. Chisels, rasps, mallets, and several sets of calipers lay scattered about. Wood shavings were all over the place, covering the ground like hair on the floor of a barbershop.

In another corner was a spotting scope and a portal through which he could see the driving range. Had he been watching Hogan?

A miscellany of artifacts rested on the walls and atop the bookshelves: old trophies and new ones, some engraved, some plain. Paintings of golf holes, of fields, of flocks, of shepherds . . . Of shepherds? It can't be. No way. Not Jones, Haig, Old Tom . . . and . . . him?

Then I realized my error. I wasn't listening carefully enough when Jones and the others were explaining it. This man is a shepherd, or at least he was in another life, and when they told me about him, I must have had wax in my ears. I heard the word "Ship" when they called out his name, but this old man was no oceangoing vessel. He has to be one of the game's originators; it was "Shep" they were saying all along. With the enormity of the moment overpowering my every attempt at analysis, I was transformed from an inquisitor into an awe-struck spectator. I stared at him, transfixed, amazed.

But I could not stand still for very long. To rouse him, I gave his shoulders a cuddly roll, praying his eyes would come open and nothing would break. He jerked slightly and shook his head to clear away the cobwebs. He was awake, and there appeared to be no aftereffects from his brief slumber.

"Oh, laddy, I'm in a state t' be sleepin'. This auld body canna go like in the days when me baffin' was t' be seen across the land. Aye . . . four hundred . . . nae . . . five hundred years. 'Tis a lang time, e'en fer an old bounder like me. But there's nae time fer talkin' abou' tha'. Ye've come here, nae doubt, t' be musin' the profundiddies wi' me."

How was I going to explain this to anyone with any intelligence? I've walked into the den of one of the original golfers, and he's still kicking, even if barely, and he's got something he wants to talk to me about. Musin' the profundiddies?

"Do you know about Mr. Hogan?" I asked in a somber tone.

"Aye."

"Are you worried?"

"Nae."

"The people downstairs are scared stiff he'll destroy everything."

"I canna say, laddy. If he's t' do it, then he's t' do it. All I know is, ye've been sent here fer a reason 'n' by a power higher than me."

"Wait a minute. Just who are you?"

"I'm an auld shepherd from the hills near t' Blairgowrie. Drove me flock doon the hillside t' Perth, 'n' when we got a chance, we'd go all the miles t' the Auld course at St. Andress. Now tha's where there's gowlfers, me boy, like ye ne'er hae seen nor can likely imagine."

"I have a better imagination than you think."

"Aye?"

"Yes, at least I think so, if that counts for anything here." I was speaking with respect, I hoped, tiptoeing with each word so as not to offend him. "Sir, the game may have changed over the centuries, but we're still baffin' at it, if I can borrow your terminology."

"Nae," he answered sternly. "'Tis nae longer the game I'm knowin'. Ye're countin' 'n' playin' by a book full o' rules. A 'cyclopedia, 'tis! Now, me boy, when we could get t' the fields, we'd be baffin' with all our might, tryin' to smash the stones o'er the glen 'n' out t' where we couldna see 'em nae more."

"That hasn't changed at all," I answered. My mind conjured up the image of a youthful Palmer at the top of his follow through, having just hammered a ball with his driver, flattening it with the club face the way a blacksmith pounds steel. I could also see my pals, the L-Man, Johnny Susko, Duke, Big D, and Tall Ricky, swinging for the downs. "It may be golf," I told him, "but we still play Home Run Derby more than once in a while. Where I come from, guys whale on it pretty good."

"Aye, of tha' ye may be able, but ye're countin' 'em," he said, growing testy.

"Maybe so. But we're doing what you and your contemporaries were doing—back when you were doing it, that is." I shrugged. "It's the same old game. It's called Hit It and Go Find It."

He looked out the window, his eyes fixed on something in the distance.

"These boys, like Hoogin, they're somethin', they are."

"Ah, yes. Hogan. What're we going to do about him?"

"Wha' are *ye* gonna do? I ne'er said I'd wrestle wi' the likes o' him. Hoogin 'n' his game . . . together as one, they're too mighty a mountain for a man o' me weariness." He shook his head and bore a look of resignation. "Nae, laddy. Unless there's somethin' special tha's needin' my attention, I'm nae gwin t' be a-tusslin' wi' the likes o' Hoogin. Can ye nae see why?"

Of course I could. But even though Shep did not look able to risk the elements at his age, and despite the fact he was no match for Hogan physically, he still could help me in a big way. The trick was to get him to drop the frustrations, the protestations, the apprehensions about the present-day state of the game and start—how did he put it?—musin' the profundiddies.

There was so much ground to cover! Where could, where should, where must we begin? At the roots? Why were the three of us drawn to golf with such intensity—him from the rolling hills of fifteenth-century Scotland, Hogan from the Depression-baked caddie yards of Fort Worth, and me from the quiet Richmond district of San Francisco? That inquiry alone could consume more time than I had, but we had to begin somewhere.

Old Shep and I spent the next several minutes talking about Hogan's obsession with the game. The discussion inevitably turned to technique. What is so all-engrossing about mechanical perfection, I asked, when it must be applied in the context of an imperfect game in an imperfect world? After all, even a perfect drive can land in a divot, a perfect approach can bounce off line, and a crucial putt, even one stroked perfectly, can go awry if it collides with a single spike mark.

"Ye're thinkin' now," he said, scratching the white mane that flowed over his shoulders. "I'm ne'er shure they matter in this, all those divots 'n' spike marks, fer once ye've learned t' cuntrull a crook, ye've learned all there is t' know abou' baffin'. Nae, laddy, a man canna ferget how t' hit once he's learned it. 'N' once he knows the way t' do it, then his mind is free fer thinkin'—'n' tha's a blessin' 'n' a curse, shackled together, for 'tis thinkin' what gets t' be such troooble."

Thinking? Trouble? Old Shep didn't know the half of it. How many times I'd felt perfectly aligned while addressing a shot, only to watch my ball fly hopelessly off line into the trees or some ungodly lie. All those days when I just couldn't get into the game. Or the days when I did get into it, only to fall on my face. Even par after fourteen, and I didn't break 80. What made me lose it? Five over after three, and I shot 75. What enabled me to find it?

"I know what you mean," I said, trying to keep the conversation flowing, my goal being to ride the current and follow Shep's river of knowledge to its source. "They say it's all mental."

"Totally," he responded, his gapped teeth forming a glowing smile. He was laboring with each breath, as if he'd started a mental hundred-yard dash. "'N' if ye can harness wha' lies within, ye canna be beaten." He paused for a moment to catch his breath. Then he pointed to his head, poking an index finger at his right temple. "This here's a cauldron," he said excitedly. "Now, laddy, sometimes she's cold . . . 'n' sometimes she's smolderin' 'n' cracklin' from the fyre. Great is the man who kin allow the flames t' be lickin' the upper reaches o' his kettle withou' bein' consumed in the process."

I began to feel my own head radiate with heat, and I pulled away from him.

"Dinye be flinchin', laddy, fer fear'll ne'er tame yer noggin'. Ye hae t' feel the flames, but ye mus'n allow 'em t' burn up wha' yer cookin'. A thinkin' man kens when t' pull hisself away from the fyre, 'n' then the stew he's boilin' will simmer wi' all the flavors mixin' together. 'Tis then he'll be smellin' 'n' tastin', laddy, 'n' if'n he's done 'er right, he'll nae soon ferget the meal."

Despite Shep's vivid imagery, I was confused and must have looked it because he pulled me to him, and when we were nose to nose, he picked up where he had left off. "Dinye be thinkin' wi' a cluttered mind, laddy. Tha's where the troooble begins."

He instructed me to clear out my mind, rinse it out completely. Keep it open and fresh, he said; in that way a man can write a new story each round. "When ye're playin' the game, laddy, ye're inscribin' yerself in the book o' life. Ye're doin' it with every swing."

Every stroke, he cautioned, is a new experience, with no moorings, no ties to the past. "'Tis a game full o' wonder," he said. "Fer in each shot there is a new opportunity, a new discovery, a new adventure. 'N' laddy, the adventure feeds the excitement, which fuels the fyre."

He explained that this excitement was a mystic power. According to Shep, excitement releases juices—"lubricants," he called them—that oil the machinery of the mind, cleaning it out as they squirt through the gears of a man's thought processes. "'N' when these juices are flowin'," whispered Shep, "they kin clear oot the dust tha's cloudin' yer vision." It was like taking care of a boat after a long journey, scraping away the barnacles, if you will, that form on the hull of the human mind.

Excitement, he said, would not only make a person's blood rush, not only clear out the obstructions that clutter the process of free and inspired thought, but it would change a person, too. "It'll hae ye seein' everythin' around ye, and when ye does tha', laddy, ye become one with yer world. At tha' very moment, ye're part o' all life, at the edges 'n' at the heart o' it all at once."

I was wondering just what this sensation felt like when Shep supplied another clue.

"When the leaves are movin', laddy, ye'll be movin' with 'em. 'N' when the planets 'n' the Earth are circlin' each other, ye'll be turnin' with 'em." A man with that sort of rhythm, he concluded, has got to be able to control a golf club. He guaranteed it.

"But how does someone actually do this stuff in real life?" I asked, concerned about that "smolderin' cauldron" and those flames. My fear was that such heat would bring danger to hands that could not control it—and the image of Hogan's bloodied hands flashed across my mind.

"Ah, tha's somethin' now," he said with a far-off gaze. "How do ye manage it? Only a few kin say 'n' fewer kin do."

He walked over to a bookshelf and began thumbing through a collection of instruction books. He had them all: the great ones, Horace Hutchinson, Sir Walter Simpson, Tommy Armour, Ernest Jones, Harry Vardon, as well as the modern theorists, Bob Toski, Jimmy Ballard, David Leadbetter. He tossed them onto the table like a Las Vegas blackjack dealer.

Then he held up a copy of *Golf in the Kingdom*. "This here," he said, "this here is somethin' special. I'm givin' 'er out the way those manufacturin' companies distribute calendars. Pretty pictures they're a-passin' on t' their customers. But ye won't be markin' down yer days on this here, 'n' ye won't be tossin' her away a' the end o' the year, neither. Not if ye ken the lessons tha' are in here." He held the book aloft again. "Nae, this here, this here's somethin' t' be readin' 'n' readin' again."

"What about the other teachers? I can't ignore them. I have to study them, too, don't I?"

"Now, laddy, dinye be confusin' them w' the likes o' Shivas Irons, fer there's nothin' t' be comparin' between 'em. Those others, they canna teach the game I know, and ye'll nae be learnin' wha' ye needs t' ken from them. They only tell o' baffin', wi' nae a word abou' thinkin'. I'm talkin' abou' real thinkin' now, laddy. 'N' if'n ye wanna be studyin' how t' think, wha' ye must do is—"

"Can't I study the players as well as the 'thinkers,' as you put it?"

"Aye."

"Where do we begin?"

"Well, laddy, there's—"

I cut him off with an idea of my own. "Jones, right?"

"Aye," he said.

"I mean Bobby Jones, not Ernest."

"Aye." He nodded approval, then put his fingers to his chin. "He's the best I've e'er seen. Haggin, now he could battle, too, but he's nae a match fer Bobby. I hae nae been able t' uncover the troo proof, but Joones . . . he 'n' Shivas, they musta had a meetin' somewhere. Once a man gains the understandin' he needs, he'll nae ferget it. But, laddy, dinye be placin' all yer eggs in one basket, neither. For as great teachin' as Shivas kin do, he canna be a sub-stitute fer livin'. Now Joones, he knew how t' live, he knew."

"But Jones was so angry as a young man. Cussing, tossing clubs, and all that. What happened to him? How did he get so good?"

"'Tis all right t' explode, laddy, fer tha' shows yer a-totin' a bushel o' the energy on yer shoulders. Ah, young Bobby . . . like a ragin' animal he was. But ye see, he learned how t' cuntrull it." Shep paused, looking for the right image. "Like breakin' a horse, 'tis. Ye love the surge of a stallion, but if ye wanna be ridin' the beast, what guid does it do ye if'n the blasted horse throws ye? All ye gets are bruises, 'n' ye'll ne'er be a rider."

"But what made Jones so special? What lifted him above the others? Did he learn something the others missed?"

"I dinna know. But I'm sensin' there was some power . . . some-thin' ye 'n' I canna see. But 'tis there for shure. I'm thinkin' Bobby was a messenger; someone sent him t' tell us somethin', fer there's ne'er been one like him e'er since. He dinna let nothin' cuntrull him . . . and yet he could cuntrull all 'twas 'round him. 'N' he did it withou' hittin' a thousand practice balls, neither. Nae like those—what did Haggin call 'em?—those roo-butts out there t'day onna toor."

"But how do you train yourself to do it? The control, I mean."

"Aye, tha's the secret. There's nae a trainin' ground, as ye de-scribe it. There's only learnin', 'n' once ye've learned the way, once ye're knowin' yerself, ye've learned somethin' ye can keep fore'er.

'N' no one kin destroy it, neither. Tha's wha makes it so powerful. Once it starts, it ne'er ends."

Old Shep is a kind, sagacious fellow, but he was playing his cards close to the vest. He spoke only with images, and that was entirely appropriate, for as he kept reminding me, these things have to be felt; they cannot be transcribed and followed like a recipe.

"Have ye e'er played a round in th' wind, laddy?"

"I hate it," I confessed, thrusting the words in his direction like an iron slammed back into the bag after a missed shot. "You can't get set. And if you put any sort of spin on the ball, even the slightest bit, the wind takes over, and you have to stand by helplessly as your shot drifts away into no-man's-land."

"Aye, 'tis troo. In gowlf, laddy, yer shots can be kidnapped by the wind. Prisoners o' the fates. But listen t' me now." Shep's eyes bored into me as if they were diamond-tipped drills. "Ye've got t' learn that fer a man who's trustin' his troo self, there's nothin' t' fear."

"But I don't know anyone who likes to play in the wind."

"Don't be admirin' 'n' adorin' their tastes, me boy, fer ye'll only be copyin' the weak ones, the ones who fear themselves. Ye canna begin t' sense it until ye feel it. But hear me, laddy, 'n' trust in me words, fer the wind is much more than a pesterin' influence. 'Tis a mirror o' yer whole self. It has the power t' strip a man naked before his enemies, make him shiver t' his bones. Tha's wha' they're all fearin'."

"I can't say as I blame them."

"But ye can harness her, laddy, if ye takes the time t' listen."

"Listen to the wind?"

"Aye. For 'tis the heavens speakin'. 'Tis the energy swirlin' around ye. Ye kin try 'n' fight her, but ye canna stop her tha' way. Ye kin ne'er stop her. 'N' ye shouldna' be hopin' t' do tha', neither. Fer the day she stops is the day yer life is o'er."

I was watching him more closely now; his message was getting through to me, growing deeper by the word. Shep's face grew taut; his brow was as furrowed as a freshly raked bunker.

"Is the wind the most important thing of all?"

"'Tis nae more important than anythin' else. Ye see, tha's the mistake they all make. 'Tis louder 'n' rages more than the other things, tha's fer shure, 'n' tha' may be, but 'tis nae more meaningful. 'Tis a symbol, one ye kin see and feel. A symbol o' the energy. The wind is wha' leads t' the energy. She's a steppin'-stone, laddy. 'N' the energy is wha' ye must be seekin', fer it's flowin' in everythin'. Ye just hae t' be lookin' fer it."

"Is finding the wind the key to the energy?"

"Nae. Many a man can do tha', 'n' there's many that has. Ye'll gain nothin' special e'en if ye're lucky enough t' be locatin' the energy. Wha' 'tis worth knowin', laddy, is wha' t' do when ye find it. 'Tis how ye *use* the energy. Tha's where ye'll see the difference in men."

His face softened, and as he continued to explain it all, the words sounded a melodious rhythm.

"Hae ye e'er seen a ship on the ocean?" he asked. "Ah, when 'tis calm 'n' the water's flat like glass, she rides wi' great balance. But when 'tis stormin', wi' the sky thunderin' 'n' all tha', the waves crashin' 'n' all, she rolls like a barrel down a hill, rumblin', tumblin', crackin' 'n' creakin', and ye canna be bettin' she'll make it t' shore. But if her cap'n 'n' his mates know the sea, they'll keep her balanced. 'N' she'll only be lookin' like she's fightin' the waves. What she's really doin' is tamin' 'em, ridin' 'em, lettin' 'em carry her forward."

"When it's storming," I inquired, "is that the time to measure the energy and use it to your advantage?"

"Yer listenin', boy."

"And because you can't make the wind stop, you might as well make the most of it. Is that what you're telling me?"

"Tha's only part o' the lesson, laddy. Fer ye must always remember tha' the wind is talkin' t' ye, 'n' the reply ye give is like talkin' back. If ye be fightin' 'n' arguin' wi' her, she'll fight 'n' argue wi' ye even harder. But if ye can talk t' the wind, ye can gain a friend, and a good friend she'll be."

"You know," I said with an understanding I didn't have a moment ago, "I've had the same feeling, that struggling feeling, whenever I start to argue with people. Sometimes I just go off, and the person I'm talking to does the same thing, but in the opposite direction. And the next thing you know, we're at each other's throats. And yet, if I can find something—anything, really—that we can agree on, we bond to it, grasping for it as though it were a lifeline. And then the discussion turns down a different path. We start moving toward each other, learning that there's more that unites us than divides us."

"Nae only are ye listenin'," he said, "but ye're learnin', too."

This last comment filled my heart with joy. But one glance at my wristwatch and I began to panic. It was getting late, and I did not know if there was enough time left for the work that lay ahead. I knew I had to ask my question directly now.

"Jones told me," I said, "about the choice. He laid it out pretty clearly. But there's something I need to ask you. Has anybody ever replayed a round?"

In an instant everything changed. It was as though I had pricked the balloon that was holding us aloft. Shep's shoulders began to slump, and he was now old again and tired. His features lost their character, and his muscles went limp. His eyes, which had been illuminated by the fire of his imagination only moments ago when he spoke of the wind and her power, now stared out from hollow sockets. His lips were no longer moist but vapidly dry. Even his hair, already ghostly white, seemed a bit paler.

"Nae," he said, his mind on Hogan. "There's been nae replayin'. And wi' guid reason."

"Hasn't anyone been tempted to do it?"

"Nae . . . nae tha' I ken."

"But why is that? Surely someone has to have been tempted somewhere along the way."

"There's a reason tha' I'm believin' in, but I canna say 'tis the thing tha's causin' players t' be shyin' away. Ye see, everyone has somethin' . . . 'n' that's the beauty. 'Tis somethin' different for everyone; 'tis like the color o' the sun after the rain."

"A rainbow?"

He sighed. Then he continued but in a cautious voice that was considerably lower in tone. "I dinna ken how ye're callin' it now, but I'm sayin' there's a time, a happenin' . . . for every pairson, there's somethin' that's so special, so peaceful, that ye wanna have it, ye wanna be with it . . . t' know well . . . 'n' t' . . . love. . . . Aye, t' love. Can ye see wha' I'm sayin' here, laddy?"

"I think so. But what's driving Hogan? Why is he pushing so hard? He knows about this place, about the pathways, the choices, the decisions that await him when the time comes. It's as if he can't wait. It's like he's already made up his mind. The man's hitting balls until his hands are bleeding. Did you see that yesterday?"

He looked my way as he walked over to his spotting scope, which he patted gently. "Aye. Wi' the help o' this, I did."

"So what about him?"

"I was a-fearin' ye'd ask me that. I canna figger him out. Hoogin's a strange one, he is."

No kidding, I said to myself.

"Let's forget about Hogan for a moment. Even if you can't figure him out, maybe you can figure me out. Tell me . . . why did you send for me?"

He did not answer immediately. For almost a minute he watched me, circling slowly, one creaking step at a time, examining my features with the greatest care as if he were looking at me for the first time, trying to read the line on a green he was unfamiliar with. What could he be thinking?

"We've been watchin' ye," he explained. "'N' we kin see wha's inside o' ye. Ye canna e'en see it yerself at this early stage o' yer life, but ye hae a feelin' fer things tha's a rarity in men. I dinna know if ye'll ken from it . . . but ye're startin' t' grab hold o' wha's t' be needed if ye're t' be harnessin' the wind the way we've been speakin' abou' here."

"But why bring me here? Why not just leave me alone, back where I was, at Lincoln Park? Can't you folks do for yourselves here? Can't you do what needs to be done?"

"Laddy, yer fightin' it now fer shure. Canna ye see it?"

"See what? All I see is Hogan out there practicing like there's no tomorrow. And then Jones and the rest of you expect me to come in and turn him around. What am I doing here, and why am I suddenly carrying this burden that you've all strapped to my shoulders?"

Shep's gaze softened, and he sighed deeply. "Those're nae questions t' be grapplin' with, fer there's nae an answer lurkin' roon th' bend. Dinye be thinkin' o' Joones 'n' the others. 'Twas the wind tha' brought ye heere, laddy, and ye canna ask the wind her reasons. Just follow her, feel her, make her yer own."

"Make the wind my own?"

"Aye, laddy." A slow smile creased Shep's craggy face. "'Tis like a long baff yer facin' when the sky's a-howlin'. There's nae a point in cursin' 'n' ragin', arguin' the wind shouldna be there. Ye've got t' accept the wind and know she's nae somethin' apart from ye. Ye've got t' get inside o' her, 'n' let her inside o' ye. When ye do tha', ye'll be twistin' 'n' turnin' with her. Tha's the heart o' the game, laddy, and tha's the heart o' all this here. 'Tis all connected. Canna ye see it?"

"But Hogan—"

"Hoogin's a part o' this, too."

I was still confused, but something was starting to take shape in the back of my mind. I asked Shep, "Is everything in the game as pure as you describe it? Is it all good?"

"Tha' I canna say, fer guid 'n' bad, right 'n' wrong 'n' such, wha' are they t' natrull things? All I ken is tha' nature 'n' her wonders in all their naked glory, they're all part o' gowlfin'. Flowin', growin', blossomin', changin' as we pass. Tha's nae somethin' guid or bad, laddy, but somethin' tha's troo. 'N' tha's the beauty o' it."

"You mean the land, the sky, the wind, together with—"

"Aye, laddy. They're all but one thing in the game, 'n' I've ne'er seen a gowlfer who isn't surrounded, battlin' it all, strooglin' t' play whilst the world's movin'. A man's thoughts are nothin' but his roots t' the ground, 'n' when he lets 'em grow deep, laddy, he'll nae be blowin' away when the storm comes."

Suddenly I began to see what he was getting at. Still, my thoughts were only fragments, pieces of thread that must somehow be woven into cloth.

"And Hogan," I said, "is he—"

Shep then preempted everything with words that made me shudder.

"'Tis nae jus' Hoogin, laddy. 'Tis Hoogin 'n' ye. Ye're both in the rushin' waters now, swirlin' 'round each other like petals in an eddy. Ye're affectin' each other," he said with emphasis. "Ye're rubbin' shoulders like ye was dry sticks startin' a fyre."

The very thought was reason to pause. I mean, talk about "musin' the profundiddies"! He was setting the table, and I was enjoying a feast with every thought. Man and nature, golf and life . . . me and Hogan? But yet I needed to know something, and almost thinking aloud, I asked him, "How can I get through to Hogan? I've got to turn him around."

"Ye canna change Hoogin, fer his roots are runnin' deeper than the tallest tree. 'N' Hoogin canna change ye, neither, laddy. Be knowin' tha'. Now, be hearin' me words 'n' dinye try formulatin' an equation, cipherin' an answer. This here's feelin's at work, laddy, 'n' when they're workin', 'tis magic, 'n nae mathematics."

"But how do I talk him out of replaying the Open?"

"Maybe ye're nae a-gonna be able t' do tha'. Maybe ye shouldn' be tryin' t' do tha'. Hae ye e'er thought o' tha'?"

"It's impossible, then, isn't it?"

"Now dinye go puttin' words in me mouth, laddy. I dinna say tha'."

"You said I might not be able to talk him out of it."

"But maybe ye can say somethin' t' make Hoogin decide fer himself tha' playin' it over again isn't what's best."

He stopped for a moment, letting the silence punctuate the discussion.

"Hoogin's a man who's knowin' himself better'n any man can hope t'," he continued. "Tha's why he dinna need ye nor Joones nor Haggin nor any man t' be tellin' him wha' t' do. He's got the

yre, aye, 'n' his burns like none we'll e'er see again. His cauldron's
-bubblin', yet he's got the cuntrull. He's chartin' his own course
»y his own star, usin' a map 'n' compass only he can read."

"Jones says I'm the only one he's talked to."

"Dinye be fooled by tha', for Hoogin's superstitions are gettin'
he better o' him. He must be thinkin' ye're in disguise. Hoogin
nust figure ye fer a messenger, a courier. He thinks he's speakin'
»ack t' them downstairs through ye."

My thoughts drifted away, returning to last night and the
Ireams. I was starting to withdraw from Shep, hoping the warmth
»f these sheltered surroundings would inspire a breakthrough that
vould enable me to reach the Hawk. Old Shep followed me as if he
vere reading my mind.

"Those dreams ye were conjurin' . . . they're a start, laddy."

"But that was only my imagination, visions while I slept. This
; the real deal. I'm eyeball to eyeball with Hogan, and I've got
) . . ."

Shep shook his head from side to side disapprovingly. The look
n his face told me he was worried. Was he afraid Hogan had got-
en lost out there? In this rarefied place, was Hogan an explorer
vho had taken a fateful wrong turn? Or had I? And how would I
ver know?

In despair, I pleaded for guidance. "You've led your herd over
he hills," I told Shep, looking directly into his weary face. "You've
riven them over mountains. You did it when you were back there,
vherever it was, whenever it was that you lived. How do I move
Iogan? How do I walk a path that he'll follow?"

"Tha's nae fer me t' be sayin'. 'Tis nae me place, laddy. There's
ae a man kin say it. Hoogin's nae a sheep, ye know, 'n' ye're nae
is shepherd. Ye've just gotta keep on lookin' 'n' hope it comes t'
e revealed so ye and Hoogin can connect wi' each other when the
ght time comes."

But how? I've read the stories, the ones about him repelling fel-
»w professionals who sought advice, turning away amateurs who
ied to befriend him; sometimes he even rebuffed his friends.

When Gary Player was a young professional, he once asked the Hawk for advice, and Hogan, a justifiably proud clubmaker as well as a sage instructor, asked Player but one question prior to dispensing advice: Whose clubs do you play, son? Player admitted to playing equipment manufactured by Dunlop. Hogan's response was classic Hogan. "Go ask Mr. Dunlop for help," he said, giving Player a blank stare. He even gave Nicklaus the cold shoulder. When Big Jack sought to canonize Hogan at the Memorial Tournament a few years back, the Iceman rejected the offer. "I don't do that," he said.

Old Shep had taken me as far as he could, and we both recognized it. Slowly, he turned away from me and returned to his putting. I left him to the sputtering playback machine, to his pebbles, his featheries, and his crook. The only thing I noticed as I left the room was that his worries seemed directed not at me or at Hogan but at himself. He may not know his future, but somehow he seemed to know what would transpire between Bantam Ben and me, and he knew it would come out all right. Then again, maybe he didn't really know at all; maybe he was just resigned to it in any event, no matter what the outcome, so why fret over the details?

Something told me I would never really know for sure. The only thing I did know was that Hogan would likely be back, and soon, and I had better be ready for him when he arrived.

·12·

My audience with Shep burned indelibly in my mind. Yet the mental pictures of it were for my eyes only, for I knew full well there was no way to explain to my friends at school or my family or even my golfing companions that I'd had an audience with a wise man who was over five hundred years old.

I knew I had to leave Shep's aerie to attend to my work with Hogan. But there were so many questions I longed to ask! What is balance, and how does one find it? How do you keep a streak alive? Can you stare down trouble and make it vanish? Can you will the ball into the hole? How do you tame a case of bad nerves? What is confidence made of? How thin is the line between playing well and playing like a lame dog? Is there a cure for the yips?

If anyone could answer such classic golfing queries, it would be the man who's seen the whole of the game grow before him. But there wasn't nearly enough time. I had made a pledge to Jones, and I would be faithful to it. Besides, it was just the way Haig laid it out yesterday: Everyone has a job to do.

There was only one place for me to turn, and it was to be found at the bottom of the stairs. I softly backed my way out of Shep's aerie and retraced my steps on the spiral stone staircase. But there was a vast difference: The climb back down the turret was much faster than the walk up. I was gone from Shep's chamber and from the mysterious cavern that led to it faster than I would have liked.

When I pulled through the doorway and returned to the bar, I was besieged by Old Tom. He wanted to know everything about my visit with Shep: What did he say? Did he tell me what to do? What was I going to do? How would I approach Hogan? Even the Haig, that master of nonchalance, was leaning over to hear my reply. Jones came to the rescue, telling both of them to leave me alone. "The young man's got work to do. I suggest we all give him the breathing space in which to do it."

Old Tom stormed off, talking to himself as he walked away. Haig went back to rubbing down the bar, but he eyeballed every step I took. Jones just watched.

The sky outside was that same battleship gray as when I first walked through the fog, but suddenly the sun began to break though the cloud cover. The first light I saw came not from the range but from the other side of the clubhouse. A vibrant multicolored beam radiated from the library as the late-afternoon sunlight burned its way toward us, wafting into our midst through one of the stained-glass windows. Which one was the magic prism? Was it Nelson winning eleven straight? Or Sarazen firing that perfect four-wood? Maybe the golfing gods had seen fit to round up all of them together, forming a veritable laser beam of memories, hoping to spear my attention and draw me to the library. Whatever the strategy and whomever or whatever it belonged to, it was working. I turned my head and saw it. Even though I was being drawn toward the books and records, toward the rainbow of filtered light, I looked at Jones one last time. I saw only the slightest change in his expression. What control the man had! He had to be caught up in this, too, but he wasn't showing it for anyone to see. Or maybe it was just not for anyone else to see; as for me, I detected his lips beginning to quiver, then I saw them break upward ever so slightly. He smiled the smile of a Mona Lisa, detectable only by those who wanted to see it, and he nodded almost imperceptibly. I was glad I could catch the subtleties and read a message into them; I felt sure Jones was telling me I was on the right track.

Once I had passed into the sanctum of sanctums, Jones closed the library doors behind me. No one would disturb me while I went about my business. If I uncovered just a single key, I knew I could unlock the puzzle, solve the riddle, and get through to the Iceman. Old Shep and Jones had been guiding me through the thicket, and there must have been something the two of them wanted me to discover. Could it be Jones's moment, the choice he made when the eternal question was put to him?

Where did he say it was? St. Andrews. Six years into retirement. He was with old friends. What was it all about?

In a corner I saw a microfilm reader, the type you find in a research library. The only time I'd used one of those things was when I took a history class at Berkeley and the professor required us to read old newspapers to get a feeling for the era we were studying. I recalled reading the business pages the day before the stock market crashed. PRESIDENT HOOVER PREDICTS BOOM TIMES AHEAD! I also remembered perusing the world news during the first days of December 1941. It was the week before Pearl Harbor. U.S. ENVOY TO VISIT JAPANESE DELEGATION TO TALK PEACE. How different history seems when you read the actual newsprint of the day. What do we lose when we glorify past events and coat them with the patina of afterthought? Were they really the way the history books tell them? Did they really happen that way? Or do we just wish they did? These old papers may not be totally accurate themselves, but at least they tell it the way it was at the time; the front page is printed long before the revisionists have any chance to set about their busywork.

What does all of this have to do with Hogan? I was already at the card catalog, looking for some helpful reference material. Once I found the card I was looking for, I could see that Jones was right: Everything I needed was here in this room.

The index card said the crucial material was on the second level.

The surprise came when I found it in its original form, not on microfilm. I quickly located the oversized volume that contained the issue: *The New York Times*, June 28, 1936. The story told it all: Bobby Jones and Grantland Rice were on their way to the Olympics, those glorious games, the ones in which Jesse Owens went *in your face* to the Führer. *Those* games. There might have been a hint in what happened at St. Andrews that June day that a remarkable athletic event would soon follow in Berlin. Something was in the air.

Jones had returned to the Old Course, drawn by the magnetism of the place and the people and the history he was a part of on its fairways. It was intended to be a casual visit and a casual round, but inevitably it was much, much more.

Jones's affair with St. Andrews was not, to be sure, a case of love at first sight. Jones's initial impression of the Old Course was nothing much—a flat stretch of pasture, he concluded. And he was right. It was a pasture five hundred years ago when fellows like Shep drove their flocks over the hallowed terrain that would later become the home of the game. And Jones's early rounds at St. Andrews almost drove him away for good. In 1921, while playing in his first British Open Championship, a young and tempestuous Bobby played fairly well for two rounds. Then the wheels came off his teenage chassis. He hit it flat sideways for the first nine holes of the third round, as the Old Course took the full measure of his prodigious talent. He shot 46 going out, and if that were not bad enough, he proceeded to double-bogey the short tenth. The steam was coming out of his ears. A "smolderin' cauldron," indeed. Then, at the par-three eleventh, the "High Hole" as it reads on the card, Jones came completely unglued. On in five, he was staring down a putt for triple bogey; he could endure no more embarrassment. He picked up his ball, tore his card to shreds, and stormed off. His explosion put him out of the competition.

In an instant Jones knew he had made a terrible mistake. Quitting under pressure was not his style, and it was nothing to be proud of. Years later he would say that his blowup on the eleventh hole at St. Andrews turned him around; it transformed him from a wild, unfinished talent into a champion's champion.

Jones returned to St. Andrews many times over the years. He played there in the 1926 Walker Cup matches, winning in four-ball competition and overwhelming the opposition in singles play. In one thirty-six-hole match he beat noted British amateur Cyril Tolley by the incredible margin of 12 and 11. Once Jones had learned to appreciate the subtleties of linksland golf, he came to love the artistry of playing the delicate, ticklish pitch-and-run shots it requires. His deft touch and his mastery of all phases of the game were not lost on the Scottish galleries. As Jones had come to love St. Andrews, St. Andreans had come to love him. They adored his tempo, syrupy smooth and almost effortless. And his flowing swing, so solid through the hitting zone, was a sight to behold.

Jones visited the Old Course again in 1927 when he defended the British Open Championship he had captured the year before at Royal Lytham & St. Anne's. His opening 68 tied the course record, and his seventy-two-hole total of 285 lapped the field by six strokes. The townspeople had waited so long for their dream golfer; in Jones they had found him. When his final putt went down, the throng that surrounded the green broke free and nearly crushed him in frenzied celebration. They hoisted him on their shoulders and gave him the ride of his young life.

Of course, when Jones next came to St. Andrews, it was 1930, and he was after the only major title to elude him: the British Amateur. Jones's failure to capture the British Amateur was not for lack of trying; in two previous attempts he had come up empty. Not this time. Jones battled furiously, winning six matches, some in dramatic fashion. In the fourth round he met and conquered his old rival Tolley. They were tied going into the seventeenth, the dreaded Road Hole, and Bobby was lucky to match Tolley's par four. They also tied the eighteenth, but Jones captured the first extra hole. All that did was earn him the right to face George Voigt in the semifinal. Jones was two down with five to play, but he played on courageously and prevailed, one up. The final was anticlimactic as Jones overwhelmed Roger Wethered, closing him out 7 and 6 at the twelfth green and carrying off the third leg of his Grand Slam. That was his last round at St. Andrews until he returned six years later.

The ensuing years had taken their toll on his game, but his love for St. Andrews was unaffected by the passage of time. His love, if not his stroke, was as powerful at the age of thirty-six as it had been at nineteen when he played in that fateful 1921 British Open Championship.

But still, Jones had not played competitively in over half a decade. His game was rusty, at least if one compared it to the battle-tested version—the one last seen on the eleventh at Merion when he vanquished Homans.

Actually, the trip to St. Andrews was something of an afterthought. Jones and his wife Mary had set out with Kate and Grantland Rice to see the Olympic Games. While crossing the Atlantic, they met up with some friends who were headed for the same destination but with one important side trip on their itinerary that Jones had not considered up to that point: They were headed for Gleneagles to play some golf. They persuaded the Joneses and the Rices to join them.

On their last evening at Gleneagles, after dinner had ended, the conversation shifted to their travel plans and how best to return to Southampton to catch the boat for Germany. During the discussion, Jones said that he could not bear to be that close to the Old Course without going over for a game. After further discussion, the group decided they would oblige Jones. The next day—June 27, 1936—they would venture to St. Andrews for a round of golf and then return to London from there. Jones would later write, with the sort of understatement characteristic of his modesty, "My intention was that we should drive over for lunch and play a round in the afternoon."

Jones, Rice, and the others slipped into town quietly. Jones kept himself busy at the hotel while one of the others went over to make arrangements for starting times and caddies. One of the young bag-toters asked with a typical sense of caddie curiosity whom he'd be caddying for. "A man who knows the game" was all he was told.

Somehow word leaked out that Jones was the man who would be teeing it up. Once loosed, the news spread like a prairie fire. When the townspeople learned that their hero had returned and was going to play, shops closed down, homes emptied, and everyone who could made his or her way to the golf course.

By the time Jones and his mates arrived at the first tee, there were over two thousand people gathered to watch them play.

Any other mortal might have turned around and gone back to the hotel. The excuse would be easy enough to manufacture: The back got stiff . . . the rheumatism flared up again . . . stomach cramps . . . it must have been something I ate. But not Jones. Even though he had been playing poorly at Gleneagles and was, in his own words, "not pleased with the prospect of exhibiting my game in its present state, especially to the people of St. Andrews," he was being pulled to his destiny by a force even he could not resist. Nothing was going to keep him from his beloved Old Course.

From his opening stroke Jones played with the keen eye of a craftsman, the hands of a surgeon, and the heart of a champion. Going out, his every shot was hit purely and sailed through the wind as if riding a string tied between his club and the flagstick. The elegant lady that is St. Andrews was his, dancing with him, following his lead, swirling around him and embracing him as if nothing could ever separate them. Thirty-two strokes was all it took to complete the outward nine. Four under.

As is traditional at courses in the British Isles, every hole has a name, usually one that stems from some natural characteristic or topographical oddity. The names are part of the lore of the game. They add spice to the cut of land nature has served up for play; they tell a player what lies ahead. The Road Hole. The Corner of the Dyke. The Spectacles. Roon-the-Ben. Woe-be-Tide. The Postage Stamp. The Railway. Luckyslap. Risk-an-Hope.

It is no different at number eight at St. Andrews, a hole known simply as the Short Hole. It is a par three of 178 yards, played to a double green that it shares with the tenth. This day the flagstick was tucked behind a mound. The shot was a difficult one, but Jones, already three under, was ready to play boldly. He played what he described as a "soft shot" with a four-iron. He cut it into a following wind, which the ball rode like a taxi all the way to the hole. Jones had faded his shot perfectly around the mound. It finished approximately eight feet from the hole.

As Jones slipped his club back into his bag, his caddie, a youngster of nineteen or twenty, said to him in a whisper only Jones could hear, "My, but you're a wonder, sir." Jones smiled and gave his looper a pat on the shoulder. To his dying day Jones would recall the moment with great fondness. It was, he would often say, the most sincere compliment he could ever remember.

The rest of the round had some twists and turns, and Jones weathered them like a champion. He parred the tenth, which years later would be named the Bobby Jones hole in his honor. But at the unforgiving par-three eleventh, which was his undoing in 1921, he again fell victim to misfortune. He had to play to a hole location he had never seen before. The flag was cut at the very rear of the green, directly behind the Strath Bunker. The wind was once again at Jones's back, but this time it trailed off a bit to the right. Although in competition he would never have played the shot he hit, this day was different: Feeling that the golfing gods were on his side, he fired a five-iron at the flag. The shot was too strong. Jones had to play out of a bunker set into the bank of the River Eden. His first recovery shot never left the sand. His second ended up four feet away, but he missed the putt. The double-bogey five shattered his dreams, but this was not the same Jones who had quit fifteen years ago.

He played onward, making a succession of fives. By the time he came to the Road Hole, Jones had dropped to one over par. But something welled up within him. He hit a rocket from the tee, his ball sailing over the stationmaster's garden, then drilled a long iron to the edge of the rambling green. Having safely avoided the disaster that lurks at every turn of the hole, Jones calmly two-putted for a perfect par four.

At number eighteen, he ran his second shot through the Valley of Sin, and the ball stopped only a stone's throw from the hole. When the putt fell for a finishing birdie, a roar went up that seemed to echo over all of Scotland. The women cried, and the men did, too. "'Tis grand, just grand," one old-timer said as the tears streamed down his cheeks, drenching his long white beard.

Jones finished the back nine in forty strokes. That, coupled with his outward thirty-two, gave him an even par total of 72. The score was unimportant, for the numbers did nothing to measure the depth of feeling, the history, the connection that existed between Jones and this special place and these special people. In front of his most ardent admirers, Jones had danced with his favorite lady and charmed her, while being charmed himself.

When it was over, the massive crowd begged him to speak, but there would be no speeches. Jones stayed among the townspeople, signing autographs until his hand grew weary, and then officials escorted him inside the Royal and Ancient Clubhouse, which stands adjacent to the eighteenth green. It had been an incredible day. The day of a lifetime.

And that was his moment, captured with every emotional strand intact, every uplifting impulse as fresh and new as if it were still taking place.

Now I could see why Jones laughed at me when I was weakly attempting to guess what he had chosen for himself. The Grand Slam? His first victory? The Masters? All fine times but mere chicken feed compared to his return to the Old Course.

I had a justifiable feeling of satisfaction in having discovered all this. This was a story for the ages, one not just to be read and told but to be reread and retold to every generation. It spoke volumes about life and the lessons to be drawn from it: humility and greatness experienced at the same time; the courage to try and the confidence to succeed; the quiet of simple companionship and the thunder that can be generated by great achievement; a crowd of people and a man who knew little about the inner workings of each other, and yet who were drawn together by the unbounded power of love. He saw in them the guardians, the protectors, the preservers of his true homeland; they saw in him a warrior, a hero, a conquering knight, a champion who would let nothing come between him and this special place.

Did Hogan ever achieve that? Did he have a moment like that? The mere thought of the Hawk caused my side to ache, the way it does when I've run too fast and not breathed the way I should. When I think of Hogan, I see perfection but also the pain that produced it. With Jones it is like drinking good port—so smooth, so rich, so . . . sweet.

It was past six o'clock, and Hogan would be back any moment. The card catalog told me they had the other reference I needed. This one was located on the first tier, not far from where I was standing. It was right under one of the blank windows, in a spot where there was plenty of light, for the sun's bright spears penetrated this part of the room unaffected by the color of stained glass.

I was turning the pages frantically, for I did not know the exact date to look for. It was the year after my brother was born but a different month. Probably in February. But was it the first or the twenty-eighth? The advertisements told of men's suits selling for under $35, and two-bedroom houses going for about $12,500 in a nice area.

There he was, on the cover of *Time*. Big and bright, Bantam Ben smiled like a champion. It was January 10, 1949, and he had just completed a staggering run of championship golf, becoming the first player in history to capture the U.S. Open, the PGA Championship, and the Western Open in the same year. The glory of his game now transcended the confines of a golf course and, like one of his drives, carried far and true. If this magazine cover was any indication, Ben Hogan's name was hurtling down the middle of that wide fairway known as mainstream America.

Sifting through the books and papers, I found a hard news story that told about the Phoenix Open. He shot 270. Lost a playoff to Demaret, but they were all saying he was starting out just like he had left off. It was odds-on he would be the leading money winner once again. The loss at Phoenix was his first defeat of the 1949 campaign; he had already won twice, at Long Beach and at the Crosby. It was a scintillating opening month, and the rest of the year held great promise.

But now, in the afterglow of his quick start, Hogan was going home to Fort Worth to rest until the Masters, which wouldn't be played until April. He was going to be ready. The Hawk had never won that one, and he wanted it badly.

Then I saw the article I had been looking for. It was all there, just as I'd heard. The place was somewhere east of Van Horn, Texas; the date, February 2; the time, about 8:30 A.M.; the weather, hazy sunshine—at least it was hazy until a dense fog covered the twisting highway, Route 80. He had just checked his tires because he suspected a flat; instead, all he found was ice on the pavement, so he cut his speed down to almost nothing. He started up again and was inching along, barely going thirty, when four headlights came bearing down on him. Two of them belonged to a huge Greyhound bus, driven by an impatient Alvin H. Logan, who was trying to pass an Alamo Freight Lines semi. The bus was barreling right at Hogan as it tried to pass the truck. There was nowhere for the Hawk to turn: A culvert was to the right, and that plodding six-wheeler was dead ahead on the left. It was his shiny, spanking-new Cadillac against a runaway bus. Fractured pelvis. Broken collar bone. Three busted ribs. Broken ankle. Bladder injury. Massive contusions to the left leg. Hogan's entire body was reshuffled like a deck of cards.

The article said he saved his wife's life by covering her body with his own. Hogan's own account of what happened was, well, classic Hogan: "I just put my head down," he later said, "and dived across Valerie's lap, like I was diving into a pool of water."

As for Valerie, it was nothing but a feeling of hopelessness. "It was the end," she recalled to a reporter. "A situation in which we had no chance." In a touch of irony, only moments before, the Hogans had been discussing the highway hazards that confront professional golfers, men who travel so much but are seldom involved in collisions.

In the early seconds after impact, the Iceman was lying so still that Valerie thought he was dead. When she felt him twitch, she knew he hadn't left her; she also knew she had to do something fast, but she was pinned underneath him. She wriggled free, after which she stopped a man and woman who were driving by.

Hogan himself would later recount the post-accident trauma in the forget-me-not parlance of a man who had just brushed off death. "I remember my leg was hurting," he said, "and I asked somebody to hold it. Then I started getting very cold and asked them to cover it. I passed out again—I guess I passed out a dozen times before the ambulance finally got there. I don't remember them putting me in it."

It wasn't like the sirens pulled up right away. The post-accident scene was horrific, the tangled wreckage blocking the highway, people milling about. Valerie said she aged a hundred years in an hour and a half. Her husband kept getting grayer and grayer. "Mrs. Hogan said it was 90 minutes after the crash before an ambulance arrived to pick up her husband," one article reported. "Confusion in the crowd that gathered was blamed for the delay, several believing that others had already summoned an ambulance."

If the Hawk had his way, they would have taken him on to Pecos, a town eighty-nine miles ahead on the route they'd been traveling. At least that's what he said to the ambulance driver after regaining consciousness. Was it delirium? Or a commonsense suggestion? The professionals were acting out of instinct. The Hawk couldn't move; all he could do was think, so that's what he did. And when he thought, he was guided by sound principles. He wanted to keep going east. Why? It was closer to home in Fort Worth. Did Hogan know they were taking him all the way back to El Paso? Not likely. "If he'd known that," said Valerie later, "we would've had real trouble with him."

The ambulance stopped briefly in Van Horn so that X rays could be taken, then continued on to El Paso, a full 119 miles distant. They checked him into a Catholic hospital called Hôtel-Dieu. The doctors who attended him were named Villareal, Cameron, Fenner, and Green.

What could Bantam Ben have been thinking about during that long ride to El Paso? About the Open and PGA Championship he'd won the previous year? About the money and the glory? The short thumb? About the fools who were standing around gawking at the wreckage, assuming someone else had made the call to the ambulance people? Or about just hanging on to the thread of life long enough for doctors to have a shot at saving his mangled body?

The newspaper said it all so matter-of-factly: "The physicians expressed confidence that Hogan would be able to play golf again." They weren't so sure, though: ". . . but would not venture a guess as to when."

Some of them were even more glib, if that was possible. It was "dollars to doughnuts he would be back on the tournament trail sooner than expected." Easy for them to say.

Reading on, I learned that two weeks after the original surgery, a nasty blood clot moved from Hogan's legs up to his chest, through the right half of his heart, and into his lungs. When the Iceman complained of chest pains, the physicians investigated and knew right away that they had another emergency on their hands, arguably more life-threatening than the accident itself. Not only was there a blood clot in the danger zone, but they detected another one, lower down. Would it move? No one knew, but they couldn't take any chances.

Knowing they needed an expert, the local team of doctors picked up the telephone and called the Mayo Clinic. They were told to find Alton S. Ochsner, a renowned professor of surgery affiliated with Tulane University in New Orleans. But there was a problem: Even if they could reach him, there was no direct flight from the Crescent City to El Paso. Hogan was fading fast. His blood count was dropping, and everyone knew the obvious: They were going to run out of time unless something extraordinary happened.

It was a desperate hour, but fortunately for Hogan, his brother Royal had an idea. He called Brigadier General David W. Hutchison, the commander at Biggs Air Force Base, located near the hospital. When he finally caught up with Hutchison, he put forth a simple question: Could the general help the Hawk, a man who had served two years in the Air Force during wartime?

The answer came with action, not words. The general put together a B-29 crew in the middle of the night—at 3:30 A.M., to be exact—and sent them screaming through the air to New Orleans. They returned to El Paso by 11:30 that morning, having touched down in Louisiana barely long enough to get Dr. Ochsner on board.

No one knew if they had acted in time. The doctors in El Paso had thinned Hogan's blood to prevent further clotting. His hematocrit was down to 17, which meant that the percentage of red cells to overall blood volume was drastically low. It was approximately one-third of normal. If the number dropped much further, Hogan's heart probably would fail. One of the wire services prepared an obituary.

The first thing Dr. Ochsner did on arrival was to order several transfusions. He restored Hogan's blood count as best he could, and although it was well below what was normally considered a safe level for surgery, he knew he could not wait any longer. For two hours the greatest golfer in the world was under the scalpel, clinging to life. The surgical team cut a wide incision in Hogan's abdomen and tied off his vena cava, the vein that feeds blood to the heart from below. If it hadn't been done, there was a danger that a third clot might form and float up from one of Bantam Ben's legs and cause a fatal lung clot. The words pulmonary embolism hung over the surgical team like a storm cloud.

While Hogan was in surgery, Valerie and Royal were in the hospital chapel praying for a miracle. She had no way of knowing what was going on in the operating room, and all she could do was look within herself and hope for the best. Finally, late in the afternoon of February 19, the danger passed. Hogan was gaunt and weak. He was twenty-six pounds underweight, but he was alive.

He required around-the-clock nursing care. Valerie actually moved into the hospital with him, and when Hogan's night nurse took ill, she filled in, dutifully staying beside him until dawn for weeks on end.

When June and the Open rolled around, Cary Middlecoff and the others were in Chicago, attacking Medinah, while Hogan was hobbling on ankles so swollen they could not be encased in ordinary footwear. A pair of unlaced G.I. boots had to make do. Hogan pushed on, walking when he could, as far as he could. The surgery had disrupted the circulation in his legs to such an extent that swelling and pain in the lower portions of his body had become a daily experience, particularly when he moved around. How would he ever walk a golf course again?

I wonder if Hogan ever read any of those articles. How could those reporters know of his pain, of the torture he put his body through after diving desperately to save the woman he loved? He was Bantam Ben, the Hawk, the Iceman, the King of the Links— and yet when the bugle sounded the call of distress, he answered the summons without hesitation, risking everything. Some would say after the fact that the leap across Valerie's body actually saved not one life but two, for the steering wheel was pushed clean through to the backseat from the impact of the collision. Had Hogan not moved quickly, he would have been back there with it.

It was a lonely time when he—and he alone—could only wonder if the touch, the feel, would still be there when the doctors cleared him to swing again. *If* they cleared him to swing again. What if he couldn't do it anymore? What then? A club job giving lessons on Tuesday morning? No, thank you. That was not for him.

He explained the problem best to Jack Murphy, a reporter for the *Fort Worth Star-Telegram*: "I don't know if I can get back to the edge I had last year. Suppose something is paining me? If I start favoring an ankle or a shoulder or something, it'll throw me off. If I get ready to hit the ball, and I'm thinking partly about that pain—well, I'll hit it all right, but not the way I would if I were able to concentrate on all the things you have to do to make your shots just right."

And then there was the matter of the short game. "Winning golf," observed Hogan, "is a matter of touch. It's something you work at and try to develop, but you don't develop it. It comes to you. It's the difference between the first-rate golfer and the fellow who scores well once in a while. Even if you make a bad shot now and then, you know you've still got it. The good golfer has the touch—he knows he can do it. I won't know what I can do until I've played a couple of tournaments, and maybe not then. It may take longer."

The first tournament on the comeback trail was the 1950 Los Angeles Open. No one expected much from Hogan; they were glad he was able to walk, to be sure, and they were glad he had found his way back onto the tour. But could he play? Anyone who doubted Hogan's resolve or his ability simply didn't know Ben Hogan. If they thought he was only going to go through the motions, stretching his atrophied muscles, walking around simply to wave at the gallery, they were in for a major surprise. Hogan played with purpose, and those who saw him those four days will tell you he had that look on his face again. He opened with 73, handling the shaky moments with great discipline and control. He knew his game would improve as the tournament wore on, and it did. He shot 69 in the second round, and when the third round was rained out, Hogan gained a precious day of rest for his aching legs, which he kept wrapped in heavy bandages even as he played. The pain and the cramps were one thing to deal with, but they were easy compared to tackling his untested confidence; after all, the last event he had competed in was the 1949 Phoenix Open, just before he and Valerie headed into the hazy fog covering that stretch of highway outside of El Paso. Could he do it? A pair of 69s to close the tournament provided the answer. Hogan's total of 280 was miraculous under the circumstances. Sam Snead birdied the last two holes to catch him and force a playoff; Hogan didn't win, but his performance sent a message: The Iceman could play major championship golf even with a half-broken body. The Hawk was flying again.

Hogan continued to play the tour, picking his spots, keeping himself in shape. The legs and his back were the major problems. Heavy bandages helped control the cramps in the legs, and a brace helped check his aching back. He played on until he came to Merion, the same Merion where Jones sent Homans to the showers early. It was there, in 1950, that one of the great chapters in all of sport was written. Playing across the Baffling Brook, over the Quarry, up next to the flagsticks with the funny baskets atop—there, from the middle of the eighteenth fairway, he fired his now famous one-iron, the shot photographer Hy Peskin captured so brilliantly for UPI. It was there that Hogan proved to the world that he had returned to the top of the mountain. It was there—after the accident—that he battled a star-studded field, eventually tying Lloyd Mangrum and George Fazio, beating them on Sunday in a playoff. It was there that he won his second U.S. Open, two years after his record-setting performance at Riviera. Bookends: one before the accident, one after.

It is easy to look back on Hogan's triumph at Merion and see the incredible, indelible mark he made on the game. What a victory! Great as it was, few accounts emphasize what he had to go through the final day—Open Saturday, as it was known then—when the field played thirty-six holes in one day. Hogan knew there was a serious question whether he could even finish under such conditions. As a precaution, each night after completing his round, he dutifully unwrapped the bandages that stretched from his ankles to his crotch and proceeded to soak his weary body in hot water. It helped, but still . . . Thirty-six holes of major championship golf in one day, one very long day, was a tall order even for a healthy Hogan. Midway through the final round, when he knew he had the lead, Hogan was struggling. His legs radiated with pain, but he pushed on, having his caddie retrieve the ball from the cup and, on occasion, having his playing companion, defending champion Cary Middlecoff, mark his ball for him on the green.

He was three ahead with only seven holes left to play, but at the twelfth tee everything almost ended. Hogan took a mighty swipe at his drive, his legs locked, and he almost fell. Struggling to hold his balance, he staggered over toward Harry Radix, a friend who was standing nearby at the edge of the tee box. "Let me hang on to you, Harry," said Hogan. "My God, I don't think I can finish." He played on gamely, sometimes hanging on to Radix, sometimes walking by himself. The gallery of thirteen thousand surrounded his every move. Step by step Hogan limped his way to the seventy-second hole, finally striking that fateful one-iron that brought him home tied for the championship with Mangrum and Fazio. It was a shot that propelled Hogan into an historic playoff which he won. More than one writer has called his finish at Merion the most gallant golf ever played. But Hogan didn't stop there, not by a long shot.

Next came the Monster, which was what they all called Oakland Hills after the Iceman gave it that name. In 1951 the USGA did a number with the rough and the speed of the greens. The grass was long off the fairways, and the putting surfaces rolled like glass tabletops. It was the toughest course anyone had ever seen. But Hogan tamed it. His 67 in the final round was one of only two subpar rounds during the entire championship. He called it one of his finest rounds ever. It brought Hogan his third Open, his second after the accident. One behind Jones. Two behind immortality.

You have to wonder what would have happened if he and Valerie had not been driving on that West Texas highway that hazy February morning, or if the Greyhound was just a little behind schedule or a little ahead. What if . . .

Would he have won at Merion, at Oakland Hills, at Oakmont? Would he have lost at Olympic? Would he have been as driven? As possessed by the game? Or would he have played for the sheer love of it, the way Jones did in '36? And would he have wanted that to be his moment? I couldn't say yet. All I knew at this stage was that something was burning inside him, and he was bursting at the seams to let it out. It was as if the man had a score to settle with somebody, with some . . . thing.

San Francisco Express
June 19, 1955

Fleck Ties Hogan!
Playoff Today
for Open Title

Classic Golf Creates Magic Finish for Unknown Driving Range Pro

They'll Meet at 2:00 P.M. Today

By Dick Yost

It was one of those moments you never forget.

It was his final hole, and he was utterly exhausted from four long, difficult rounds of competition. But Ben Hogan was still on his feet. The Olympic Club's Lake Course, which has proven itself a heavyweight contender all week, had failed to knock the wee Iceman down.

But it had certainly made him weary. Hogan walked slowly up the final 100 yards of fairway, limping with every step. He was tired, but his work was done. When he putted out for a final round 70 and a four-round total of 287, the entire throng of 10,000 people, many of whom had waited all day for a good vantage point to watch him finish, gave Ben Hogan one of the greatest ovations of his career.

For what seemed like 10 minutes, they clapped, whistled, and shouted their approval. After all, it isn't every day a man wins the United States Open Championship for the fifth time—or so it seemed.

A Crowd to the Rear

Hogan had weathered the challenge of Open Saturday, shooting a seventy-two in the morning round, which moved him into the lead going into the final 18. Sam Snead was on his heels, having come all the way back from a near-disastrous 79 on Thursday. He was only one back at 218. Tommy Bolt, who had been leading all the way until Hogan passed him, fell back to 219, while Jack Fleck, who had played so well in the second round, dropped down to 220 and three behind Hogan after struggling with a 75.

The final round was one of firsts for Hogan. It was the first time he had parred the seventeenth hole all week. And it was the first time he had matched Olympic's impossible par of 70 in the championship. His nines were as symmetrical as bookends: 35 on the front, 35 on the back. Three bogeys and 3 birdies. He bogeyed the thirteenth but made up for it with his final birdie of the day at the short fifteenth when he nailed a 35-footer for a 2. The thunderous ovation rattled the trees. Hogan was playing his best golf when he needed it the most.

A WELCOME OVATION

Hogan stood on the final green for what seemed like an eternity. If ever a player deserved a lingering look at his own destiny, he was the man. The crowd indulged him as he took it all in, saluting him enthusiastically as the sweetness of the moment became evident on his often stone-cold face. When he took off his characteristic white cap and waved to the fans, it caused the noise level to rise by a factor of at least two. If there is a roof on the sky, it got raised a few feet yesterday afternoon at Lakeside.

Gene Sarazen, rushing to get the story to the nationwide television audience, congratulated him near the scorer's tent on the apparent victory. Hogan, ever the serious, studious competitor, begged off. "There's still some golf to be played," he said. But a few seconds after they went off the air, he turned to Joseph C. Dey, Executive Director of the United States Golf Association, and handed him his golf ball. "This is for Golf House," he said, dedicating the ball to the USGA's museum.

He walked off to more applause and made the climb to the locker room where he would relax and soak his aching legs.

Then the drama really began.

JACK WHO?

While Hogan was soaking, an unknown driving range pro named Jack Fleck was quietly making his way around the turn, playing brilliantly in near isolation as the massive crowds were swelling to watch Hogan finish. But someone should have had the binoculars focused on the man who plays out of the Duck Creek Golf Club, located near Davenport, Iowa. Oh, yes, he also lists an affiliation with a place called the Credit Island Golf Club, which he described for the world today as a driving range.

It may have been unlikely, but that's why they call it the United States Open. Fleck easily moved past Snead, Bolt, and Julius Boros when he posted three straight birdies early in the round. He made threes at the sixth and seventh, then deuced the short eighth. But mishaps along the way held him back. He turned in 34.

Then he birdied the tenth. And while playing number 12, he could hear the roar from the clubhouse. He knew Hogan was in, but he didn't know with what. When a marshal told him that Hogan had shot 287, Fleck knew what he had to do to tie him.

FOUR HOLES TO GO

By the time Fleck reached the fifteenth hole, he was facing a mountain of a challenge. He needed two birdies on the final four holes in order to catch Hogan and force a playoff. Many in the gallery thought it impossible and began the long walk back to the hillside adjacent to the clubhouse behind the eighteenth green. That would be where the USGA would present Hogan with the trophy.

Those who left Fleck hadn't taken too many steps when he gracefully played a six-iron to the fifteenth. The hole is short and tight, a par three with an island of a green set between tall eucalyptus and pine trees. It is surrounded by deep-walled bunkers. None of that was a problem for Fleck, who split the flag with his shot. His ball obediently put on the brakes and came to attention eight feet from the hole. He made the putt, and when he did, the gallery let out a roar that echoed through the trees.

The doubters who had turned their backs on Fleck quickly turned themselves around and raced to the sixteenth tee. He was only one behind now, and there were still three to play.

Pars at sixteen and seventeen left Fleck with one hole to play and only one way to play it: birdie for the tie and the glory, par or worse for a ticket back to the driving range.

HOGAN WAITED; FLECK SWEATED

By the time Fleck reached the final hole, Hogan was well aware of what was happening. He had been sitting silently inside the massive Spanish-style clubhouse dreading the possibility of a playoff. His battered body had taken enough punishment for one week.

The eighteenth hole at the Olympic Club is one of the finest finishing holes anywhere, but not because of its length. It is only 327 yards long, steeply downhill off the tee into a narrow valley of fairway, then just as steep a climb to a thimble of a green. And getting home in regulation is the easy part. Putting on this sidehill house of horrors is no fun. But Fleck would have to find a way, or else he would be going back where he came from, his name the answer to an obscure question: Who finished second to Hogan when he won his fifth Open?

At about the same time that Fleck was walking to the tee, Hogan broke the tense silence that was paralyzing everyone around him. "I hope he makes two or four," the Hawk said softly, referring to Fleck's potential score.

Fleck took a long time to play his tee shot, finally hitting a three-wood. Clubbing down did not help him; he pulled the shot to the left, and the ball finished in the rough. The gallery let out a collective groan. But the lie wasn't bad, and he had a shot at the green. Fleck was between clubs, finally selecting a seven-iron over an eight. He swung smoothly, and the ball flew perfectly, high and soft, right at the flag. When it stopped seven feet to the right of the hole, he knew he had a chance. It was his turn for the ovation.

PUTT OF A LIFETIME

But there was still work to do. The green was as fast as lightning and just as dangerous. There were players who had 4-putted from only a little further away; some had even putted off the green entirely. Fleck looked over the putt, giving every inch of the line a good look. He addressed the ball and tapped it lightly. The ball rolled so slowly, it was agonizing. It was like watching an old man climb down a rickety ladder. But the ball found the hole, and when it did, there was bedlam.

The unknown driving range pro had tied the immortal Hogan.

Inside the clubhouse, Hogan turned to his caddie, Tony Zittelli, who by that time was sitting beside him on one of the locker room benches. "Better unpack my gear," Hogan said. "Looks like we'll be playing tomorrow."

Hogan had shaken up the press corps an hour earlier by announcing his retirement from competitive golf. He was well aware of the fact that there was still some golf to be played. "I don't intend to play in any more Open championships. I may try a few tournaments now and then, but I intend to become a weekend golfer and devote all my time to my clubmaking business."

If Hogan does retire, he will have a lot to look back on. The glory will linger, and his miraculous record may never be matched.

"Boys, if I win it, I'll never work at this again. It's just too tough getting ready for a tournament. This one doggone near killed me. Besides, I don't think it's fair to drag Valerie around and put her through this every time. It's time to settle down, get to enjoy a regular life, make up for some of the things we've missed."

Hogan is definitely the sentimental favorite in the playoff. He's the prohibitive betting favorite as well since few are predicting much from Fleck, who must now face the Hawk one-on-one at Lakeside.

They will play a full 18 holes today at 2:00 P.M. The winner will pocket $6,000. The loser gets $3,600.

·13·

MY RESEARCH CONSUMED THE ENTIRE AFTERNOON. BY THE TIME I had finished reading about Hogan and his doctors, I was conversant with a host of medical terminology such as clavicle, talus, and the union of the ilium, ischium, pubis, and sacrum. I felt as though I'd read enough to become a physician. It was past seven o'clock, and while I wanted to read more so that I could complete the circle of knowledge, time was too short for any such luxury. I hurried back to the bar, to the window, to see if the Hawk had returned.

The range was empty. No one, not even little Eddie, was out there. Where the hell was Hogan?

I sat and stared, hoping my luck would turn and the chance to talk to the Iceman would present itself. I could sense that the few club members who had come down for a late-afternoon nip had fixed their eyes on me. When I looked about the room, I knew my sensation was real. The wrinkles in their brows told more than their stares. The air was heavy with doubt.

I was full of nervous energy, surging with anticipation, when Jones stopped by. Unlike the others, his face was calm, and the even tone of his voice conveyed the confidence of a man who knows not only what lies ahead but also how to go about getting the job done. He offered encouraging words.

"I thought it best to leave you alone in there," he explained. "None of us here can rightfully steer you any more than we could steer one of our mashies. You can't hope it into the hole, you know."

"Yeah, I know."

"He won't be back here today, at least that's the word Haig's getting from Shep. He's going to make the play tomorrow morning, sometime after the sun crests over those trees." Jones looked benignly at the forest beyond the range. A sixth sense told him Hogan was in there waiting.

"Do you mind if I accompany you to dinner tonight?" he inquired.

Do I mind? No, I don't mind. The man has thirteen major championships and the Grand Slam under his belt; between 1921 and his retirement nine years later, he won more than half of the national championships he entered. All I had was the team title of the San Francisco Academic Athletic Association. Fifth man for the Washington High Eagles. Kid stuff.

"I read about your visit across the water," I said to Jones, letting him know that at least part of the homework was completed.

"And what did you learn?" he asked.

"There's something to be said for a round with old friends."

Now he knew that I knew. "So you think you understand why I selected that occasion to settle down with? I'd like it if you'd kindly share your insights with me. Would you do that?"

I told Jones that the articles were superficial, but the sense I got was that he played so far beyond expectations that there must have been a guiding hand, a divine presence, in what happened that day.

"Why . . . it wasn't witchcraft, you know."

"It was a pretty good brew of something that made you perform like that."

"I wasn't performing. I was just having some fun. You know, Shep's right about the feel. Once you learn it, it never leaves you.

That's why a man of seventy can still lay a shot struck with a nib-lick onto a green as softly as he could when he was twenty. I know because I've done it. The years piled up on me like leaves falling in September, but I still got out there as long as I was physically able to swing the clubhead. I didn't hit it as far as I did, say, against Homans, but the game was still enjoyable for me. And on a very significant level, I might add."

"But you weren't exactly playing from the senior tees that day at St. Andrews, Mr. Jones. You were playing like a champion."

"It wasn't anything like that. Didn't you read those articles? I was just out having a good time with some old acquaintances. There was no pressure. I was as free as a bird. It was so different from the championships. I wasn't expected to do it; that's why they wrote so much about it. Heck, if I was back there in 1930 and I played the same round, they would have written about how I really should have shot thirty-one or twenty-nine or some other such nonsense! They would have drained all the joy from the round by talking about what might have been."

Jones had certainly given me something to think about. "What if you had shot twenty-nine? Now that would have really been something!"

Jones stared off toward the driving range. His tone of voice softened and the words came out slowly. "Had I shot twenty-nine, it would have been just as you said. Really something. But it would have been something very bad. Because twenty-nine leads to twenty-eight, and on down the line. The whole reason I quit the game was to get off the stage, so I could enjoy the game for its own sake and for my own sake. What made that day at the Old Course so meaningful to me is that I *did* enjoy it for what it was. I didn't have to dwell on what might have been. I could bask in what really happened."

"And it has stayed with you over the years, hasn't it?"

"You'd better believe it, son."

"Do you still draw pleasure from it today?"

"That's such a small part of the picture. I draw not only pleasure

ut inspiration and knowledge from that round every time I think
bout it. The experience was a gift; I can't say from whom, but it
vas bestowed on me by some . . . force . . . that has enabled me to
lay and replay it again and again. And each time there is a new in-
ight, a new lesson to be gleaned. Relax over the ball. Don't worry
bout where it's going, worry about how you've aimed. Take it
ack slowly. Let the club do the work. Exhale on the downswing.
Jon't think while you're swinging, just coil and release. Stay
vithin yourself. Be true to your feelings. Always think it over, con-
ider the options, but make the play you feel is right. If you have
oubt, resolve it, pick a club, and stick with it. Worrying about the
hot won't help you hit it."

All I could do was listen.

"Son, these thoughts have kept coming at me for years. And
hey'll keep on coming until the end of time. This is a form of en-
rgy that recharges itself every time it cycles through my mind."

"All of this from just one round?"

"Son, one good round can lead to a lifetime of creation."

"Do you think I'll ever have a round like that to draw from?"

"Everybody does, son. Oh, it doesn't have to be a round of golf,
nind you. It can be anything—an act, a deed, a gesture. It's just
hat golf is such a special game. It gives us all a fresh look at our-
elves, an honest look. And if I've learned anything, it's that a
nan's game is a signature that can't be forged."

I began to see that Jones was the living embodiment of the
hings Shep was talking about.

"Trust me, son, the pages you write on the golf course will be
vritten by your own hand and no one else's. If you give the game
alf a chance, it'll unlock the innermost thoughts that live behind
he walls of your mind."

"How do you do that?"

"There's no book, no lesson that can be taught in this area. You
ither see it or you don't. The trick is knowing it when you see it.
f you're lucky enough to see these things when you're in their
nidst and if you have the courage to trust your vision, you'll derive

an inner strength that can't be duplicated. What I'm talking about here can't be manufactured. You either feel it or you don't. And you won't find it by looking. It finds you."

"You know, I've had that very sensation before. At Berkeley there have been times when I felt as if I was experiencing something to remember, something very special, and I stopped dead in my tracks so I could sit and contemplate it. I did nothing physically, but I could feel it seeping down inside me."

"That's what I'm talking about. Have you ever tried explaining it in words?"

"Yes," I replied eagerly. "But there was no chance. Every time I tried, I lost the feeling entirely. I became so protective of it that when I came across those special moments, I just lapsed into silence, alone, and drifted off into this . . . space . . . where I could experience the feeling again. And once I grabbed onto it—or once it grabbed me—I just hung on and rode it out as far as it would take me."

"Have you ever tried that on the golf course?"

"I once meditated on it so hard during a round that I think I hypnotized myself. I don't even remember the shots I hit, but friends told me I was firing at the stick all day. Shot something like sixty-six. And I can't even remember how I did it. That's more than a little bit frustrating, let me tell you."

"It can be like that. But don't let it stop you. Keep at it. You'll get better the more you practice."

"Practice? I can't exactly go to the driving range of the mind, can I?"

"Well, no, but you can keep striving for that state of mind where nothing bothers you. Let me give you an example. Ever play a round of golf where everything was just *off*? I mean, the lie didn't look right no matter how positively you tried to approach it? Then on other days, no matter how badly you hit it, the grass was always perfectly matched for the type of shot you wanted to hit? Now the question is, what makes one day so right and the other so wrong? I've concluded that it's not anything physical. You don't get all the bad bounces one day and none the next. You get a little of each every day of your life. But if you look at it the right way, the bounces won't matter. All that will matter is your attitude."

"But Hogan," I interjected, bringing us back to reality for a moment, "he says you have to master the physical technique in order for the rest of this stuff to fall into place."

"Ask him about the days when he hit it pure but couldn't make a putt. Go ahead, ask the man. How physical was that? Shoot, I've seen him complain about the yips—well, there's nothing physical about that at all. If you think you're gonna miss it, you're likely as not to live out your thoughts. On the other hand, if you're convinced—really, truly, totally convinced, with every squeaking part of your body—that you can't miss, well, you won't. Ever get over a putt and become convinced it was going to go in the hole? I mean, really know it's going to go down from, say, thirty feet or more?"

I nodded, a quiet smile bursting on my face at the very idea.

"Sure you have. We all have. I've seen days when the world was an ocean, swelling and foaming all around me. And then all of a sudden in the thick of the battle I found I could make the water lie as flat as a plate, so smooth I could skip stones across it. And I was able to draw that putterhead back and stroke the little jessie right into the heart of the hole. But why and how did it happen? How did I know ahead of time what was going to happen?" Jones was talking like a swami, connecting with another world, one filled with dreams and hopes and thoughts of peaceful valleys and waterfalls that never run dry. "Son, it happens because our minds allow the stroke to be pure and unhindered by doubt. We let ourselves believe in it. And we do believe in it. This isn't physical at all, son; it's mental, that's what it is, pure and simple. The power of the human mind."

"Do you think Hogan can cure his yips?"

"From what I can see, he's got more than the yips. Something has grabbed ahold of him, something fierce. No matter what it is, it can't be healthy. That much obsession blurs the mind and renders it powerless to see all there is to be seen. Do you know what I'm talking about?"

I thought I did, really, but I'd never be sure until I confronted the Iceman.

We talked on through the afternoon, sitting at the fringe of the dining room, near the bar, in large overstuffed chairs. We were next to the windows, and we both looked out at the range, waiting for Hogan to return.

Jones did not wait idly. He offered me his discourse on the game and the vicissitudes of playing it at the championship level. What a tutorial this was! He told me what it felt like to compete for a national open championship, at stroke play, when the course is a veritable forest of dangerous predators who can eat you alive, talented players who are trained to attack and who are capable of striking miraculous shots at any given moment. A roar is heard from some far-off corner of the course. What has happened? Who did it? Is he on your heels or has he overtaken you? Is it the time to press, or should you lay back and bide your time for a better opportunity?

Jones told me how the imagination can run riot on you in situations like that. In the Open, he said, you constantly feel you're running from something without knowing exactly where the trouble is—or worse, what or who the problem is. It's eerie, he said. "Like walking through a haunted house at midnight."

He told me of the dangers of letting one shot, no matter how small, get away from you. "One shot carelessly played," he opined, "can lead to a lot of grief." No kidding, I thought to myself, recalling my personal mastery of that concept.

"You'll never do it all at once or all with one single shot," he taught me. "Keep hitting it, keep plugging, and don't worry about what the other fellows are doing. All you can do is your best, and if you're out to impress and rattle your adversaries, the best and surest way is to make sure that what you do *is* your best. Be resourceful, use your head, give it your all. If you do that, the rest will take care of itself."

"What if your best isn't good enough? I mean, you don't exactly like to lose, do you?"

"No, I don't, but I learned one fateful day on number eleven at St. Andrews that losing can teach you lessons, too. Don't let anger blind you to the wisdom that can be distilled from your deeds. If you let your temper destroy your equilibrium, you'll deprive yourself of the capacity to learn. Hell, you can blow off some steam—that's a perfectly healthy thing to do now and then—but remind yourself that there are things to be observed which will enable you to discover something about yourself that will be helpful later on. Pick up the crumbs. Harness the anger. Channel it into something productive."

I sat soaking up these drops of knowledge and experience like a sponge.

"You know what happened to me that day when I walked off back in '21?" Jones asked. "I was so damned embarrassed that it made me into a champion. That's what unleashed my string of championships. I was so ashamed of myself that I just had to do better. It wasn't the anger that fueled it but the understanding that I could never go down that road again. And I never did. And look what it brought me. Fifteen years later, in 1936, well into my retirement, I had the greatest moment of my life. And it happened just a few yards from where I had my worst. Live and learn, son. Live . . . and learn."

I could only wonder at the way he must have used his mental skills to battle syringomyelia, the muscle disease that bent him over and crippled him late in life. Talk about pain! It was a double dose. I mean, cutting a man down was bad enough, but for the world to see a champion laid low like that was unbearable. But not to Jones.

"It was painful, I'll tell you that," he explained after I summoned the courage to ask him about his later years. "But you know what gave me strength? I vowed not to let it beat me. I said to myself that if I'm to die, even if it's to be a tortured, agonizing demise, I'll carry myself with grace and dignity so there'll be something for others to look up to. It was a bit like playing cards. You can cry over what you've been dealt, or you can make the most of your hand. I've always wanted people to say that I played the devil out of what I held in my hand. I wanted to amaze them with my ingenuity. And even if I lost, bitter as that could be at times, I could still see the sweetness in the experience, as long as people knew— if I knew—that I'd gone further, done more, tried harder, and flat out showed 'em that if I was to be beaten, it would take a mountain of a man to conquer me. And when it happens, as it will to anyone, take it like a man and hand over the reins to the fellow who's going to drive the carriage. Thoughts like that propelled me, moved me, enabled me to fight that dreadful sickness. It was match play and it was all I had to work with, but it worked. And you know what? My last years were as good and full to me as my twenties were."

"How did you handle those seven lean years, between 1916 and 1923, when everyone expected so much of you? When you never won though they all said you would?"

Jones shook his head, laughing. "I was burning like a furnace, son. Shoot, I was so damned hot, you could have fried eggs on my forehead. But then it all snapped for me that day at St. Andrews when I stormed off."

"Forty-six blows on the front nine is something to snap about."

"Yes, but it didn't snap apart. Just the opposite—everything fell into place. I saw it all at once. My whole life raced by right in front of my eyes. I saw my family, my friends, my home, the whole field competing against me, everything. They rushed by, then they came back. And you know what? They flat out surrounded me. I felt them all walking with me as I stormed back to the clubhouse. I was trying to shake 'em, but they stayed on my tail. Step for step, they were with me."

"Jesus."

"I'm not just whistling Dixie, either. I mean they were *there*. It was as spooky as midnight. And you know what? I suddenly realized they were not just beside me but inside me as well. We were one. There were no opponents, no gallery, no one else. Just me. I had to do it for me, not for them. If the others won out, I was part of their victory; I could share it with them. It was like looking at the world from the entrance of a doorway. I was inside looking out. And you know, sometimes it was hard to see, son, because all the others were trying to get inside and stand beside me."

It is impossible for me to convey the enormity of what he was describing. If what Jones was telling me was true, he transcended his body that day. He stepped outside of himself, and when he climbed back inside, he brought the whole world with him.

"Don't you ever encounter people who don't believe any of this? People who not only don't accept it but who actually resent a man like you, with all your success?"

"I've met them, yes. But, son, it's like trying to move into a new neighborhood. If they don't want you there, move on. And if that sort of thing happens to me, I'll keep walking until I find a place where I want to be with them as much as they want to be with me. That's the only way to find harmony."

"You mean a man of your character would let some small-minded creep kick you out of the neighborhood?"

"If it would destroy my equilibrium, yes, I'd move on. But if I could connect with him and change him, then hell no, I'd stay right there. Son, you have to learn that you can't lay down rules like they were railroad ties. You have to . . . How can I say it? You have to learn to live for yourself, to hear your own song. You have to sing that song, too."

"Mr. Jones, you're talking more about living than you are about playing golf."

"Playing *is* living, son. And living is like playing. Not for amusement, not for laughs, not for a pastime. You're building something out there. Not a game or a round or a score. You're building a life. You see, when you learn how to play, you learn how to live. Unless you understand that, it's all for naught. It's just a crop that sits in the field rotting through the winter. You have to harvest what you've grown, son."

"How in the world did you keep it all under control? Old Shep says that's what separates people. What did he say? 'It's not finding the energy, it's how you use it.' "

"Let me tell you one thing I've come to know," Jones offered. "It's as true as the line on that putt I nailed to tie Al Espinosa."

I moved to the edge of my chair.

"The sweetest sound is silence. And, son, you have to listen for it, have to know it when it hits you, for if you can hear the heart-beat of inner peace, you'll be so tranquil, so sure of your bearings that even a clap of thunder won't make you jump. You'll be able to endure anything the world sends your way. And the slightest noise, the simplest of things, will have the intricacy and elegance of a symphony."

"That's so beautiful." His words were like paint, his canvas a masterpiece. Even so, there was still a reckoning point. "What's Hogan apt to make of all this?"

"Son, you have to stop worrying about what others think and start worrying about what *you* think. That's what's important. I wish I could give you the words to say, but I can't. I wish there were a way to say it, but there isn't. Not that people haven't tried. Some call it beauty or grace or goodness. You can call it that. Or you can call it energy, as old Shep does. But it doesn't matter what the label is because it's there. And what there is in the air, on the ground, in the trees, in the eyes of others, it'll stick to you like glue if you just let it. Son, if people would only realize what's right there in front of their noses, why we'd patch up all the rips and tears in the world in no time at all. It's just that simple."

I did not hear any bells sounding from the sky. There were no cymbals crashing against each other, no waters parting, no visual miracles revealed. But something had happened right there in that room. The air was warmer around me, and I could feel it against my skin. By the light of the golden sunset, I saw the detail in the bark of the trees just outside the window. The clouds were moving to the east. I saw a pattern in them, and I noticed the shadows they cast on the grass. When I looked down at my hands, I saw every pore on the skin that covered my wrists. I had never noticed these things before, but I surely saw them now, and they bore a crispness, a clarity that was breathtaking.

When I looked over at Jones, even he looked different. Suddenly, as if the forces above had bestowed upon me the focus of a microscope, I could see every stitch and loop in his light brown cashmere pullover. His barrel chest, the broad back, those massively muscled legs. I could see it all. He was a locomotive ready to leave the station.

Jones's hair was parted a bit off center, to the left, and his skin was well tanned. He was not as dark as Hagen, but he bore the look of a man who had spent more than his share of time outdoors. Yet there was not a wrinkle of worry or doubt anywhere on his face. And his eyes. Oh, those eyes! The pale blue-gray of the irises was as cool and soft as water. Even with the energy boiling inside him, it was easy to see Jones was at peace.

He must have had the Hawk on his mind, yet he wasn't talking about him at all. Still, I could not resist asking the question that loomed in my mind: "Will Hogan ever come to think of these things the way you do?"

"What makes you think he doesn't already? If you haven't talked to him at length, how do you know?"

"How will I ever know? Hogan's so tight with his words, you'd think they were pennies and he was flat broke, afraid to spend them on something that wasn't absolutely necessary."

"That doesn't sound like a bad approach to me. Especially if you are broke."

Jones got up and looked at me with a smile. His face was full of confidence, and it told me he knew I was close to figuring it out.

I believed then that I had nearly assembled the tools to deal with Hogan and his obsession with the '55 Open. Jones's words, coupled with Shep's and the articles I'd read, gave me a fresh look at the game and the lives it parallels. Jones's life. Old Shep's. Hogan's. I had seen a great deal and had come to know firsthand the frenzy of a puzzle maven, scrambling amid the scattered pieces, trying to put them together in sequence. I was close. Very, very close. Even so, there was a place I had to revisit to test my knowledge against the beguiling aroma of the game that was now swirling around me. It lay just beyond the clubhouse windows.

The sun had tiptoed offstage, the only remnant of its glow the amber spears of dusk that crisscrossed the range, draping the grassy peaks and valleys of the landing area with an irregular patchwork of light and shadow. No one was out there. The air hung still and warm, and the only sound was a soft crinkle of ashes 180 yards away. Hogan's message still loitered in the milky stillness that hovered between late afternoon and early evening, the smoking numbers a scary reminder of his determination to correct the past.

But if Jones was right, if his message had tangible meaning beyond the mental gymnastics I had just practiced, if I was truly to connect with the Hawk, then I had better put the master's teaching to work. And so I headed out the door, ready to apply Jones's lessons to a fresh sack of practice balls. There was still time. As long as there was light, I could swing and watch the results of my effort.

Being alone on the range was an eerie feeling. I sensed a clubhouse full of greatness peering down at me, waiting to see if the kid from Lincoln Park had been listening or whether only his body had been present while his mind had cut class.

A simple rack at the end of the range was filled with practice balls. There were spheres from every age, even a sampling of featheries, ready for anyone who cared to let them fly. I passed over an array of featheries and gutties, past the Sure-Flites, Sure-Shots, and Kro-Flites, even skipping the chance to experiment with something as exotic as a St. Mungo's Water Core. Nor would I stretch the limits of my distance with a Penfold. I left that to Vardon and Ray, who could have all the small balls they wanted. One point sixty-eight is my diameter, and it was to that part of the rack that I devoted my attention. When I found a sack of shiny new balata beauties, I grabbed hold, pulling the bloated pouch up to eye level as if it contained gold dust.

When I dropped the balls to the turf, I saw a glimmering collection of Titleists and Maxflis. The balls glowed in the golden light of sundown and even seemed to move among themselves, elbowing one another, begging to be hit first. I peeled off a pellet with a borrowed iron, and as I hovered over it, I visualized a shot that would cut through the air with the silence and grace of a perfectly crafted paper glider plane. But I couldn't get the shot off, for just as I was ready to hit, I heard the soft timbre of bagpipes, which broke my concentration. The sound was no ordinary procession of notes; it was an incantation, a calling, an aural incense that drew me away from the ball.

I looked back at the clubhouse, but there was nothing to see other than the stately building and its backhouse standing motionless. The muted lighting of the dining room framed a tableaux; no one was moving, not even Hagen, who stood like a statue before a barful of members.

To the rear of the clubhouse was the road we traveled to Pebble Beach. Titanic Thompson, the crashing sea, that roaring gallery— they were only memories now, the smoky penumbra of the day's action having been pushed aside by an invisible hand that had fanned the air to dispel the mystic vapor where dreams live.

I spun around, still searching for the source of the sound. There was a shaft of light at the left edge of the range, piercing the dusk at a place where a gap in the trees seemed to lead to a fresh green field. I blinked, but it was still there. There was no one to ask, so I didn't feel the need to pose a question. But this was very, very odd. Earlier in the day, when I was watching some of the fellows practice, there was no space between the trees. It was a solid wall of bark and greenery.

My first few steps toward the light were short and halting, an indication that my feet were not nearly as curious as my eyes. Within seconds, however, my entire body was in sync, every pore anxious to discover what awaited me at the gap in the trees.

When I was ten feet from the opening, a blast of wind all but knocked me over. It ripped through my hair, pushing it backward, away from my face. It caused me to huddle in an effort to conserve my body heat. The temperature was dropping quickly, yet despite the change in weather, I sensed I was on the right path. The sound of the pipes grew in intensity with each step.

I could see an adjoining fairway, rolling and folding as though it were a down comforter of emerald and auburn, tossed casually to cover an unmade bed. A purple spray of heather led me through the draw where the pine, cypress, and juniper trees had parted. The fairway had a shopworn presence, the way an old carpet looks when laid on a creaky hardwood floor. Tall whins and prickly gorse bushes lined the short grass. Out past the rumpled creases of fescue, a town sat with a harbor behind that was calm and quiet. To the left and right, isolated cottages dotted the border of this well-walked stretch of muted green. Families were inside, awaiting nightfall.

Now that I was here, the pipes faded into nothingness, and the only movement, aside from the stiff breezes, came from the draw-holes of nearby chimneys. Fires had been kindled, and the scent of burning logs and dinner roasting drifted upward and outward from the brick towers that spouted from the rooftops.

After several minutes I heard a grunt, and then I felt something buzzing past my ear. When I turned back to see the end of the fairway farthest from town, I spotted old Shep flailing away with one of his crooks. Frail as he was, he was out there, gunning pebbles and featheries as if they were Titleists, sending his missiles hurtling through the air. They didn't fly with the aerodynamic draft of a golf ball, but those mothers moved once they were hit. And his distance wasn't bad. From what I could see, the darn things were traveling upward of two hundred yards.

Physically speaking, Shep may have been only a will-o'-the-wisp, yet he seemed to generate enormous power when he cranked up. Even with the wind forcing his ragged robes to flutter, he remained steady. His swing was quite short, with a release that carried him into his follow through with the purity of dynamic motion. It was hard to believe, but the old fellow never seemed to miss a shot.

I wasn't certain an interruption would be appreciated, so I remained off to the side observing. Finally, after several shots had flown far to the right side of the fairway, Shep looked up and motioned for me to walk over.

"I was hopin' ye'd come," he said. His voice was husky, its muffled tone rubbing the wind like sandpaper.

"Are you practicing?" I asked.

"Nae."

"Playing?"

"Nae."

"Well . . ."

"I'm baffin', laddy. 'N' as ye can see fer yerself, 'tis nae an easy task I'm takin' on here."

"I can see that. I saw those last few shots trailing off to the right. Maybe you ought to take a rest for a minute or . . ."

"Laddy, ye're lookin' withou' seein'. There's nae such a thing as yer sayin'. I'm aimin' o'er there. Canna ye see wha' I'm tryin' t' do?"

Embarrassed, I took another look at the fairway. The featheries and pebbles were arrayed in distinct circles, long and short, left and right. Shep appeared to be writing a message of his own.

"You're just hitting to a spot, then moving the spot. Just like Hogan."

"Laddy, 'tis is nae a game I'm playin' here. Me flock'll be grazin' doon from Perth 'n' the Midlands, 'n' all I'm doin' is selectin' where t' nestle 'em, before gwin' t' town."

He was bringing golf's history to life. Up to now, I had only read stories about the origins of the game, about how ancient shepherds, first in Germany, then in Holland, then across the North Sea in Scotland, selected grazing lands by hitting stones out across the vale. A man won grazing rights over all the land covered by his shot. Even in those days it paid to be a long knocker.

When I took another look toward the town, I realized this was not a golf hole as I knew it. There was no flag off in the distance, no green to aim at, no cut line to distinguish rough from fairway. This wasn't a golf course at all but a pasture. And Shep was not out here for golfing or practice; what we've come to know as a game was once just a natural part of a shepherd's life.

A startling thought traveled through my head: If this is a pasture, if Shep is a shepherd, if . . . *when* the heck am I? There were no clues, no markers, no convenient newspapers to pick up and read.

The only thing I could do was observe the surroundings. But how can you mark time by watching the grass or the gorse, the heather, the whins? Even the pipers, whom I could not see, had laid down their instruments.

Off in the distance, the town's chimneys continued to transport the scent of dinner upward into the sky. A fully rigged schooner pulled into the harbor, its only sign of lineage a red flag hanging limply from the main mast. Old Shep stopped to watch me take in the scene. When I looked back at him, he smiled. "She's from Flanders by way o' Holland, laddy, bringin' o'er a load o' cheeses 'n' spices 'n' maybe some featheries, too."

"That ship," I said, agape at the sight of a fifteenth-century vessel, "she's—"

"Aye, laddy, she's a seagoer. Now dinye be worryin' abou' the year, fer tha's nae a worthy question in these parts. Ye'd be better off if ye were baffin' yerself."

On the ground beside Shep lay several crooks of varying lengths, fashioned out of different colored woods. I picked up one, hefting it like a baseball bat. My grip was surprisingly light. The polished shaft was full of gnarls and irregular bumps, but somehow they seemed to fit my hands with a friendliness one rarely finds in a club that is held for the first time.

"Gae on," Shep said. "Ye can take a bash if ye wish."

He reached down and opened a sackful of featheries.

"I can't. I'll tear these things apart."

I looked down at the featheries spread on the ground, afraid that one swing would cause an explosion and the two of us would choke to death in a cloud of stuffing.

"Oh, laddy," he said with a laugh so deep and hard that it caused him to cough violently. When he regained control, he stared into my eyes with the same intensity he had displayed upstairs when we first met. "Gae on," he repeated. "Show me wha' ye kin do."

My first attempt reminded me of what it was like learning to play the game. The first few swings were taken far away from the ball, with enough firmness and speed to give me a feel of what the club could do. Trying to flex the shaft was a waste of time, for these crooks were miniature tree trunks. They were considerably heavier than what I was used to, but I made the most of it. After a few passes, I began to feel the air rush as I completed my downswing.

"Wha' 'r ye waitin' fer?" he asked.

"I don't exactly see a foursome yelling at us because they want to play through."

"These balls, laddy, they're ne'er gwin' anywhere till ye hits 'em. 'N' I'm nae gwin' t' stand here 'n' let ye pass up the baff, nae in a gloam like this tha's so full o' excitement tha' she's curlin' me toes upward."

His impatience to see me take a whack forced a swing before I was ready. My thrashing motion missed entirely. I mean, we're talking cold whiff. I was embarrassed but undaunted. I struck another blow, and this time the ball bounced meekly ahead, a feeble grounder that, if this were baseball, would have come to rest quietly around second base. My frustration grew by the moment, the stalk of its ire climbing as if this putrid display were a magic fertilizer. Shep's gaze twinkled upon me, but his benevolence was no help. I continued to scratch out timid ground balls.

When Shep grabbed for my arm, my first instinct was to resist. "Leave me alone," I said in protest. "I'll get this if it kills me."

"I'm nae worried abou' ye, laddy. 'Tis this poor patch o' thistle ye're choppin' up tha's causin' me the concern. I've ne'er felt a man could kill the earth, but, laddy, ye're gwin t' change me view."

He had a point. The ground was succumbing to my mediocrity as I took my cuts. Blades of grass, chunks of turf, and the dusty earth beneath them were flying with each swing. And the feath-eries! The blasted things were shooting off to the right. And these babies weren't just slicing, they were pure laterals. For crying out loud, how bad do you have to be to shank a crook? There wasn't even a hosel on the darn thing.

When Shep gently nudged me aside, I peacefully submitted to his command. I was anxious to see how he did it. After he pow-dered one of the featheries down the fairway, I complained that there was no way such a grandfatherly reed of a man could do that. "Laddy, can ye ken the lesson I'm givin'? Can ye feel the surge?"

When he took the next swing, I began to notice what he was talking about. His entire body, if not his whole self, was melded to the crook in his hands. When he connected with the ball, his body seemed to leap down the fairway, giving chase to his stroke. "Cast yer body after the ball, laddy. Chase her wi' yer arms. 'Tis the only way t' feel a part of it."

He handed the crook back to me.

My next swing started to produce results. At least I was starting to get the thing airborne. First one shot, then another. They began to fly off into the purple haze that hung like a curtain above the still water of the harbor. My shots were not monstrously long, but they were getting out there.

"Now ye're gettin' it," he said.

But my golfing wallet was not thick with prosperity. Just as I began to power the ball, my swing quickened and I lost the sense of timing it took to make a crook work the way it was supposed to. My immaturity was fertile ground for impatience, and it caused me to give up the chase. Exasperated, I conceded defeat. "I don't think I can do this."

"Laddy, there's much t' ken abou' baffin'." He curled an outstretched arm around me and pulled my body so close that it was cupped within his, sheltered from the cold. "Here ye're tryin' t' do it all in a day. Dinya ye be worryin', boy, fer ye're only takin' the first few steps o' the journey, 'n' they're the most important steps, fer they're the ones that'll lead ye t' the next ones. If ye're t' do anythin', laddy, jus' make sure ye keep on walkin'."

"Would you mind if I took another shot?"

He looked up to the sky, then off to the town. I knew he smelled a meal about to be set on the table. He could easily see that there wasn't much light left. And the two of us would have to shag the balls when we were done. But he didn't care about the time. "Take yer best shot, laddy."

I acknowledged his encouragement with a nod. I was considerably more deliberate with this attempt, making sure that I was ready to hit before taking the gnarled crook away from the ball. Even as I waggled the bulbous shillelagh, I knew something good would come of it. The shaft, stiff as a telephone pole a few minutes ago, now felt as flexible as a flyswatter. My practice swings made a wind of their own. When I swung into the featherie, I could see it compress against the outstretched face of my club. Then it rose slowly, burning a hole into the wind. I watched it for what seemed like an hour but in reality was only a few seconds. By the time gravity overtook the shot, the ball was over two hundred yards distant. Alive with success, I exclaimed the call of victory: "That baby's got some sore stitching!"

"Nae," he answered. "She's sleepin' in the fairway, tha's all."

"Are you kidding me? I put a major hurt on that thing. It's out of round."

I must have said the right thing, for Shep was beaming with accomplishment. The teacher could see that he had imparted his lesson. And yet he was not entirely certain. He measured me with his eyes and ran his fingers through his beard like a rake. Then he issued a challenge: "Laddy, let me see ye repeat yer magic."

With the sensation of pure contact still dancing inside me, I selected another ball, separating it from the litter of spheres the way a cowboy cuts off a calf. The ball sat innocently on the turf, a help-less victim awaiting a violent assault. Two practice swings were plenty. I tore into the shot, bringing every ounce of effort to the task. My eagerness to excel overpowered my ability to control the motion I had started. I lost my footing on the downswing, tripping over my feet as I approached impact. It was fan city, sit-down time, strike three. A whiff that was as cold as winter.

Impulsively, I reacted. Whether it was caused by frustration, anger, embarrassment, or a little of each was no matter. Disgusted, I slammed the crook into the ground. "Dammit!" was all I could say.

Old Shep watched closely, shaking his head.

He stepped over and stood beside me. He picked up the dis-carded crook and inspected the bumpy surface for damage. He was looking close, checking for hairline cracks. "Ye've bruised her, laddy. She'll need tyme t' recover. Nae more baffin' fer her fer at least a fortnight 'r two. Now step aside, laddy, 'n' take a peer at this. I'm gwin t' show ye somethin'."

Shep pulled out a velvet sack that had been stashed in of one of the nearby gorse bushes. He loosened the golden thread and ex-tracted a club crafted from ebony but bleached the color of bird's-eye maple. His eyes shimmered with delight. "Isn't she a beauty?"

The grain curled down the shaft and spun a web in the center of the long, narrow club head. The knotted burrs that jutted out from the surface would have been, in any other context, a mark of de-formity, evidence of contortion, the sign of some wicked spell cast to bring pain where once there was beauty. But here on the time-less wooden skin of this club, they were badges of distinction, not bumps of ugliness. Shep rubbed each one with care. "She's alive w' feelin', she is."

Shep picked three featheries from the pile and told me where each would go. "The first one, laddy, she's gwin' throo the glen, cuttin' into the strath 'neath tha' far hillock. Then th' second, she'll be like a cannonball, shootin' th' wynd 'tween those trees o'er there." He pointed to a narrow alley of grass that blanketed the furrow between the neighboring trees to the left of us. The gap he'd be aiming for was, at most, only four or five feet wide. "'N' this last one, laddy, she'll sail like an angel, floatin' free all the way t' Dundee."

I gave him the blank stare of unknowing youth.

Shep shrugged with laughter at my inability to decipher his prediction for shot number three. "Wha' I'm sayin', laddy, is tha' once she rises, she's ne'er comin' doon."

Three quick pops were all he took. No warm-up, no prelude, no fanfare, no practice swings. Shep just stood up to the ball and bashed. His approach was somewhat uncharacteristic, given all his talk about getting the body ready to partner the mind. Perhaps he was showing me that if you are ready, you don't need a lot of folderol. Just grip it and rip it. Whatever the technique, it worked. The sound of the shots was deafening, each one roaring a dragon's fire as it spun off the burled club face. The night, which had grown dimmer, loitered in abeyance, the remaining light lingering with curiosity as if it, too, wanted to watch the old man work his wizardry.

The first featherie started out low, veering its way through the dusk. Then it cut softly to the right, never losing velocity as it crossed over a small valley that transected the fairway. The ball came to rest atop a humpy swale. Ball number two did just as he predicted, shooting straight down the tight hallway of grass, never threatening to touch the walls of trees that bordered it on both sides. The ball threaded the needle, traveling so fast that the echo of its whine hung in the air like the searing exhaust of a race car.

The final ball was hit so high and deep into the sky that it wouldn't come down until the middle of next week. Shep mentioned Dundee; I did not know how far away that was, but what I saw told me it must have been in another time zone, for that was where this thing was going. It was, without question, the longest shot I had ever seen. I lost sight of the ball after it passed over the chimneys of the town. It was still going upward some four hundred yards distant. It faded from view, but then suddenly, with a muffled explosion rumbling through the clouds, I saw it again as it burst over the harbor like a gigantic flashbulb, the sparkling remnants of the leather cover falling harmlessly into the sea beyond the moored ships.

"You really hit that thing!"

"Laddy, dinye be lookin' a' me like I'm a freak o' nature or a beast o' myth. 'Tis only simple baffin', and any man has th' ability t' ken it. But the distance 'n' the power, they're nae important if ye've nothin' t' tie 'em to. Baffin's jus' baffin' means nothin' withou' somethin' t' hitch it to. Ye must find th' connection if'n yer baffin's t' have meanin'. Troo meanin', tha' 'tis."

Before I could ask another question, he spread his guiding hands over my shoulders and set me up to take a final cut. With him to place me in position, I felt like a new man. Now I dispensed with the warm-ups. My backswing was smooth, and I felt my arms at full extension when something told me it was time to bring her down. My arms felt as if they were crashing against my left side, and the club felt as though it was crashing into and through the ball. Impact was a thunderclap of energy, which caused my body to feel as if it were being carried away, following in the wake of the shot, which soared out into the fading light. I had done it, on cue. One shot left, and I nailed it. Old Shep watched for my reaction, and when he saw the fascination in my face and the jump in my step, he returned a look of approval.

Arm in arm we walked together to fetch the featheries. It took some doing, but we corralled every last ball, save the one he obliterated over the harbor. After the roundup was complete, Shep stuffed the bulging ball pouch into the long duffel that held his crooks.

"Laddy," he said as we turned back toward the clubhouse, "there's so much t' learn, so much t' teach, so much tyme t' devote t' these matters. . . ."

He let out a deep breath, heavy with concern that what he'd taught me so far would not be sufficient to deal with Hogan.

The old man was concentrating so hard that his head was vibrating. His entire body was a knot of muscle, punishing itself in an effort to squeeze out the juices. He looked like a weightlifter trying to press twice his body weight. If I hadn't known better, I'd have said Shep was trying to will something to happen.

The wind had stopped, and the air was thickening with heat. The very last slivers of daylight were fixed on the horizon, as if Shep had refused to let them leave us.

Only when Shep exhaled did I hear again what had summoned me to join him. The pipers had returned. As the final strands of sundown burned golden across the treetops, I could hear their high, reedy tones playing faintly across the hills, too far away to be distinct but growing stronger the more I listened. I heard ancient and emotional strands of music that carried special significance in this special place.

Shep stood apart from me now, watching as I drank it in. When I turned to find him, he raised a hand and pointed off down the fairway. There, to the side, stood two men practicing. The taller and younger of the two beat down with a wooden-shafted play club, propelling gutties, one after another, into the void of early evening. The shorter fellow, apparently his teacher, made a few adjustments, and the shots zinged away with added crispness. The two of them laughed with delight as they watched the balls tear into the twilight. After a few more swings, the younger man stepped aside to let the older one hit. The old man's swing was choppy, perhaps a concession to age, surely not a sign of clumsiness. The older man pointed out the flaws in each shot, then reset his address position. I saw the moment of impact before hearing the crack of it, but hear it I did. How sweet the sound!

And then I heard a voice calling after a shot that was winging its way through the curtain of emerging moonlight. It was a voice I had heard before, but never without timbres of strain and concern. Somehow, even at this distance, I could tell that the harried, worried look was banished forever from the old man's face, and why not? For there was Old Tom Morris standing serenely in the gloam, reunited on the links with his beloved son. Champions both, they stood before me comparing skills: father and son, together once more, sharing all the joy the game has to offer.

It was an incredible scene, one that opened a floodgate of emotion. I could hear the pipers getting louder, their notes beginning to vibrate inside my head as I watched the reunion of this grandest of golfing families. I was being pulled toward them by an invisible, indescribable force.

Old Tom launched another rocket while Young Tom watched admiringly. Then Young Tom picked up the club, and everything reversed. Shep looked on with pride even though he surely knew this had been coming all along. I, on the other hand, sucked in the thrill as fast as I could inhale, but still I was breathless.

"Wha' ye're lookin' a' there, laddy," said Shep softly, "tha's gowlfin' in her purest form."

The look in Shep's eyes could not have been clearer. I knew now that the wind that transported me here had made no mistake. And as the intensity of the bagpipes grew in the falling night, the song they were playing carried up into the sky, a smoky incense in the Scottish air, drifting north toward the highlands. It was "Amazing Grace" as I had never heard or felt, and it had never seemed more appropriate: "*I once was lost, but now I'm found/Was blind but now I see. . . .*"

San Francisco
Express
June 20, 1955

FLECK WINS OPEN PLAYOFF; HOGAN RETIRES

UNKNOWN IS OPEN CHAMP; HIS 69 BEATS HOGAN'S 72

By Dick Yost

The playoff ended as strangely as it had begun.

The same doubters who said on Saturday that Jack Fleck couldn't possibly birdie two of the last four holes to tie the immortal Ben Hogan were out there again yesterday, except this time they had 18 full holes to talk about Fleck's chances. There was no way he could do it. Not two days in a row.

But do it he did. Playing controlled yet dynamic golf, the nobody from Duck Creek became a somebody in San Francisco. Jack Fleck, a man who had not won anything in his life, became the champion golfer of the United States of America. Ben Hogan, the man who has won everything there is to win, will play no more. In a dramatic announcement at the trophy presentation, Hogan, his voice breaking with emotion, announced his immedi-ate retirement from competitive golf.

It was Fleck's day from the start. Although the battle-weary Hogan outhit his younger challenger often, Fleck's hot putter proved the most potent weapon in either player's bag. Fleck took only 30 putts in the pressure-packed playoff. Hogan, meanwhile, struggled with many of the short ones, letting Fleck off the hook more than once.

Hogan seemed to be fighting something all day long. Whether it was Fleck or the pressure of winning a fifth U.S. Open, surpassing the legendary Bobby Jones, is unknown. But something was affecting the Hawk. He wasn't flying as free or as high as we've come to expect.

They parried with each other for seven holes, then Fleck pulled away for good with three straight birdies at the eighth, ninth and tenth.

What could Hogan have been thinking? Here he was, playing on a course that had proven to be impossible throughout the championship. It was crunch time, he had a huge edge in experience, the heat was on, he was even par, and he was two down.

Fleck was walking on air, his arms falling loosely to his side. In contrast, it was Hogan who seemed tense, his muscles curling back on themselves like a strip of wet rawhide left to dry in the sun. The fatigue of the long practice sessions and the four arduous rounds that preceded the playoff was plainly evident. Hogan had to be aching all over, exhausted from weeks of climbing up and down the Lake Course's many hills and valleys.

ROLE REVERSAL?

How ironic the scene had become. Just a day before when Fleck approached the fifteenth tee, he was two down with four to play. Today, as he stood on the same spot, he held a two-shot lead in a U.S. Open playoff against the greatest talent in the game. It was Hogan who would have to pull off the miracle this time.

When both men parred the fifteenth and sixteenth, it was apparent that the sand in Hogan's hourglass was quickly slipping away.

SOMETHING SPECIAL

But at the seventeenth, Hogan gave us a powerful look at what makes him so great. As he left the tee after driving, he was slump-shouldered. His walk was deliberate, as though he were measuring the amount of energy each step would require before allowing his weary legs to move forward. With the clock running out, Hogan was trying to save himself for what lay ahead.

Then suddenly he seemed to get swept up by a wave of force. He began to walk faster, as if the wind were behind him, carrying him with it.

His diminutive body seemed to grow with each step as he limped his way along the slanting fairway of the Lake Course's hardest hole. Anyone who heard his comments in the press room Saturday about "squirting a little adrenaline into a crucial shot" knew what he was doing. He was pumping himself full of the stuff, knowing that he would need every ounce of strength to reach the green on this monstrously long, 461-yard, uphill par four.

As Hogan stood over his three-wood second shot, the air was as still as the spectators. There was no sound, not even a cheer to encourage him. They were all just watching, in awe that he was still out there, doggedly pursuing his dream.

His swing unfolded in slow motion for those lucky enough to see it. The ball exploded off the clubface, the crack of impact echoing through the trees like a gunshot. Ben Hogan, the man who couldn't get home here during six practice rounds and three more in the championship, had just hit the green for the second time in a row. And this time he was only 14 feet away.

Everyone knew there was a very real possibility of a two-shot swing, for Fleck played the hole with the tentativeness of a man starting to unravel. His second shot was short and in the rough, and his third, pitched over a bunker, left him with a 6-footer for par. The distance must have seemed a mile to him as Hogan lined up his try for a birdie. There was a real possibility they might be going to the home hole all even.

Hogan, however, could not convert. His downhill putt took a look into the hole as it trickled by, but it wouldn't fall. Fleck, after taking a look toward the clubhouse, realized how close he was to the championship. He pulled himself together and quickly stroked his par-saving putt. It rolled almost two feet past the hole. He had missed.

Now Fleck was only one up. It was either player's championship to win, and Fleck would have to stand with the gallery and watch as the greatest pressure player in the game drove first off the final tee.

ONE TO PLAY

Hogan waited patiently at the eighteenth tee for the crowd to

settle in. He pulled a wooden club from his bag and surveyed the landscape. The pencil-thin green was 327 yards away, with four bunkers around it. The hillside behind the green was packed with people, 10,000 strong, waiting, wanting to see some history.

The tee itself had been freshly covered with top dressing, an attempt to repair a week of damage and have the hole ready for the playoff.

Hogan set himself firmly and checked his alignment. His quick, compact swing lashed out at the ball, but his right knee gave way on the downswing, causing him to slip on the loose soil. The shot showed the full effects of Hogan's disrupted swing. The ball spun out of control to the left, diving out of view and burying itself in the deepest part of the jungle rough.

Fleck drove safely and reached the green in two.

There was no hope left in any rational mind. But Hogan refused to quit. He flailed at his second shot, knowing a superhuman swing was his only chance of getting home.

Try as he might, Hogan couldn't do the impossible. He moved the ball only a foot. Then he tried again. This time he did better: three feet. A third slash at the bulrushes got him out of trouble and onto the fairway. His next shot took off, sailing past the hole by 40 feet. He was a mile away in five. It was all over.

Then Hogan sent the world a message. He stood frozen over his ball for what seemed like minutes before he gave it a gentle stroke to start it downhill toward the hole. The ball took a long time to travel the distance, but when it fell in, there was an explosion of noise.

Hogan had made the final putt of his career. It may have been for double bogey, but it was a coast-to-coast, long-distance snake. It was one for the books.

When Fleck lagged up for his par, it was anticlimactic. Though the crowd cheered wildly, it was hard to tell who they were yelling for: The new champion or the aging hero who had played so valiantly?

UPSET OF THE CENTURY

Regardless of the identity of the crowd favorite, one thing is clear: This was one of the game's greatest upsets, reminiscent of Ouimet at Brookline. It also produced one of the all-time great unknown champions, right up there with Sam Parks and Tony Manero.

Hogan, however, knew all about Fleck before the championship began. Fleck plays clubs manufactured by Hogan's new company. Hogan himself delivered Fleck's wedges to him earlier in the week. In the end, Hogan had been beaten with his own weapons.

Fleck started loose and stayed that way until the knot got tight at seventeen. His throat may have narrowed, but he didn't choke. He won it with a game that, for one very special week, was better than everyone else's.

Hogan acknowledged Fleck's prowess at the awards ceremony. "He's one heck of a player," he said. "But I guess all of you figured that out by now." Hogan then waved his telltale white cap like a fan over Fleck's putter, a belated attempt to cool it off.

The Father's Day crowd gave Hogan an extended ovation, fearing they might never again get the chance to salute one of the game's greatest players. Fathers and sons, entire families, covered the hillside behind the Olympic Club's eighth green, where the trophy presentation took place. Groans of "Come back, Ben," could be heard as Hogan formally announced his retirement.

Hogan, who has no children, looked out on the families sitting before him. He slowly shook his head when the crowd seemed to be collectively begging him to keep playing competitively. "Golf is my life, and I love it," he told the throng. "I'm sorry to say I'm through with competition. I came here to win. I worked harder than I ever have in my life. Whether I won or lost was incidental. I wanted to make a good showing, and I hope I've done that."

Hogan acknowledged the crowd's farewell ovation as his wife Valerie stood by his side. Fleck's family, which includes his wife and young son Craig, were back home in Iowa. They got the news by telephone from the new champion just moments after the playoff ended. Fleck's son, who is an ardent Hogan fan, robustly proclaimed he "was pulling for Daddy, but I didn't like it that Hogan lost."

In the end, one can only say the future has confronted the past. What Jack Fleck will achieve from here on out remains to be seen. About Hogan there is no such mystery. What he has done in life and in golf will never be repeated.

·14·

THAT NIGHT I ATE SUPPER AT THE CLUB FOR THE LAST TIME. THE dining room was full. Little Eddie hustled to cover all the tables, attending to tastes that ran from caviar to nachos, lobster to fish and chips. I made the rounds after I had finished eating, sharing light conversation and enjoying good company. I visited with everyone from golfing stevedores to Dwight D. Eisenhower himself. These people were all gracious hosts even if they happened to express their feelings differently, explaining their games through their varied experiences and careers; they were like an explosion of color, a kaleidoscope of life that enthralled me.

Across the room I could see that Jones had a special fondness for Lema, much the same way he fancied Hagen. Come to think of it, Lema and Hagen had a lot in common, and not just when the cork popped, either. They were both from modest families, they both set out early in life to become professional golfers, and to their respective generations, they were both symbols of dashing, swashbuckling greatness. Jones must have loved watching them beat the pants off players who had a more pampered upbringing, who were privileged and advantaged. Lema and Hagen, in their own way, were the great equalizers. They put things on a level of achievement, where one's ability counted more than a pedigree. And then there was Hogan; he could deal this stuff in spades.

A small crowd spent several hours exchanging ideas on the perfect swing. Feeling at home with the group, I easily joined in the discussion. I talked expansively of my own game, particularly about my swing, how short and compact it is and why that has special benefits. There is not much that can go wrong when you take it back only three-quarters, I said like a professor. "I can coil like a tight spring," I said proudly, "and I can whip it around at a hundred miles an hour." Jones laughed, and the others followed his lead. The whole room rocked when Jones asked me, "Is that on your backswing or downswing?"

I laughed, too, and then explained that of course it was the part of the swing where I'm lashing into the ball, not pulling away from it. They still laughed. I calmed them down by explaining my game is patterned after that of Doug Sanders. Hagen stopped the giggling when he told the group he liked the idea, especially if I dressed like Sanders. "That old Sanders," he said, admiring my taste. "He sure knows how to use color."

The crowd dwindled one by one until they were all gone. By the time the last diners departed, it was just Jones, Hagen, and me. The bar was ours for the night, and we continued to argue about the nuances of the backswing, the downswing, grip pressure, the proper alignment of the vees, and all of that. I thought of beating balls, but my drooping lids told my mentors I'd sooner hit the sack than a five-iron. They left me quietly in peace. Alone in the dining room, I gazed out at the range, wondering when Hogan would be back. I was asleep in my chair before I knew it.

I jolted awake at three in the morning. I was scared that I had missed him, but when I realized it was the middle of the night, I calmed down. The Club was fast asleep, and no one was about. The moon hung over the range like a light bulb strung over a workbench. All was still and quiet except for the crickets, their legs working overtime to punctuate the darkness with their twitching sounds.

Something, I don't know what, prompted me to find the locker room. Once I did, I kept walking, half asleep, on through to the storage area where the members' bags were kept. So that's where they were! I slung my clubs over my shoulder and made my way out behind the clubhouse to the range. Someone must have known I was headed that way because a pile of balls was waiting for me. Bright and new, they looked like a batch of fresh eggs waiting to be scrambled.

Fortunately, the moon was still full and bright. I could easily see the balls at my feet, but following them once they were hit was another story. My first shot was a weak effort, sailing low and dying weakly to the right. Too thin. Another swing produced a high fade that went off into the trees, nowhere near the target. I don't know exactly where it wound up, but I knew it was a goner when I heard it ricocheting among the pines. Number three was better, but it, too, sank faster than it rose, a fat shot that came off the club face like a knuckleball; it dropped to the ground well short of where I was aiming. I kept at it, not letting the initial discouraging efforts sink my spirits. I can do this, I told myself. Finally, by the eighth or ninth swing, I connected. I felt solid contact, and when the ball whizzed off into the cold air, I heard the sound of a properly struck seven-iron. My divot was sharp and not too deep. Just right. I hit another and another. Hey! I had found it! They were going where I was aiming, and the hang time was pretty decent even for me. If only Hogan could see me now!

Captivated by my ability to rifle shots off into the night, I quickly went through the entire bag, forwards and backwards, hitting every club I had. The slowest swings were with the sand wedge, the balls floating easily to a flag that was only fifty yards away. By the time I worked my way up to the driver, my hands were starting to tire. As I addressed each new shot, the soreness in my fingers crept up into my forearms. My grip got tighter and tighter. Convinced I could mash one beyond the end of the range,

I cut loose with a mighty thrust, only to hit the damn thing off the heel; the ball squirted sideways to the left, directly between my legs. I spun around before the ball had even stopped rolling to make sure no one saw my feeble effort. To my great relief, the entire club was asleep.

I continued to bat out shots, some better than others, until sunrise. I paced myself, pausing between swings to regroup my thoughts, making sure I was aligned correctly and my backswing wasn't too fast. Taking a break between shots worked to my distinct advantage. My strength lasted longer, and the shots were much more consistent.

I was doing everything right. Knees over the balls of my feet, I sat down at address just like the great ones teach. I bent from the hips, and my navel turned away from the target, transferring my weight to the right side. My back was taut at the top, the club pointed down the line, and when I came through to impact, I was as solid as a rock. I could feel the shaft bend when I hit the ball, and the feeling was so pure, I'd swear I could picture the ball climbing up the grooves on the club face as it spun backward during the first nanoseconds of its flight.

The lighter it got, the better I seemed to strike the ball. I concentrated on my four-iron, firing off slow-rising beauties that seemed destined to end up right where I wanted them. Slowly but surely I was creating my own ball pattern in the landing area. Hell, I said to myself, I'll write Hogan a message of my own!

One temptation that got the better of me was to see how far I could belt that little white sucker with my four-iron. With each shot the effort was a little harder, the grip a little tighter. I was almost to the point of grunting at impact. The swing might have been wilder, but the contact was still good. My shots were still flying high and true.

He must have been over there in the trees, watching me, thinking, analyzing—probably laughing—as I progressed from a controlled backswing to a frenzied slash, trying to outhit myself.

"Don't worry, son," Hogan said to me. I nearly jumped out of my skin. He must have sneaked up from behind while I was mopping the sweat from my brow. "You keep swinging it like that and whatever it is that's ailing you will tire itself out. Once it does, you can get back to work."

"You . . . you've been watching?"

"Yes."

"Why didn't you just come over and straighten me out?"

"I don't do that."

"But you came over to make a comment. Why did you wait so long?"

"It hasn't been that long, really. Besides, at this stage I have plenty of time."

Great. He has plenty of time. What about me?

"Do you think I should keep at it?" I asked.

"That depends."

"On what?"

"On whether you want to play golf."

"And if I do?"

"Then you'd better keep at it for a long, long time."

"Will it take me that long to understand everything?"

"No."

"Why not?"

"Because you're never going to understand it all, that's why. It's too damn complicated. All you can do is understand a few basic principles, and then if you're fortunate, you'll come to understand yourself. You do that, and you're over the biggest hump of all. We don't all play the same, you know. We just apply a few fundamentals, then rely on ourselves to carry on. You want to know what I'd do if I were you?"

"Sure."

"Just play the game for its own sake. Simple as that. Let it get down inside you, deep inside. Let it consume you. It'll power you to new heights, you know. Now let me see that swing of yours again."

He wanted to see my swing? I couldn't believe it, but it was true.

The Iceman was going to give me a lesson! I swung, and I made what I thought was good contact, but the only sensation I could feel was my heart pounding against the outer wall of my chest. "How's that?" I asked him.

"Weak. Try it again."

Weak? I thought I hit it pretty darned good. The next shot sailed even farther and straight on line. He said nothing. I hit another. Same thing. I didn't fish for compliments; the way I figured it, if Hogan didn't walk away in disgust, at least I could tell someone someday that while I hit balls, *he* stopped by to watch. That was the best I could hope for from him, I guessed.

"You look like you're starting to sense it," he said with an approving tone. "You can feel it, can't you?"

"Yeah," I replied, although I did not look up. My swing was slower now, more controlled, with Hogan shooting confidence into my veins. Another shot zinged away.

"Now try shortening your thumb. Draw it just a touch outside going away—then lash at the back of the ball."

I did as he said, and it produced a high floater that landed and backed up. Perfect!

"You don't need me, son. Not anymore. Just play the game."

Hogan set his gear down by the bench and started to loosen up. It was daybreak, and there were just the two of us on the range. Our shadows stretched like rubber bands, drawn long and tight in front of us. I felt stronger just looking at the black silhouette of my body ten feet tall, draped across the grass. I popped three drives down the middle. They were frozen ropes, bouncing at least thirty yards after they landed.

"Whoa, son. Take it easy." Hogan turned toward me. "Don't use a golf club like a machine gun. Hit 'em slow, one at a time. Take a moment to watch the flight pattern of each shot. We've got all day out here."

Easy for you to say, Ben.

His first swing was a soft pitch shot that went barely twenty yards; it was a soft floater, struck perfectly. He hit about one ball a minute, eventually settling on a five-iron with which to hone his skills. I have always learned more by watching, so I quietly made my way to the director's chair and watched Hogan work his magic.

Nothing had changed. Every shot, whether a flip wedge or a full-dress middle-iron, was hit squarely, so squarely that the ball had no chance to think for itself. It was going to go where Ben Hogan directed it to go, like it or not.

I gave him an hour to unwind and shed the cobwebs. It was a quarter to nine. Time to do what I had to do.

"How did it feel at Riviera?" I asked him.

"Quite frankly, I don't remember much about that."

"Is it because of the accid—"

"No, not that," he interrupted coldly. "It's just that when you play that well, you tend not to recall the shots with much particularity. When you're in the zone, when you're really concentrating, there isn't any room upstairs for the memory to record anything."

"But what does it feel like?"

"Remember when I told you about it yesterday? It's . . . it's total control. You don't worry about each swing or that much about mechanics. You have that programmed in already. You just swing—and it goes where you want it to go."

"Was it like that at Olympic?"

"No. I played well, but I was struggling all the way. The course was hilly, which tired me out, wore down my legs. I was hanging, hanging, always hanging, hoping, looking over my shoulder. Praying I could get to the clubhouse before the other fellows. For a while I thought I had made it, too."

"You want number five, don't you?"

"Number five? What are you talking about?"

"The fifth Open Championship. You want to have five of them under your belt so you can beat Jones."

"Beat Jones? Whatever for?"

"To be the best of all time."

"Son, I don't bother to worry about that. I can't control that. That's what people like you want to think about. You want to analyze it, argue about it. Was Jones better than me? Was I better than Nicklaus? Was Nicklaus better than Jones? For crying out loud, you guys manage to do everything but play the game for its own sake. You know something, son? If I stopped to worry about beating Jones, I'd be chasing a myth I could never catch. Was Hank Aaron better than Babe Ruth? Let Jones have his glory and leave me to mine. Besides, I did win five Opens."

I gave him a spacey look, trying to draw it out of him.

"Didn't you do your homework?" Hogan was half asking, half scolding. "Ever hear of the 1942 Hale America Open? It's listed in black and white in the official *USGA Record Book,* right next to the other Open Championships of the forties. You can't get more official than that."

"I know all about it," I said, hoping to impress him with my knowledge of his career. "But there are some who say it wasn't the Open, just a substitute tournament during wartime, not everyone was there, that sort of thing. The fact is, Mr. Hogan, not everyone agrees with you."

"You're missing my point entirely. I can't control people, especially all you golf historians. You folks can disagree all you like. I don't bother worrying about things like that. You know, they had sectional qualifying for that championship, just like the Open."

"Yes, and they had more entries for it than for any previous Open."

Hogan looked at me with surprise; he didn't expect me to know about that.

"They were all there," he replied. "Demaret, Nelson, Lawson Little, Mangrum, the Turnesa brothers."

"Snead wasn't there."

Hogan looked at me sideways.

"Of course, the Open wasn't exactly Snead's cup of tea, was it?"

His eyes flashed with annoyance. "Don't you say that, son. Sam was a great competitor in the Open. Should have won it a couple of times at least. Now about this Hale America business, there was a pretty good reason Sam wasn't there in '42. It's called the U.S.

Navy. There was a war going on, one that guys like me and Sam remember."

"All I'm saying," I pressed, "is that people have raised questions. The field was a good one, but it was full of players who were well past their prime. For Pete's sake, even Jones competed, at the age of forty-two, a full twelve years into his retirement. And so did Sarazen, ten years after he won his second Open, twenty after his first."

Hogan nodded, and a subtle smile came to his lips.

"You played the last two rounds with Jones, didn't you?" I asked.

Hogan nodded again. He knew I had done some serious cramming to keep up with him. He pointed a finger at me as if that gesture would poke a hole in the argument against the 1942 Hale America National Open Championship being regarded as the equivalent of the U.S. Open.

"Young man," he said with emphasis, "I shot sixty-two during the second round. Sixty-two! One of the best rounds I ever had. Crimony, it was one of the best rounds anyone ever had. And let me tell you something, young fellow. That course, Ridgemoor in Chicago, was no pushover. No one else came close to my number that day. You gonna take that away from me? Gonna wipe it off the books?"

"Why, no. And I know they gave you a medal identical to the ones you won during those four Opens. But aren't you getting ready to go back to Olympic?"

"Maybe. I haven't decided yet."

At last, an opening. "I read a lot about you last night. You saved your wife's life out on that Texas road."

"Valerie is the finest companion I've ever had. I couldn't afford to lose her."

"You could have lost your own life in the process. Do you ever think about that?"

"Never. Son, there were four headlights coming my way. Two of them belonged to a Greyhound bus that had my name on it. Let me tell you, when something like that is bearing down on you at fifty miles an hour, in your lane, you don't think, you react. Protecting Valerie was instinct, pure and simple."

"But they let you lie there for an hour and a half. What was that like?"

"Confusion. Valerie said half the bus passengers thought the other half had called someone. It's just one of those things that happen, I guess."

"You guess? That was your life, your career they were messing with. Didn't that mean anything to you?"

"Of course it did. But what was I supposed to do about it? Get riled up? Get mad? I was in shock, dammit, so I couldn't exactly lecture them on the fine points of emergency road procedures."

I was sorry I had gotten sidetracked on the ambulance delay issue, but it didn't appear to be a fatal blunder. Hogan was talking fluidly, letting me see a side no one else had seen for over forty years.

"How was rehab?"

"What?"

"Rehabilitation. How was it getting ready to come back?"

"At first we weren't sure what to think. The doctors were positive, and that helped a great deal, but you have to remember, I almost lost my life that day. You don't forget about something like that so easily. I don't know if you can ever forget it. These things take time, lots of time. I didn't just jump up out of bed and start twisting and turning, getting ready for a comeback, you know."

"I read where the USGA sent you a telegram telling you they were looking forward to seeing you on the first tee at Medinah."

"Yeah." He laughed. "Those crazy, blue-blazered— How'd they ever figure I'd be playing in the 1949 U.S. Open four months after I just missed getting crushed to death by the steering wheel that was thrown back through the driver's seat of my Cadillac?" His eyes twinkled in the sunlight. "I was lucky to be walking, let alone teeing it up with Middlecoff and the rest of them. Those fellows were dreaming when they sent that wire."

"When did you know you'd be at Merion?"

"As soon as I could move around."

"Did you have something to prove?"

"I don't put labels on these things. And I wish you wouldn't, either. I just went out there and shot the best score I could. I won at Merion in '50 and then again at Oakland Hills in '51. That's three in a row if you're counting the ones I was physically eligible for. In 1952 I had the lead at Northwood after thirty-six holes, but I couldn't hold it. Shot back-to-back seventy-fours on Saturday. Boros passed me like I was standing still. Got it back at Oakmont the next year. Took Snead by six, Mangrum by nine, Demaret and some other guys by eleven. That's four Opens in five tries. Show me a man who's ever done better."

I couldn't do that because no one ever has. If Hogan really feels this way, why the display the other night?

"Your message really shook up the folks on the second floor," I commented, pointing to the clubhouse. "They're convinced you're gonna chase Fleck around the Lake Course again."

"Don't get ants in your pants, son. I said I haven't decided yet."

"But why?"

"Why what?"

"Why the obsession with '55?"

"Never tried so hard to win something in my life."

"So why are you so anxious to go through all that again?"

"I don't like leaving projects unfinished."

"But that project is finished, Mr. Hogan. It's over. It's part of golf history, part of the game's mythology, part of the legends—part of your legend. You know, whenever someone says 'Olympic,' they don't think of the others. They think of Hogan and Fleck. And let me tell you something else, Mr. Hogan"—I said every word, every syllable, with emphasis. How in God's name did I get the nerve to lecture the Iceman?—"when they talk about Hogan and Fleck, they don't spend all that much time on Fleck. They're really thinking about you. And it's you they talk about, you they analyze. There's never been anyone like you, before or since."

He smiled.

"You know what I like to think about when I'm thinking of you, Mr. Hogan?"

"What's that, son?"

"The grace and beauty of your swing. How you could turn it loose, let it happen, release the power, deliver a blow that a golf ball would respond to. I mean, you were a player's player, especially when you had it moving."

Hogan paused to think about what I'd said. "They were watching my little show the other night, weren't they?"

"Boy, I'll say. Little Eddie never saw anything like it. Haig's been looking for some of those—what did he call them?—glowworms. He wants to use them one of these nights when the scotch has warmed his belly and loosened his backswing."

"That's carny stuff, parlor tricks, something for a Monday exhibition. I was just curious to see if they'd watch, that's all. It's fun to strut your stuff every now and then. You know, let go, just fool around."

"You mean you weren't serious about two eighty-six?"

"I didn't say that. Didn't say that at all."

He walked away from me shaking his head. Damn! Just when I thought I had penetrated his armor, he repelled me! But I could see that Hogan enjoyed conversation. It's the people who extrapolate, who hypothesize, who assume what he's thinking whom he dislikes. Play the game for its own sake.

He was hovering over his practice balls once again. Hogan, the Iceman, the Hawk, Bantam Ben, was cranking it up. He checked his hands, his stance, his alignment, then let it go. Bam, bam, bam! The shots exploded like bullets fired from a .44.

"How can you hit it any better than that?" I asked.

"You can't," he said. "All you can do is hang on to it once you find it."

"But how do you know when to hang on and when to keep looking?"

"Oh, you know, son; you know."

"You mean like when I was firing it a few moments ago, Mr. Hogan?"

"How did it feel to you?"

"Well, actually, I don't really remember too much. It just . . . worked."

"That's it, kid. You were there. When it's working, don't fight with it, and for Pete's sake, don't flirt with it. Let it work. Let it flow out to your fingertips, then try to capture the feel. Try to understand what it's like to be in control. You'll notice how your eyes can see the tiniest gradations, the most minute variations of color in the things around you. And you'll also be able to see every mound, every dip, every little change in elevation in the fairway. I mean, you'll see everything. And you'll hear it, too. Every sound, every rush of air that filters through the trees. Everything. You'll be part of everything around you. Total consciousness, that's what it is." He looked around to make sure we were alone. "Jesus Christ! Can anyone hear me?" He looked over his shoulder again. "I'm afraid I'm starting to sound like a swami or something. You know what I mean, though, don't you?"

"Was it like that for you at Augusta in '67?"

Hogan smiled. He looked back fondly on that day in the spring of his fifty-fifth year when he turned back the clock during the third round of the Masters. Here was a man who had played with the greatest players in the game since the 1930s, proving once again that he could still keep pace. Hogan, the years having taken the smoothness out of his putting stroke, returned to the time when everything was effortless and pure. He took but thirty strokes to traverse the back nine—that day he needed no prayers at Amen Corner—and his 66 is remembered as one of those rounds marked by magic as much as by mastery. Wherever Hogan's game had been lurking over the years, he found it for a brief and glowing moment. His 66 was the low round of the Masters that year, lower than Nicklaus, Palmer, Player, Floyd, Casper, and all the rest. It was a round for the history books.

"You had it working then, didn't you?"

"Yes, but you see, it was different. It was my day, don't get me wrong, but something kept tugging at my shoulder, pulling at me, forcing me to look back. It was a long, slow walk, one that I'll never forget, but it was painful. And you know, pain is a funny thing. You can deflect it and you can overcome it, but it's there, nagging at you wherever you go, whatever you do. It's a drain on you to have to fight it constantly. I was forced to, and I did. But that isn't to say I liked it. I just did what I had to do. Son, do you have any idea what those hills do to legs like mine? They kill them. So let me give you some advice if you want to win the Open at a place like Olympic: Don't ever get old."

"But didn't your swing, your stroke, take over and make you forget about all that? Isn't the game what propelled you? Weren't you playing the game for its own sake?"

Hogan stopped again to think. Musin' the profundiddies. No, it wasn't the game, he realized. It was something else, something deep inside him, that made it happen. "I can't really explain it," he confided. "It's all of these things we've been talking about. All of it rolled together, so you can't tell one element from another. You know, if you stop to pick it apart, you'll lose it. That's why I just like to stop and savor the good moments, let them just sink in . . . and consume me." He shook his head. "There I go again."

"But you weren't too old to play, Mr. Hogan, not if what you and Jones say is true. As long as you can feel it, you can hit it. And as long as you can hit it, you can play, can't you?"

He looked down. "Who can say?"

"Maybe I can. I mean, you must have felt it at Augusta that day, the same way you felt it at Riviera in '48. You don't remember because, as you said, when you stop to cut it up and chew on it, you lose it. You know what I mean?"

"At Riviera there was no pain." There was a glint in his eye. I saw it just the way I saw it in Jones when he talked of St. Andrews, and Old Tom Morris as he hit his shots out there in the golden gloam with Young Tom.

Hogan returned to the balls and launched more rockets into

dawn's first light. I wasn't entirely certain, but something was different about him now. The water in his eyes dangled like dewdrops, and the look on his face had changed. It wasn't the grim stare of a coal miner but the contented glow of an accomplished conductor listening to his favorite symphony. All of the notes were in sync, and Hogan's five-iron was his baton.

I sensed I had connected—somehow, someway. I had the eerie feeling that there was now a bond between us, as if Hogan knew that I understood the excruciating details of what he had gone through, that I knew how difficult it had been, that I wasn't taking him or his achievements for granted, and, most important of all, that I wasn't bugging him for *the secret*.

Hogan paused and toyed with the range balls, rolling them into a little circle around his feet. Then he broke it up and rolled them into a different pattern. I watched and waited for him to speak.

"You know what would be nice?" he asked, looking up at the clouds forming in the early morning sky. "To be left alone, to be out here just beating on it. No legends, no myths, no ghosts to chase. Nobody asking me what I think or how I did it or how I'm going to do it. Let's just hit it and get after it, all the way into the hole.

"And you know what? Maybe once, that's all, just once I'd like to step out of my body and watch the action. Not in a movie. Not watching a picture. I mean in *real life*. Wouldn't that be something? To stand beside yourself and watch your swing? You could see it all: Your hands folding together on the club as one and then moving slowly to the top the way they're supposed to. And, oh my goodness, to see 'em cocked and ready to explode halfway down!"

"Man, oh, man!" I said as the power of his image swept me away.

"You know what I'd do?" Hogan asked. "I'd wait until the right moment, the last possible instant, when I knew everything was in place, in the right sequence and all, the shaft responding to me the way I wanted it to. Then I'd jump back inside and ride it out, knowing what was about to happen would be perfect, just the way

I wanted it to be. There'd be joy in that, you know. The joy of flow-ing motion, of leverage properly directed, of a golf ball propelled in the right direction, with the right flight pattern, headed straight at the target."

Hogan gazed contentedly at the far end of the driving range. "Just once," he said, "that's all I'd need. The surge of impact would rip through my body like a hurricane. Oh, to hit your best shot and know it was the best you had in you! Give me that, and you can keep the photographs, the books, the articles, all the sto-ries they tell. Just give me that. It's all I could ever want. Good heavens, it would fill my cup for a long, long time. Do you under-stand me, son?"

Hogan looked my way with the intensity of a man possessed. The demon, his demon, was now floating free, inside and outside his body. He was on a transcendent plane, one where he didn't care what people thought because he knew everything was right, that he was right, that he was where he ought to be, where he wanted to be.

"And you know what else?" Hogan asked.

I shrugged—not because I was tired of listening but because, if I had learned any lessons during my brief visit, the first and most basic was that it was not my province to invade Hogan's thoughts, especially at this juncture.

"When you hit a shot like that," he said, "one that's just ab-solutely perfect, well, it's yours. No one else can ever know you've done it, that you've hit it the way you planned. No one can take it away from you, either. It's yours to savor in your own way."

"That's the way it should be," I answered, somehow finding the words with which to respond. "After all, Mr. Hogan, they're your shots. They belong to you."

Hogan said nothing. He curled a range ball under his five-iron and rolled it away from the other balls and onto virgin turf. It sat up, a tiny white dot shining brilliantly atop a bed of close-cropped green grass. The Hawk addressed it slowly and methodically. His alignment was perfect. At address, a stunning calmness pervaded him, every muscle in his body poised, ready to be unleashed but disciplined to move as he, and only he, could direct. In one slow and flowing motion, Hogan delivered his blow. The ball shot off his club face, spinning violently as it began its ascent. It arched to its apex, then fell gracefully to the earth. No yardage markers or flagsticks were relevant to this shot. The only thing that mattered was that Hogan knew it went where he wanted it to go and, equally important, that it traveled in the manner he directed.

This one majestic five-iron was Hogan at his best. He gave it a lingering look, pausing to admire what his unparalleled talent had produced. Then, and much sooner than I had expected, he was done. He carefully removed his telltale white cap. He dried his forehead with a terry-cloth towel, the initials *BH* scripted in royal blue at one of the corners. Then he turned to ask a favor.

"Drop these off for me at the club room, will you, son?"

"Sure," I said, tingling at the thought of being asked to carry Hogan's sticks.

I reached to pick up his bag, but my attention was diverted as I saw him reach under his shirt to undo the corset that had been supporting his sore back. He placed it into a satchel, which somehow already contained the braces he had been using to shore up his aching legs. He stretched once, and then, as he picked up the satchel and began to walk away, I glanced at his golf bag again. Hanging off it was a round tag made of plastic, one like a thousand others I'd seen and read over the years. But this one gave me goose bumps. It read:

CONTESTANT

FORTY-EIGHTH UNITED STATES OPEN CHAMPIONSHIP

RIVIERA COUNTRY CLUB

LOS ANGELES, CALIFORNIA

JUNE 10–12, 1948

So that's where he's going. Back to the scene of one of his greatest triumphs, to a time when his face was young and new, when his star was still rising, when his shoulders and his back could rotate without discomfort, without the fear of something snapping or some soreness bursting through to the point where he had to will his mind to suppress it. Back to a time when he could walk without a limp. He's headed for a time when the feeling, the force, the whatever-it-is-you-call-it flowed through him like an electric current. Back to the time when the greatest mechanical master of them all had it working.

Hogan, now several paces off to the side of the range, suddenly stopped. Then he turned and came back to me.

"Here," he said, handing me the satchel containing his gear. "I won't need this stuff where I'm going."

"No, you won't," I said, taking custody of his possessions. "This stuff didn't come until later, after the—"

"Let's pull off the road at Riviera," he said.

He walked with a freer gait now, as if in an instant his body had shot back seven years, from 1955 to 1948. He was upright and bouncing as he took each step. Leaving the range, he looked back at me with a different sort of stare, not the eyes of the Hawk but something softer. It was a hopeful glance, looking ahead to his future and to the choice that he had finally made. Then he spoke words that to me were as special as any I had ever heard spoken. "Son, will you be here when I come back?"

"I hope so." My voice was calm, but I was trembling at the very thought, for I was in the process of working up the nerve to ask him the same question. Now, knowing that our thoughts and dreams had grown from the same seedling, I fixed my gaze on Hogan with a new focus. His image was burning itself into the lining of my soul, an indelible portrait that would have to sustain me as I awaited the possibility of our reunion one day.

Hogan began to depart, and, instinctively, I followed him toward the trees.

"I'd really like that," he said as he walked. "You know, all those years on the road, all that time we spent chasing the sun and the glory, Valerie and I never had the time to settle down. Then that damn accident. It took all I had to battle back. We never had time to . . . never had time to . . ." Hogan's loneliness was overwhelming, and it was wrapping itself around him like whipcord on a driver.

Hogan was looking, searching, stretching for something to hang on to, for he knew he was in danger of being swept up by the current of emotion that was swirling inside him. He wanted desperately to keep his footing. For a man like Hogan, there is nothing scarier than the thought of losing his balance.

This time, however, it was I who broke the silence. Hogan had his dreams, but I had mine, too.

"Mr. Hogan, if I come back to this place someday . . ."

"Son, you don't need to call me Mister."

"Well," I said, dreaming the impossible, "I mean . . . I'd like it if you'd . . . you know, if you'd be the one I never had. I mean . . . I'm afraid I'm not very good at this sort of thing." My voice was breaking up like a weak radio signal that fades in and out of a mountain pass. I could feel Hogan's loneliness and a good deal of my own tugging at my sleeve. A tear began to fall down my cheek as I watched him. I saw the circle of his life being completed and mine still being drawn. My mind wandered back to the library where I had read everything there was to read about the Hawk. The words of the *San Francisco Express* walked a tightrope across my memory. "The Father's Day crowd . . . Fathers and sons, entire families, covered the hillside . . . Hogan, who has no children, looked out on the families sitting before him . . . In the end, one can only say the future has confronted the past."

Hogan's voice snapped me out of it and brought me back to the present.

"There's this fear I have," he said with hesitation. "How can I explain it so you'll understand?" Hogan looked fondly at his weathered hands, those callused, bleeding paws. He made fists, released the tension, and looked over at me. "All of this practice leads to something. You see, son, I've discovered the way to find it. The feel, I mean. But it scares the blazes out of me because once

I've got it, what do I do with it? Keep it? Hoard it? Let it go? And if I give it up, if I release my grip on it, will it be gone forever? That's my fear, that's what I'm afraid of—that the feel will leave my fingers and never return. And all those folks, the ones who ask, who have asked, who will continue to ask . . ." He let out a deep sigh. "They want me to give it to them on a silver platter. They don't even begin to understand the thrill of the exploration, the experimentation. I don't think they'll ever be able to grab ahold of it. They'll never really know the feel, not the way I do. It doesn't take a genius to see that, and I'll be doggone if I'm going to let go of everything on their account."

Hogan had constructed an island green for himself, and he was safe there, protected from invaders by water and sand. He may have deterred the others, but now that I'd come this far, I had to strike the final approach.

"It doesn't have to be that way," I said, trying to lift a shot over the many hazards that guarded him. The trouble around him was ominous, and the hurt of his pain was lasting. It was etched into his face. The thought of what Hogan had endured sparked my fear that his scars might be too deep to heal.

"The way you describe it, Mr. Hogan, it's a one-way street. Someone always loses in that sort of exchange. I can't say for certain, but I don't think life has to be like that. From what I've seen around here, it's possible for two people to give at the same time. At least, I think they can. Besides, you don't need to worry. There isn't a man anywhere who can pick you clean."

Hogan turned toward me, his wet eyes glistening in the sunlight.

"Do you know how nice it is just to hear you talk, son?" A broad smile dominated his face. "Here we are, just you and me. No one watching. No gallery. No press. No one keeping score. And you, you're not trying to beat me out of anything. You don't even seem to want anything from me. All the others, they kept asking for the secret, as if I could dispense it like a pharmacist. Then you came along."

He was looking right through me, his eyes fixed on the trees where he knew he soon must go.

"You just watched and tried to understand," he said plaintively, not knowing how to complete the connection, perhaps unsure of how to start trying. "Somehow, you got inside me, son. Did you want that to happen?"

"I don't think that's the right question. This isn't about me, Mr. Hogan. I think it's about you. And I don't think it's about what you want, either. I think the issue is, did you *need* for all of this to happen?"

Logic was taking over again, creeping across the pesky grain of Hogan's mind like Poa Annua. Then he turned to me, deflecting the ultimate question. "I can see we have a connection of some sort here." He was still pushing the plate over to my side of the table. "Why do *you* need that, son?"

Finally I summoned the nerve.

"I guess . . . well . . . I don't have a father, Mr. Hogan. At least, that's why I think I might have—"

"What do you mean? You're here, you've been born, you have parents, surely—"

"He died when I was just a baby. I never even knew him. My only connection was through the stories my mother told me. About him, them, the life they had planned. And then, boom, he was gone, just like that, dead before he was thirty. And that was it. My mom said he was the only man she ever loved, but he was just an empty chair to me. Do you know what it's like growing up like that, without a—"

Before I finished the question, I could see I had awakened something deep inside Hogan. He knew what I was talking about, and he knew more about it than I ever would. And yet something prompted me to keep talking.

"I didn't have what most kids have," I said. "No dad to play catch with, to teach me stuff, that sort of thing. It was hard, but I kept on going, grinding, really, hacking my way along, taking my cuts as best I could. From the first moment I saw the films of you playing, I started to dream. One day, I dreamed . . . one day—"

"And so you—" Hogan stopped in mid-sentence, realizing why the two of us were there, why we had found each other.

The moment he saw it, we were bound together, our individual memories, our parallel experiences, choking us up. Hogan and I had led each other to confront the past—and it all flashed by for each of us. The good times, the bad times, the times that never were. Promises made, promises broken, promises unfulfilled. Promises that went unstated, never heard, because no one was there to complete the connection. Nobody at one end to speak, and nobody at the other to listen and respond.

"All those lonely miles you racked up, always on the road, going from one tournament to the next. Your speedometer lapped itself more than once. There wasn't any time, was there?"

Hogan was nearly bleeding from the thought of it, but the question was his to grapple with. He must do so however he saw fit.

The two of us were just standing there, looking at each other. There were no more words between us, and I doubted either of us would hear them if there were. It was just Hogan and me, both of us falling apart and falling together at the same time.

"You just be here, son." Hogan pulled out a handkerchief and daubed his eyes. His motion was as precise, even under these circumstances, as when I first encountered him in that bathroom. After he regained his composure, he let out a sigh. He knew it was time to depart.

"See you around," was the last thing I heard him say as he headed off toward the fog, which hung low along the tree line. He said it with a quiet, hopeful voice. *See you around.* And to think it all started in that bathroom, with me wearing spikes where I wasn't supposed to, searching for a shot I had toed sideways, dead right, into the darkness of the Monument.

Hogan was walking away slowly. For him the driving range was a friend to whom he could not bear to say good-bye. When he neared the tall pines that bordered the practice area, he turned back to me. One last lingering look. And then in an instant he faded from view, disappearing as he became one with the trees.

• • •

Several minutes after Hogan vanished, a sixth sense told me someone else was on the range. Sure enough, from down at the other end came the sound of someone beating balls. Even before I turned to see who it was, I knew. It was Jones. He was down at the section of the range that lies closest to the clubhouse. He was whipping a hickory-shafted iron around the way Obi Wan Kenobe wielded a light saber. The motion was fluid, as if the club were part of him. The energy built around him in the form of a halo. To this day I've never seen anything like it. It was as if some eternal, supreme power had kindled a flame within Jones, the glow emanating outward, drawing everyone in the Club to him.

His shots flew long and high. They landed one on top of another. Haig stood closest to Jones, and he watched closely, with glee. Then he asked Bobby if he could hit a few. Jones obliged and Haig drilled them like a carpenter. There was no wasted motion. For all his frivolity behind the bar, Walter Hagen was a different man out here. He was strictly business. I got near enough to see his face after a shot. He watched it intensely, as if the ball were his only daughter out on a first date. The shot dared not stray off line. I wandered even closer, thinking that an intimate look at the swings of Hogan, Hagen, and Jones wouldn't be bad for one morning's work. God, these guys are good.

Jones walked over to offer his hand. He looked at me, at the clubhouse, all around the place. "You and Hogan," he said longingly.

"We both got the same jolt at the same time," I said. "It was something, I'll tell you that."

I gazed wistfully beyond the trees, out to where I saw the Haig and Titanic Thompson tee it up. Hogan's image quickly came back into focus. "I think he was training for you all along, Mr. Jones." I shook my head. "Not for Fleck or anything else. I think it was you he was after. In the end you guys really didn't have all that much to worry about."

"Oh, really?" said Jones. "You know, son, the way I had it figured, he was training for *you*. And quite frankly, I think the two of you will be a team to be reckoned with. I can only speculate, mind you, but I suspect he's been wanting somebody like you to come into his life for a long while. The two of you have been waiting for the same thing." He looked up to Shep's aerie. With his head cocked in that direction, Jones said, "He knew that, too."

I swallowed hard, knowing the full impact of what Jones was telling me. "I can't wait to caddy for him," I said. "From what my mother's told me, my father never even played the game. But I never got to know him. I mean, he was gone before I even had a chance. It was always my mom and me, trying to make our way. I'll never have a chance to do any of this back . . . over there." I looked to the trees, at the fog rolling in. There may have been melancholy floating between us, but in the mystery of the mist there was excitement, too. "Looping for Hogan!" I exclaimed as the thought overtook me. "This is going to be like making up for lost time!"

"Take it easy, son. Remember, we're not about to be rushing around here. Time's a bumper crop on this farm. That's why I reckon you and Hogan'll be all right. But keep one thing in mind, will you? Ol' Hogan, he isn't a replacement for anybody, if you know what I mean. And I'll tell you something else, son. Neither are you. This here isn't a second chance, and it's not a fresh start either. It's just another fork in the road."

Jones paused.

"You and Hogan," he said once more, with emphasis. He turned and looked directly into my eyes, firing a final message like one of his mid-irons. "My goodness, you boys are gonna be playing down a whole new fairway."

Jones quickly disengaged. "Let's just wait and see what develops," he said softly. He patted me on the back and returned to beating balls. Within moments he had broken a sweat. He had fire in his eyes. He was going after it like nothing I'd ever seen.

It really was a surprise to see him practicing with such ferocity, not because the heated energy followed so closely after the sensitive discussion that preceded it, but because I knew about Jones in his younger days. When he was winning all of those national championships on both sides of the Atlantic, Bobby Jones was not much of a range rabbit.

He looked up from the balls, and his eyes reflected a sparkle of anticipation. "Hogan's coming," he whispered. Then he toyed with a couple of practice balls. "And I want to be ready for him."

Now I watched in awe. I suddenly dismissed the thought of Hogan and me. It was Hogan and Jones that I thought of now, and the very idea made me tremble. Jones with something to practice for! He must have been waiting for Hogan, too, hoping he would choose a path that led to the clubhouse.

Haig rejoined the practice session, and he quickly ran out of ammunition. He eyed Jones's balls with envy and asked permission to scrape away a couple more. Jones nodded. Haig snagged a few balls and promptly powdered them with a wood-shafted spoon. "Let's see the Iceman hit one of these babies," Haig chuckled, clutching his trusty weapon.

The two of them couldn't wait. A crowd gathered around, buzzing with excitement, for they, too, knew that one day the man with the golden swing would be among them, ready to make new friends, to finally settle down with Valerie, to share his gifts, to teach, to practice, to compete, to battle—to join them.

By the time Jones paused for a break, the sun had reached its midday zenith. The air was clean and crisp, with the breezes of springtime drifting in and out, cooling us off as we studied the divot pattern Jones had cut out of the sod. "This one's not deep enough," he said, pointing out a thin sliver of turf cut off to the left. "Pulled it." He made several more technical points, and those of us around him hung on every word. We were watching the greatest of them all prepare for something special. His faults corrected, Jones began launching shots that flew like guided missiles.

After a few more moments, Haig put his hands in his pockets and sneaked off, back to the bar. He had work to do. This was a club, after all, and people needed to have their whistles wetted. I could see him staring at us while he wiped down the mahogany counter.

From his spot on the range, Jones looked up toward the second floor. Old Tom was watching, Young Tom at his side. Jones nodded to them, the signal that all was well. High aloft in his chamber, Shep watched, too, then grabbed hold of a pewter tankard filled with the brew that Little Eddie had delivered to him. Then Jones looked at me.

"It's time," he said.

"I know," I said, dreading the moment. I had no idea what to say, how to end this liaison. The truth was, I didn't want to end it. For all I'd said about wanting to return home, something had happened to me here, something I could never hope to explain.

But I knew there was no way I could remain in their midst. I shook Jones's hand firmly. "This has been some adventure." I sighed. That was all I could muster at this awkward moment.

"Well . . . I, for one," Jones said, "am glad you stumbled upon us."

At this point all I could do was look back at the clubhouse and wave a final good-bye. Haig saw me and motioned for me to come inside. I ran all the way to the bar. "How about one for the road, junior?" he offered.

"Set 'em up, Haig," I said, just like one of his regulars.

We slugged down the brown stuff, and I learned that despite my journey through this philosophical par five, little had changed during the past three days. Haig took down the hooch as if it were cough syrup; the way I reacted, you'd have thought it was turpentine. I got it down, but I coughed madly as though the bogeyman had my throat in his clutches.

Haig patted me on the back and said, "Don't worry, junior. You keep at this business, and one day you'll get the hang of it. Just remember, don't worry, and whatever you do, don't hurry. Stop and smell the roses while you're walking along." I shook my head, trying to dispel the alcohol that was clouding my brain. Haig reassured me. "Easy, junior. You think swallowing the sweet heat is something you're gonna master in one sitting? Junior, even I had to start somewhere. It wasn't too many years back . . . '09 or '10, something like that . . . it was . . ."

I looked back at the range. "I'd better grab my clubs," I said, parting company with my suddenly long-winded friend. Jones was out there waiting for me. So was Old Tom Morris. And little Eddie, too, with my bag slung over his shoulder. I rushed to be with them, and was surrounded before I knew it.

"Laddy," said Old Tom, "this here, 'tis fer ye. I'm auld, but I still kin make 'em. This one 'ere, she's tight 'n' troo, 'n' hard as a chuckie stane. Like a little rock she is."

I looked down at the palms of his hands, and there he cradled a small leather sack. He handed it over, his eyes looking up into mine. The leather was as soft as butter, and inside I felt the round object of his handiwork. It was imperfect, as a featherie by nature must be, but it was one crafted by a grand master.

"Gae on," he implored, " 'n' put her aside fer when ye might be needin' somethin' t' propel down the fairway at a special tyme."

There would be no refusal of this present by me. My bag hung down from my shoulder and with my left hand I unzipped the ball pouch and stowed Old Tom's featherie for a rainy day.

"Play 'er wi' caution," instructed Old Tom, " 'n' she'll return the favor." He hugged me so tightly, I could barely breathe. The tears in his eyes met mine, and I looked at him and at Jones and thanked them both. Then my mind started to wander, roaming across the practical problems that lay ahead like a rolling fairway in the afternoon shadows, full of enticing landing areas but at the same time laced with potential bad bounces.

"Who can I tell?" I wondered aloud. "And what can I tell them?"

"Don't worry about any of that," said Jones. "These things have a funny way of taking care of themselves."

"Is this place real?" I asked.

"There's no way I can answer that for you," replied Jones. "Anything I say is just my word against everyone else's. I must tell you, son, that there's some measure of controversy about places like this. There are people—quite a few of them, in fact—who just plain don't believe in this sort of thing. I'm apt to answer your question one way, and another person, someone out there"—he motioned to the trees—"might dispute my every word. I don't want to get you into trouble."

"Play it as it lies?"

"That's usually a good approach."

"But how do I find my way back home?" I asked.

"Hangtown will escort you."

And so he did. The grim-faced sheriff was at my side, arms folded across his chest, a timepiece in the palm of his right hand, attached to his vest pocket by a gold chain. "Time to go," he said like a foreman calling an end to my shift.

The full impact of leaving this place and returning to my world was upon me. In the short time I'd spent here, I'd been somehow transformed; I felt attached to it, and it was not easy to pull away. My eyes clouded with mist, and a great sadness welled up within me. "I . . . I don't want to go." The words came out in a stutter.

"You must," said Hangtown, softly but with caution.

I looked away from all of them, out to the far end of the range. The balls I had hit two hours ago now lay inert, still and silent reminders of what had happened this morning. But even in the stillness, my memory lived. God, I had it moving out there today.

I caught it. I know I did. Even if for only a moment, the game belonged to me, the swing was mine, the shots I hit were obedient servants. Was it Hogan or Jones or Hagen? Or was it the lessons imparted by Shep? Maybe it was all of them together. Who knows? And who knows if I'll ever catch that feeling again?

All I could do was be grateful for having experienced it and for having the ability to know I was experiencing it. Jones understood this better than the others.

I knew only one way to properly thank him. It could not be done with a gift or with a gesture. There were only words, simple ones that he had heard before, ones that no doubt he heard from time to time from those he encountered here as well as from those he met in real life. It wasn't the same as the first time he had heard it, but it was the best I could do under the circumstances.

"Mr. Jones," I said as Hangtown headed me off into the fog. "That young man at St. Andrews was right. You *are* a wonder."

He smiled. Then he nodded. Then he set down his club and walked toward me, following my steps into the fog and the overhanging branches. He stopped well short of the trees, of course. The halo around him was iridescent, a rainbow pulsating outward. He waved good-bye, and as he did, I swore I could see his lips move. I've never been a lip-reader, but this was one day my eyes were seeing things they missed other times. "Fairways and greens," he mouthed. It was a message, a greeting, an instruction. Perhaps it was his hope for my future.

Fairways and greens. Those words and the vivid images of Jones, Haig, Old Tom, and Hogan are the last memories I have of the special place where the ball flies long and true, where one's mind and body seem to work without effort, where people from everywhere are at once kind and keen, connected to one another and the world around them, at ease and at the same time ablaze with the fire of imagination. There is a message here, one that I may never figure out—one that I don't really care to figure out, for every time I pause to think about it, I lose the image of Jones and his rainbow; of my good friend Haig regaling a crowd with tales of his exploits as the Houdini of match play; of Old Tom Morris glowing as he stood on an enchanted fairway alongside Young Tom; and, of course, of Hogan drilling shots on the range, wearing the grooves off his five-iron, searching for that special something, that magic feeling. I want desperately to retain those images, particularly Hogan's, for they provide something warm, something I cannot describe in words. It is not serenity, nor is it solemnity. I wouldn't exactly call it peace, either, for my mind jumps whenever I see Hogan there at the edge of the fog. Wholeness? Maybe that's it, but what does that mean?

I have analyzed quite enough for the time being; my journal is finished, the essentials of my strange travels written down for any who wish to share in them. I shall stop now and depart with a final vision of Hogan in the mist, for that is what I best remember about the place; that is what I want to remember, that is what I must remember, and that is what I will remember.

• Postscript •

As you can imagine, I have spent a good many hours pondering just what it was I experienced on the fateful day when I hit that toe job into the trees at Lincoln Park. There was much work to be done before I could let the tale be told. The first item on the agenda was obvious: I had to answer the final question I had put to Jones. Was it real?

I spent several months after my return grappling with the issue. I lacked the nerve to discuss it with my friends, particularly my golfing friends, for I feared they would dismiss me as deranged. Back then, and I suppose even today, golf was a pretty straitlaced pastime. *We can't have a lunatic on our golf team, son.* I could just hear my college coach telling me that after word spread that I was talking strangely.

Convinced no one would understand, I kept my mouth shut. But that did not prevent the vivid images of the Club from ricocheting in my head. I could see Jones watching Hangtown escort me back through the trees, a rainbow of energy surging outward, sparkling anew with everything it touched. And there was Hogan striding confidently into the fog after choosing Riviera. Was it real?

One pleasant convenience of having stepped through the Monument was that I returned without a trace of my absence. I can't explain it, but there was no time gap, no "missing three days" that had to be explained, however lamely, to a friend or relative. But the inconspicuousness of my adventure was no salvation; quite the contrary, it was a lead ball chained to my ankle. I was bursting to describe what I had seen, but without proof, my ramblings became a captive experience, imprisoned inside me, unknown to the outside world.

My first six months back on this side of the trees were pitiful. I became a fitful recluse, too scared to acknowledge what had happened. I drew inward as I scrambled to sort things out. My imponderable dilemma was the mental equivalent of a six-footer for par, with the match dormie. I had to get the ball into the hole, a task that would require enormous faith and confidence. Alas, I lacked the tools. Despite old Shep's teaching and the lessons I had learned from Jones and Hogan, I was too afraid of missing. So I convinced myself it was only a dream.

I was afraid to even walk on a golf course. The notion of revisiting a fairway after an adventure like that was overwhelming. The idea scared the pants off me, for I did not want anything to disturb that memory. I knew time would wash it away soon enough, but until then I was determined to hold on to as much of it as I could. I was clinging to the recollection, trying to hold it within me as a personal treasure for as long as possible.

But I knew that approach could not last forever. I simply love the game too much to let my clubs stand idle for very long. So the following summer, after I had at long last summoned the courage to venture out to play a round at Tilden Park, located above the Berkeley campus, a stone's throw from Strawberry Canyon and Memorial Stadium, it happened: I was talking casually with a couple of friends, off to the side of the first tee, when I began to rummage through the ball pouch on my golf bag for something to play with. The moment my fingers touched the soft leather sack, I knew. As I came to realize what was in my hand, my friends noticed the troubled look on my face. The inquiries came at me from all sides.

In an act of instinctive defensiveness, I deflected the conversation to safer subjects. Even though I had a featherie to substantiate it, surely no one would believe my story. Instead of the truth, I explained what I had found in my ball pouch as a gift from an uncle who knew nothing about golf. "He actually thought I'd be playing with it," I said. "Can you believe that?" I spoke in a monotone, as dispassionately as I could, and used my best poker face. No one batted an eye, even though a bumper crop of goose bumps had sprouted on my arms.

I beat a hasty retreat from the golf course. I didn't own a car in those days, so buses and trolleys were the only way I could get back to Lincoln by myself. I decided to go it alone, to take a shot at retracing my steps. Crossing the Bay Bridge, I had hope; the fog had already rolled in through the Golden Gate, and as I sped through San Francisco on public transportation, the sky overhead was changing from a sunny blue to the battleship gray that is Lincoln Park's hallmark.

But I had no luck. The Monument, the trees, the fog, the eerie stillness were all there; gone were the rumble, the tile floor, the bathroom . . . the Club.

I may not be able to physically revisit that special place, but my thoughts can wander where my feet cannot. I have played many a round of golf since my rendezvous with Hogan, and I must say something has been qualitatively different about my manner, my psyche, my mood, my feel for the game. My shots have become explorations, adventures about myself. Trouble? There's no trouble on a golf course unless you make some for yourself. If you have learned the lessons I have, you will never be bothered by hazards or bunkers or blind shots. Even the wind can be harnessed and made to follow you from behind; its finicky disposition can be tamed to do your bidding.

How does this happen? It happens just the way Jones and Shep and Hogan said it does: through the limitless power of the human mind. The smolderin' cauldron. Musin' the profundiddies. Playing the game for its own sake.

Since my return I have played literally hundreds of rounds in a trance, talking to Jones and Hogan as I walked down the fairway. From time to time my playing companions have asked me what I was doing, and the inquiry usually breaks the spell. It is like a hypnotist snapping his fingers, bringing his subject back to normal.

Ah, yes. Normality. The most remarkable thing about all of this is that now, after having immersed my every living fiber in this experience, having extracted from my thoughts a thick and lasting layer of memories, I find myself surrounded by a state of "normality" quite different from before. Of late there is no snapping out of the trance. In fact, it is as if there is no trance at all. I am in a state where inquiries from others don't matter. They cannot penetrate the power of the force that guides me. Indeed, more often than not I find that I draw those closest to me into this rarefied atmosphere too. As a group, we catch the feeling, and it binds us together.

I have experienced this most often with one particular golfing partner, who for the sake of privacy will go unnamed. He and I have a unique form of synergy. As a team we are unbeatable—at least we think we are—and our achievements in competition have borne this out. We have shot some remarkable scores, and we have done so consistently. Perhaps the greatest validation has been from our opponents, who have remarked on more than one occasion, "You two guys have something going out there." They can't figure it out, but we know. You see, this particular partner is the only one to whom I have dared disclose the details of my visit to the Club. Fortunately, he has never questioned the experience, nor has he gone out to Lincoln Park and searched the trees for the passageway. To his credit he has left himself open to its possibility—and in doing so he has seen, felt, and experienced the special sensation that comes over a person when everything is right.

I probably think more about Hogan than any of the others. And what about him? Is he a messenger? Is there a spirit that surrounds him, that emanates outward, grabbing hold of anyone willing to stand close enough to be touched by it? Who knows? There are no burns, no marks on my body to show where the lightning struck. But I know it did.

Have you ever listened to a discussion about great golfers? The same question arises every time: Who was the best? It is an unanswerable query, but one that continues to stir both emotion and debate. The names are all too familiar and new ones are added every few years: Jones, Hagen, Sarazen, Snead, Nelson, Palmer, Nicklaus, Player, Trevino, Watson, Ballesteros, Faldo, Norman. The list goes on and on. But have you ever noticed what happens when Hogan's name is mentioned?

Sometimes it is more subtle than at others, but it happens every time without fail. There is a hush, a silence, a pause; people look at one another, waiting for someone else to speak, to offer comment. It is as if people are afraid to cross a threshold, afraid to reach out and touch the legend. Sometimes it lasts only a second or two, but it is a palpable moment, as tangible as if carved in stone, fixed and frozen for all to witness.

What does this mean? The only thing I can figure is that Hogan *is* a messenger. Not in the religious sense, for Hogan is neither a prophet nor a savior. But what is he? He is in every sense a teacher, one whose lessons are deep and powerful. His approach to the game and his golfing achievements are like perpetual motion; they will live forever, and they will constantly renew themselves, imparting a fresh dose of wisdom to each new generation of golfers that takes the time to study them. The same thing can be said of Hogan's life itself.

The history books tell of his exploits after those four fateful days at Olympic. Despite his declaration of retirement following the playoff with Fleck, Hogan played on, and his moments continued to sparkle and radiate glory.

There was Cherry Hills, of course. It would not be an overstatement to describe the final day of the 1960 United States Open Championship as a golfing vortex, as three generations of greatness swirled around one another. Many have written how the lives of Palmer, Hogan, and Nicklaus intersected that day, like three mighty rail lines crossing one another at the same train station.

To be sure, the world's eye was fixed on Palmer as he slashed, scrambled, and stampeded to that wondrous 65, which catapulted him all the way to the top, past no fewer than fourteen other players. In one incredible run, the king was born.

But Hogan was there, too, playing quietly and deliberately in the twosome in front of Palmer. He was paired with a promising young amateur, a fat kid from Columbus named J. W. Nicklaus. After sixty-nine holes, Hogan was tied for the lead. He was still tied when he reached the seventeenth hole, which was his thirty-fifth of the afternoon, seventy-first of the championship. He had hit every green that day, thirty-four in a row. All this at the age of forty-seven—ancient by the golfing standards of the day.

The seventeenth at Cherry Hills is a 548-yard par five, straight as a shaft, with an island green at the end. The water surrounding the green means that only the longest players can hope to get home in two. In 1960, Hogan, at his age and having endured eleven pain-filled years after the accident, was not one of those players. He hit a solid drive, then laid up just short of the water with a three-iron. He was only a stone's throw from the green, but there was a twelve-foot-wide strip of water to contend with. Hogan's putting had been unsteady all day, so he knew he had to get close. He needed two pars for 280, which he figured might be good enough to win. His lie was immaculate. "I could have hit a driver off the fairway," he would say later. "It was so perfect."

Hogan puffed on a cigarette, then pulled out his pitching wedge. He hit the ball flush, sending it directly on line to the flagstick. It hit on the front of the green, took a hop forward toward the hole, then spun backward violently. The shot backpedaled down the embankment fronting the green and dropped into the hazard. Hogan's chances of winning disappeared with his golf ball.

Hogan could judge talent as well as display it. Although he concentrated on his own game that June day in the Rockies, his eye was turned by his playing partner. After finishing the round with young Nicklaus, the Hawk told the assembled reporters, in words that only a man of his experience could utter, "I just played thirty-six holes with a kid who should have won this thing by ten strokes."

In 1966, Hogan returned to Olympic. The USGA extended him a special exemption, and he took advantage of the opportunity, finishing twelfth. It was a fine finish for a fifty-three-year-old man with bad legs. Then there was Augusta in '67, Hogan's third-round fireworks lighting up the sky like a Roman candle. In 1970 he shot 287 at Champions to place ninth in the Houston Open, his first professional event in almost three years. It was a remarkable showing at the age of fifty-seven, one so remarkable, in fact, that his gallery was swarming with other professionals, craning like rubber-necked celebrity watchers, desperate for the chance to watch the Iceman's magic.

Hogan stopped playing in public in 1971, and I can only assume, wherever he is, that he still loves and appreciates the feel of doing it right. Even though he may now be confined to the intimacy of his own shadow, I am certain Hogan's soul still yearns to hit balls at his special spot at Shady Oaks, at his own pace, to his own liking, to the standards that only he can know. Perhaps if he were to do it, he'd select a pitching wedge; perhaps short shots are the only part of his game that is left. But I'll bet my name that if Hogan were to swing even once, he'd still feel the thrill of the energy his body can transmit to the clubhead.

While it is true that Ben and Valerie Hogan have no children, it is equally true that they have no regrets. The Hawk has been asked countless times whether, given the chance, he would change anything. His answer is as unwavering as one of his five-irons: "I'd leave things just as they are." He is a man who knows himself and the journey he has taken. Like anyone, he must have his own set of needs and wants, his own hopes and dreams. But they are his and no one else's. He, like everyone else, has the right to keep them to himself.

Even if Hogan were to dismiss my ramblings as the oddball

spouting of a crank or the careless prying of a sycophant, it cannot extinguish the memories that have traveled from his life to mine. Like many others, I have been his beneficiary. Whether intended or not, Hogan's image and that of Jones and the rainbow power my engine now, and it runs smoothly. It requires little maintenance and has the remarkable capacity to regenerate itself from time to time, and even when it appears to be flat out of gas, bone dry empty, running on fumes, something happens to charge it anew. The force that drove Hogan and Jones has somehow, someway, gotten inside me and taken hold of my every impulse.

It is an amazing feeling, one that goes on and on and on. It is difficult to quantify with a formula or qualify with words.

As I have written this passage, my hands have grown lighter and the words have come to me in whole sentences. I will not tamper with the syntax or with the choice of adjectives. I will let them stand, just the way Hogan stands, for all to see.

Hogan's deeds and the choices he made? They are Hogan's and Hogan's alone. What did it feel like to do what he did, to live the life he lived? That is Hogan's personal treasure, for him to gaze upon fondly, proudly, to cherish and contemplate in the solitude of his own mind. He is the only one on Earth who knows what it was like to come back, to triumph, to make it work, to get it right, as no one has ever done before or since. The memory of all that is the special richness nature allows a man like Hogan to keep after the action ends.

It is not for any of us to ask Hogan to explain anything or to lay himself on the table so that we, like scavengers, can pick him apart. We can and will draw inspiration from his public record, which is substantial. But the rest, all the rest, belongs only to the Hawk.

As for me, I have more than my memories, as vivid as they are, for I possess a tangible memento that resides in the ball pouch of my golf bag. It is at once a silent passenger and a worthy companion. I don't know if I will ever have reason to take a swing at Old Tom's featherie, but every so often I stick my hand in there just to feel it. At times it seems to pulse with energy, as if a part of Old Tom Morris himself is encased within the tightly stitched leather cover. One touch of that imperfectly shaped golf ball warms my heart and lights my face with a smile. It may be an odd pellet, but it is a beautiful and compelling reminder of an astonishing journey, and a fertile seed for golfing dreams.

• Acknowledgments •

No work is complete without saying thanks to all those who helped along the way. First and foremost, I thank my immediate family, especially my mother, Roslyn; my late father, Milton (oh, how he would have loved all of this!); my brothers, Rich Links and Don Yost; and my dear cousins, the Cohns. Your love and support kept me going from the start.

To all of my "readers," upon whom I laid the earliest chicken scratches that later evolved into a finished manuscript: You mean more to me than I can ever tell you in words. To my oldest friend, Andy Colvin; my best golf buddy, Larry Cerf (The L-Man): my fairway pals Butch Berry, Therese St. Peter, Chuck Diakon, Dave Roberts, and Richard R. Ross (R³)—you read, smiled, corrected, suggested . . . and I'm better for it. To my literary critics, Linda Gallanter and Natalie Levy, thanks for your unique insights; to my "medical team," Al Oppenheim, Merton Goode, Rob Margolin, and Arthur Cerf, who all came to the rescue when called; to Brian Duffy (the original "smoulderin' cauldron"), who turned out to be the best proofreader I know; to John Blankfort, for the superb collection of Hogan articles which were instrumental in verifying research; to Bud Brody, for helping me locate a very special caddie named Tony Zitelli who, in turn, took the time to tell me about the man who employed him during that fateful week at Olympic; to Paul and Mitch Leiber, Mike Karasik, Sandy Kosman, Don Friend (Big D), and Mark Dukeminier (the Duker) for always being interested in this crazy adventure; to Rick Lawence (Long Ricky), for Scotland, where all of this began; and to one of my favorite touring professionals, Ben Crenshaw, for setting down his putter long enough to take a read and drop me a line.

The debt I owe to the United States Golf Association can never be repaid, except perhaps in service, and for that I stand ready to leap into the breach. The USGA's extended "family" has become mine, and the names are not mere titles in a telephone directory; they are trusted, lasting friends whose support and goodwill I count among my blessings. They include Karen Bednarski, the world's greatest curator, to whom I have to deliver a very special thanks for opening up the museum and smiling my way; to Larry Gilhuly, for letting me come along on some memorable journeys; and also to Pat Gross, Tom Meeks, Paul Vermeulen, the late David Earl, Pamela Emory, Ron Read, and Tim Moraghan. Lastly, and most importantly, to C. Grant Spaeth, who read one of my early drafts: thanks for your note of encouragement. Your kind words were the helping hand that inspired me from the start and carried me through to the finishing hole.

To Mr. Hogan's good friend, Martha (Marty) Leonard, and to his wife Valerie, thanks for taking the time to read over the manuscript and for giving me a call to help me out.

To my colleagues at the San Francisco law firm of Berger, Nadel & Vannelli (and the former firm of Dobbs, Berger, Molinari, Vannelli, Nadel & Links), thanks for giving me the space to do all of this, especially to my simpatico *artiste,* Joe Nadel, who knows what the joy of writing is all about. And I must mention the late Harold S. Dobbs, friend and benefactor to an entire generation; I know he's up there smiling down on me with intense pride.

To my agent, Jacques de Spoelberch, you are an agent's agent and a memorable partner on the links. Thanks for believing in me.

To Jeff Neuman, you understand all of this better than anyone, and it shows. My, but you're a wonder.

Finally, to my darling A.J.: Honey, this book was written for you, so that hopefully, one day, you will fully understand what makes me tick, what moves me, what makes my juices flow. Please know that wherever life leads me, I'll always have you on my mind.

The next time you look toward the trees, think of me. I'll be in there, searching for something, trying all the while to hitch a ride with the wind.